Scott Miller spent 22 years as a college wrestling coach at Eastern Washington University, Campbell University, Syracuse University, and Pacific University, 18 of those years as a head coach. After retiring from coaching, Scott went into mental health services and served as a CBRS, SUD case manager, and anger management specialist for 10 years. Currently, he is an emotional regulator and victim's advocate in Wallace, Idaho, and continues to coach wrestling at the high school and middle school level. Scott is married to Amy and has one daughter and three stepsons.

To Ben

Scott Miller

REBECCA

AUSTIN MACAULEY PUBLISHERS™

LONDON • CAMBRIDGE • NEW YORK • SHARJAH

Ordering Information
Quantity sales: Special discounts are available on quantity purchases by corporations, associations, and others. For details, contact the publisher at the address below.

Publisher's Cataloging-in-Publication data
Miller, Scott
Rebecca

ISBN 9781645757856 (Paperback)
ISBN 9781645757849 (Hardback)
ISBN 9781645757863 (ePub e-book)

Library of Congress Control Number: 2020909904

www.austinmacauley.com/us

First Published (2021)
Austin Macauley Publishers LLC
40 Wall Street, 33rd Floor, Suite 3302
New York, NY 10005
USA

mail-usa@austinmacauley.com
+1 (646) 5125767

Thank you to my friends and loved ones that supported the book and urged me to get it published.

Prologue

I hate this car, it's old and rusty, but that is not why. I hate it because it continually brings me closer to that which I fear. I'm not what I used to be but maybe that is for the best. I find myself craving to be the young man I once was when everything was simple and my life lay before me, but instead I am simply older and have wasted most of my gifts. Like many men my age, I seek something mysterious that will make me feel new and vibrant again but I fear that even if found it is out of my reach.

I drive through a typical neighborhood in an unfamiliar town. The houses are older and some, like me, no longer hide their age well. It is a brisk spring morning and the sunlight brings the fresh hope of a new day. Still, I find my anxiety remains and my hands quiver as I work the steering wheel of this blasted car that carries me closer to the one I have long searched for yet fear.

I see her house and I pull over. Invisible pins prick my back and neck and the cotton in my mouth makes it difficult to draw a breath. The structure is nothing special; in fact, it looks much like the other houses of this neighborhood. I can see that it has stood many more years than I have but still, it continues to project a certain dignity. It has gone through many reincarnations and now it is gray. In front is a small lawn that cries for a cutting. Leading to the weathered porch is a cracked sidewalk that somehow holds steady for those who walk over it each day.

In the yard are toys of a child, most likely a girl, but in today's world who really knows. Maybe I'm an 'old school guy' but I remember when it was boys who played with boy toys and girls with girl toys. I've been away for a long time and things changed without asking for my input. It's probably for the best but I can't help hoping fervently that they are played with by a girl.

I turn off the engine and I stare at the house that is northwest of me just fifty yards away. I don't see the house as it is but instead, I picture another one from forty years before. It is my house in another city in a more innocent era. I remember those mornings so long ago and it brings a smile to my lips. Now I am in another place, remembering boys playing football and girls playing dolls. The neighborhood was a community then. A brother resided in every house and the girls were necessary evils that dotted the landscape.

When one moved away it seemed like a death in the family but soon another would move in and assume the mantle of the recently lost. My smile disappears as I wonder why I no longer see such things. Have we changed that much? Are we really that afraid? And then I remember that it is me that they are afraid of and I feel the guilt of a life gone awry.

As the sun climbs in the sky, shadows from trees begin to shade the front of the houses. Doors open and children come out to begin their day at the school that is only blocks away. I sit low in my car, afraid of being spotted. It seems as though it has taken a lifetime to get to this place and I do not want it blown by the arrival of one who serves and protects. I am sure they would not view me as I am so I lie low, cursing myself because I am afraid though I do nothing wrong.

The door of the little gray house I have been staring at opens and an angel emerges. She has pigtails with yellow ribbons tied to them and she bounds with the joy of youth. Behind her is the young woman I should have adored so many years before. I have waited long for this moment and now that it has arrived, I am petrified. I shrink in my car as my heart races. I feel chest pains and wonder if I am having a heart attack. My hands grip the steering wheel and momentarily I think of starting the engine and fleeing.

Yet something strange happens. I do not start the car and my hands loosen their grip. I strain to get a better look at the one I abandoned so long ago. They walk away from me and for a moment I think of getting out of the car and calling to them, begging them to stop. The child suddenly stops and turns around and I swear she is looking at me but she is now a hundred yards away and I am so low in the seat I know she can't see me. Her mother catches up to her and gently nudges her forward and they continue their walk toward the school that is just beyond the park.

As they fade into the distance, I open my door and slowly step out. I feel a hundred eyeballs on me though no one is around. After years of being where I have been paranoia dies slowly. I quietly close the door and walk toward the park. Distant shouts of children filter toward me from the school grounds and it relaxes me. I begin to feel that maybe it is all right that I am here and I continue toward the empty park.

I see a bench by the swing set and I approach it and sit. My heart continues to beat through my chest and I feel sweat forming on my forehead despite the coolness of the morning. It is peaceful here, something I admit to myself I know little about. As I fight the anxiety of rejection, I am thankful for a calmness that quietly begins to overtake me.

In the distance I see the woman walking back from the school. I try to be nonchalant as I watch her. As she comes closer, I get up and begin to walk to the other side of the park. I don't want her to notice me because I am ashamed and scared of the child I left behind so many years before. As I reach the sidewalk on the other side, I steal a glance toward her and see that she has not noticed me. I feel relief but also a pang of regret. Now she is out of sight and I walk back to where I was sitting in the safety of the solitude of the park.

The air is warming as the sun continues its climb but I feel frozen, unable to move yet my mind continues to race. I glance for eyes that I know must be staring at me. I want to move, get up, and head toward the little gray house but instead, I sit paralyzed to this wretched bench. I know what it is that keeps me here instead of where I should be. It is fear, unadulterated, and all-encompassing. I am more scared than I have been in many years. I think of the irony of this for I have recently returned from a hell that I alone put myself in. I suddenly realize this is worse, for in hell I knew what the dangers were and how to protect myself from them. Here I feel as though I am a lost child and I realize it is the unknown that has me terrified.

I look at the cheap watch on my wrist. I have been sitting here for over an hour and somehow I find the will to stand up. I must follow through on what I have started. I have spent a lifetime blaming others for my undoing, but this time it is only me that I can blame if I choose not to finish.

My legs are heavy as I begin to walk slowly toward the gray house. I stare at the cracked sidewalk as I force myself forward. I am closing in on my target and I am petrified. Suddenly to my chagrin I am crossing the street, heading away from where I should be going. I try to stop myself but I can't. My pace quickens and I silently curse myself. I don't know how this has happened but I'm again in this hated car and I am feeling the rumble of the engine coming to life. I put it into drive and the car lurches forward and I feel a sense of relief, but it is only momentary. I turn right on the next block, and then take another right and another and I am back where I belong. I park in the same spot I just came from and I turn off the engine, angry at myself for being the coward I have become.

The house beckons me and I stare at the door. I wonder what is happening behind it right now and I know that the answer I seek is approaching. Can I do it I wonder to myself? Am I man enough to face my consequences and try again or will I always be the coward? I know that if I get out and walk over there my life will never be the same. It may be better or it may deteriorate, but it won't ever be what it was. I open the door remembering that to risk for the better is always good. I will take the chance.

I force myself out of the car, my courage built up. I silently pray that it will stay with me for the next few minutes. This is my moment and I am ready to seize it. I am likely facing devastation but I will accept it if that is what is meant to be. I don't remember crossing the road or walking up the steps but I am now in front of the door of this little gray house.

I am ready, I have yearned for this moment and I no longer fear the outcome. My hand reaches out and I knock on the blue wooden door.

BOISE, ID
1982

Chapter 1

The football hung in the drizzly sky as the red-clad receiver sprinted desperately toward an opening between the two defenders. At the last second, he thrust his body into the air, arms outstretched as his fingers strained to feel the leather of the ball that was rapidly descending. The player skidded forward on the damp grass as the ball bounced just beyond him and he lay still for a moment as the official signaled the incompletion. The down marker up field changed from three to four and Boise High School was down to one last shot to prolong their magical season.

On the sideline, the coaches chaotically conferred with each other and then sent in the designated play runner with their strategy.

"Jesse, coach wants XY sprint flag left," the runner said to the quarterback as he entered the huddle.

Jesse Rayburn, a head taller than everyone else in the huddle glared at the coaches on the sideline with his hands on his hips. He knew that the defensive backs would be waiting to swat the ball down and end not only the game but for all intents and purposes, the season.

"No," he said defiantly as he ducked back into the huddle. "They're clogging the sidelines and we don't have time for more incompletions."

"Jesse, coach says—"

"Shut up, Allen," the quarterback barked. "We're going to do it my way. Allen, you're my safety. If it goes to you, get your ass out of bounds."

"Tommy, I want you to go up 20, fake in and sprint out," he said as he looked toward his receivers. "You have to get the free safety to bite and clear the middle. Jackie, the play is to you. Go up 25…you have to get past the DB so the strong safety takes over coverage. When he does, cut inside to the middle. Line, I need four seconds from you. I'll buy the other second or two. Everybody got it?"

The players looked around to each other and nodded.

"Don't screw up. On one…break!"

They broke from the huddle as one and went into their stances at the line of scrimmage. Jesse quickly scanned the defense. It was as he expected. He barked out the signals, all eyes on this damp, late fall evening on him. The spectators, many under blankets to ward off the cold, held their breath. Those wearing red prayed to the football gods for another miracle from the best quarterback the school had ever produced while those on the opposite sideline wondered if the clock was ever going to hit zeros.

The center snapped the ball and Jesse faded back five steps. The two lines violently collided against each other and the sounds of the night became hollow in Jesse's ear until all he heard in his concentration was the breathing and grunting immediately around him. The defense began to close in on him as the offensive line cracked from the oncoming force of the invaders. Jesse ran to his right, away from the pressure. His eyes continue to scan downfield and he waited for the strong safety to bite on the fake. Suddenly Jackie bolted toward the center of the field and Jesse instinctively cocked his arm and threw to a spot thirty-five yards up the field where he knew his receiver would be.

The ball whipped through the air and descended toward the target. Jackie looked over his shoulder and put his hands up just as it arrived. It landed lightly in his hands and he cradled it and sprinted forward as two defenders tried desperately to tackle him before he crossed the goal line. The chilled crowd erupted in a frenzy as the players in red jumped in joy while the vanquished hung their heads in anguish. As chants of "we're number one" filled the night air, the quarterback unsnapped his helmet and casually jogged past his waiting coach.

"What was that?" asked the coach to the player who had just delivered him his first league title.

"Touchdown, Coach."

"You're the best I've ever had, but you're a pain in the ass," the happy coach laughed.

"I know, thanks, Coach," Jesse replied with a toothy grin as the victors continued to hug and dance around them.

*

A foggy steam hovered in the air as the gleeful players cleaned up from this, their greatest, conquest. Towels snapped against backsides and howls of pain and laughter filled the tight-fitting quarters. In a small office adjacent to all of the hoopla stood the coach quietly conferring with a man in a red sweater with silver letters outlined over his chest. The coach pointed toward Jesse who was watching with interest from his locker with only a towel wrapped around his midsection.

The man in the red sweater shook hands with the coach and then stepped out of the office and walked toward the hero of the game. He was tall and angular and carried a serious look behind the spectacles that made him look older than his true age. They began to fog over from the humidity of the locker room and he pulled them off so he could see. This was his last trip of the week and he was anxious to get back to Las Vegas to see his wife and brand-new son that he hadn't seen in a couple of weeks.

"Hi, Jesse, my name is Scott Tyler. I'm from the University of Nevada at Las Vegas, UNLV for short. We've been following you this year and really like what we've seen," he said. "I want you to know that I've been authorized by our coaching staff to let you know that we will be offering you a scholarship to play for us." Jesse smiled and eagerly shook the outstretched hand. "We would like for you to come to Vegas and visit our school after the state playoffs so that we can show what we have to offer."

"Thank you, Mr. Tyler," Jesse replied as his smile grew wider.

"You're a heck of a player. That last play was something else. What do you guys call that?"

"Touchdown, sir. We put it together in the huddle."

"Seriously?"

"Yes, sir."

"Well I'd like to see a lot more of those, but only if you're wearing a Rebel uniform. Here's my card," Tyler replied as he handed it to Jesse. "Call me if you need anything. I'll take good care of you, best of luck in the playoffs, and stay healthy buddy."

"I will sir, I promise. Thank you, Mr. Tyler."

Jesse looked at the card, the one he had been hoping to get for the past year. UNLV was big time, a place where NFL scouts went. They wanted him and at last, he knew that all the sacrifices had been worth it. As the recruiter left the locker room, his teammates quickly congregate around him.

"I'm going to Vegas, boys," shouted Jesse. "I'm going big-time."

His teammates mobbed him, mussed his hair and patted him on the back. Good-natured kidding bombarded him about being a hick from Idaho going to Sin City. He smiled and laughed. This was how he dreamed it would be though he had always harbored secret doubts it would actually happen. A glorious future awaited him and his teammates feted him for his success.

The players eventually settled down and slowly began to leave. Jesse took his time and after getting dressed sat down at his locker and stared at the business card Mr. Tyler had given him. It was a typical business card but it signified to Jesse a validation of who he was and what he had accomplished.

He had never wanted to be ordinary even though his life had been. He was a typical kid from a middle-class home. His dad, George, owned a garage just outside of the University District and made a nice living. He was known for doing a good job and the customers tended to spread the word that a person could get a quality job done on their car for a reasonable price from him. Laura, his mother, ran the household. They were much like the rest of the parents in the neighborhood, attended church on Sundays, and were generally God-fearing and devout. Jesse was the apple of their eye and was perhaps a little spoiled because he was their only child. Though they weren't rich, Jesse always had the money for gas and his clothes were the current style that teenagers wore.

In return, he followed his father's rules. His size and prowess on the field made him a leader of the boys at school and the object of desire for the girls. He was handsome with chiseled features and his lanky body showed no signs of fat. He was easygoing and was as comfortable talking to the dopers as he was the jocks. He was probably the most popular kid at school, but the status didn't seem to affect him.

Outside the locker room, Karla Thompson sat with some friends talking about the things girls in high school talk about. She was still wearing her cheerleading outfit with BHS stenciled across the chest. Karla and her friends talked about their boyfriends, some lamenting about the latest unsolvable issue their beau had invoked while others spoke of their undying love for their current. Karla smiled and nodded and offered her insight when asked. Eventually, the conversations turned to the dance that would be starting momentarily in the school gymnasium which in turn led to gossip about possible new relationships or the ending of current ones.

Karla was a junior with sharp features, smooth skin, and long blonde hair with the bangs feathered to the sides. Her mom and dad were hippies from the '60s and tended to believe that the best way for Karla to develop into a young woman was through a relaxed, nurturing existence. Karla was popular with girls her age or younger, but the senior girls didn't care for her because of the interest she conjured up with the senior boys that they coveted. Karla's parents, Hank and Corrine, had lived the free-love lifestyle of the '60s and had met in San Francisco at the beginning of the 'Flower Power' period. Even now they liked to share the occasional joint and let their minds expand. They had a small business selling natural supplements, organic food, and incense that nobody in town admitted buying, yet their business had flourished for years.

Karla was the opposite of them. She was also an only child and her values sometimes led to conflict with her parents. She thought free love was disgusting, wanted no part of illicit drugs, and longed for her parents to be 'normal.' What she did not understand was that this made her like everyone else that she knew. Though her parents were extroverts she preferred a more private existence and could best be described as shy.

She was the secretary for the school DECA club and a photographer for the yearbook. She volunteered at the local senior center and made extra money working at JoAnn's Fabrics. She loved to collect stuffed animals and even now slept with a Teddy she had cherished since early childhood.

She had noticed Jesse two years before when she first entered into the halls of Boise High School and had carried a crush for him secretly for over a year. He was tall, athletic and everyone liked him. Though he was a year older than her he didn't seem stuck-up like other boys his age. She had gotten the nerve to tell a friend of her interest in him during the spring of her sophomore year who had told a friend who told a friend who told Jesse. Unbeknownst to her, Jessie had been fascinated by her all year and soon they were a couple.

For both of them, this was their first love. It had sprouted without either knowing it would happen and seven months later they couldn't imagine life without each other. Karla's parents were indifferent toward Jesse, figuring that this would be a good experience for their daughter but were becoming more concerned as the relationship grew. Jesse's parents wanted to like Karla, but in truth didn't care for her much because of her parents' reputation and were concerned that she, though sweet, would be the demise of their son. Like all teenagers in love, Jesse and Karla lived in an alternate universe and were determined to have the fairy tale of living happily ever after, even if the price for this was the breaking away from the safety of their families.

*

As Jesse walked out of the locker room, Karla spotted him and ran to him, draping her arms around his neck. She smiled happily as he bent down to gently kiss her on the lips.

"That was so exciting," she said softly. "I never had any doubt."

"Really?" he asked sarcastically.

"Maybe a little," she giggled.

"Me too," he admitted.

They grabbed each other's hands and walked toward the gymnasium where the victory dance was now in full swing. He tried to be nonchalant but he desperately wanted to share the good news he had received from Mr. Tyler with her. She sensed he had something he wasn't telling her and for a moment was afraid that maybe he had grown tired of her and was ready for a new girlfriend. She looked at him and the fear disappeared because he gave her a loving look back that was filled with an unknown excitement.

"What is it?" she asked.

He stopped and again kissed her, this time with more intensity. He led her to the parking lot and they kissed again behind a green Chevrolet blazer, away from the prying eyes of others.

"Karla, I have some great news," he said excitedly. "I'm getting a scholarship from UNLV. I just met the recruiter…" He reached into his pocket and pulled out the business card to show her.

She looked at it and felt an ache in the pit of her stomach.

"But I thought you were going to go to Boise State."

"Baby, this is a big time. Bowl games, big stadiums, NFL Scouts, that won't happen at BSU."

She wanted to be excited for him but instead felt fearful that soon she would be losing the boy she loved.

"Don't worry, it'll be great and we'll make it work," he reassured her.

She felt guilty because she knew how much this meant to him but she also realized that in a way she was angry with him. They had talked of going to Boise State together all through the summer. BSU had football, good football. They had won championships and the stadium was the largest she had ever seen. Now he was telling her everything was going to be different and he was leaving. He didn't care about her; it was only about him. His look showed the hurt he was feeling and her anger began to dissipate and guilt replaced it.

"I know, I'm sorry," she said quietly. "I'm so proud of you."

He smiled again and pulled her close. He was happy again and she knew that she had been convincing but the ache in her stomach continued and she sensed the end of the relationship slowly approaching. They walked silently toward the dance in the darkness of the night and he did not notice the tear that slipped from her eye.

At the dance, they went their separate ways to be with friends. He was enjoying the celebrity of being the star who had led the team to a championship and earned a scholarship to the school of his dreams in the process. She went to the bathroom and powdered her face to cover the tear stain the news had brought. Later in the evening, they held tightly to each other through the slow dances and she contently slipped back into the comfort of being the girlfriend of the most popular boy of the school. For the moment she could pretend that all was normal and the future still held the same promise as before.

As the dance came to an end, the boys made plans for conquest and the girls prettied themselves for their upcoming expressions of true love. Jesse waited for Karla by the trophy case and looked at the greats that had come before him. He knew that at some point soon his picture would be there also. Karla came up behind him and put her hand in his back pocket, lovingly looking up at him. He smiled and they walked out into the misty evening toward his '74 Mustang that he had cherried out with mag wheels, wide tires, and a fast motor. She climbed in and scooted to the center as he sat behind the wheel, turned the ignition, and quietly enjoyed the purr of the motor as he always did before squealing the tires and heading for the outskirts of town.

The canyon was toward Idaho City and the twists and turns of the old road had become almost second nature to him. They arrived at their regular spot and he turned off the engine and turned the radio on to the local soft rock station. It wasn't his kind of music, he was more of a Def Leppard and Loverboy fan, but she loved the ballads from Journey and Air Supply and since it was her pants he wanted to get into he put up with the slow beats that she adored.

They kissed and his hand began to slowly massage her as the windshield and windows steamed over from their heavier breathing. She gently rubbed his face as they kissed and he became bolder. He reached for the side of his seat and lowered the back and then his hand gently moved over her breast and, when she didn't protest, moved further down. Her breathing increased and he clumsily tried to unbutton her pants. She grabbed his hand and pushed it away. He tried again and she pushed his hand away again, this time more forcefully, and stopped kissing him.

"No. Jesse, not here."

"C'mon, baby, tonight was a big night for me, I want to celebrate."

"I'm not ready yet," she protested.

"Baby, I'm not going to hurt you, you know I'd never hurt you."

"I know," she murmured, knowing it was true.

"Then what's wrong?"

"I don't want to do it in a car," she replied tersely.

"Why not, this is a nice car you know."

She glared at him but saw he was only joking and began to giggle.

"Yes, it is," she finally relented. "But it is a small car and quite uncomfortable, to be honest with you."

"What if I found a more comfortable place, a place nobody would bother us?"

"I don't know, Jesse, I'm scared. I'm afraid that you'll think I'm a slut and won't want to be with me anymore."

"I wouldn't feel that way, honest. Let's go somewhere else, where you'll feel more comfortable."

"I'm not promising anything, OK?"

He grinned and nodded and felt the anticipation that maybe he would finally have all of her tonight. He started the engine and gunned it toward the highway. She rested her head on his shoulder as he drove toward town and wondered if she could really go through with it. So many things had changed this evening and she wondered if maybe this would keep him for her. They drove silently into the city and he quickly drove to the University District and pulled into the garage owned by his father where he had spent countless hours at, but never at night. He parked in the back so no one would know they were there and they walked to his father's small office in the corner of the building. The place smelled of oil and grease but the office seemed clean. He laid a blanket he had brought with him on the oil-stained carpet and the two were soon atop of each other, kissing and moving their hands about each other's bodies.

He was soft with her and her inhibitions dropped as he gently caressed her neck with his tongue. She did not notice that articles of clothing were slowly coming off the two of them and suddenly they were together as one. His excitement increased as they became entwined and all too soon the act that had started as love became hardened and animalistic and then it was finished.

He rolled off of her and immediately felt different toward her. He had long dreamed of this encounter but it had not been as he thought it would be. She sensed his disappointment and immediately felt degraded and dirty. She suddenly realized she was nothing more than what she had abhorred about her parents and it made her cringe and truly feel the nakedness of her character. She grabbed her clothes and began to dress in a frenzied manner.

"What's wrong, babe?" he asked as he watched her and he grabbed his own underwear.

"Nothing, I'm fine," she lied.

"Come on, tell me. I know there's something wrong. Didn't you like it?"

She glared at him and continued putting her clothes back on.

"Talk to me, baby."

"Guys are all alike," she snapped.

"Whoa, where'd that come from? What's up with the sudden attitude?" he demanded.

"Attitude? Is that what this is? I'm sorry, Jesse, but I thought things would be different. I thought we'd make love our first time someplace special, not a garage office...Just forget it!"

He sat up and pulled his pants back on angrily, but then he sat back and reflected as he stared at her. Maybe she was right. Maybe that was why it hadn't been what he thought it would be. He moved toward her and gently caressed her hair but she pushed his hand away and walked to the door.

"I'm sorry, Karla, honest. I really want to know what's wrong and I have a feeling it's more than just this. You're my girl and this was a big night for me but it doesn't mean anything if you're mad."

She looked at him and her eyes softened. "I'm not mad...I'm sorry...I don't mean to ruin it, I'm just scared." He walked to her and gently grabbed her chin and slowly rubbed it as he looked into her deep blue eyes which were now teary.

"What is it, Karla, why are you scared, tell me."

"It's just...well..."

"Just say it, babe."

"Alright, I'm happy for you, I really am, but I thought you were going to BSU. I'm afraid that if you go to UNLV, you'll find someone else."

"Find someone else? No way. I only have eyes for you." She wanted to believe him. Maybe she was wrong and it would be fine but the familiar doubts crept back into her mind.

"We'll be apart and you'll lose interest, I know you will." The tears finally won the battle and began to trickle out of her blue eyes. "I love you, Jesse, I don't want to lose you."

He smiled and lightly kissed her on the lips and then with his thumbs gently dried the tears that were now rolling down her cheeks. He looked into her eyes and felt full of love for her. She was so vulnerable, no longer the strong, confident girl that didn't seem afraid of anything.

"Baby, listen to me," he said quietly. "I love you too. I'm crazy about you, but UNLV offers more opportunities. NFL scouts are always there. They run a passing offense which the scouts love. Randall Cunningham is their current quarterback and he's supposed to be a high pick in the draft. I could be him...don't you see? If I'm in the NFL, we're set for life. I'd be doing this for us baby because I love you."

She stared at him and her tears finally stopped as her lips turned into a smile. He had said it, he had really said it. "You've never told me you love me before," she said as she ran her fingers through his hair.

"I do, more than you know," he replied.

"Do you promise?"

He gently kissed her again.

"Do you promise?"

"I do," he replied as they slowly lay back on the blanket.

*

The weekend had brought momentous change and though she did her best to pretend that nothing was different as she went to school on Monday, she knew everything was. After school, she kissed Jesse goodbye as he went to football practice and she wandered aimlessly to the cafeteria for cheerleading practice. At practice, she had seemed preoccupied with her friends and had struggled through the practice. Afterward, she sat against the wall next to her friend Deena Jacobson.

"You're not yourself today? Is it because Jesse's going to UNLV?"

"Kind of, but it's more than that."

"Oh, do tell."

"It's not really something I can talk about, Deena."

"Come on, Karla, we're best friends. Of course, you can tell me."

"Not really…"

"Karla, you have to tell someone. Something is really bothering you. You know I won't tell anyone and the curiosity is killing me. Now speak sister."

Karla looked at Deena seriously and then her friend made a face, lightening the mood. Karla giggled and Deena scooted closer to her friend.

"Jesse and I made love on Friday for the first time."

Deena exhaled slowly and wrapped her arms around Karla's elbow as they rested their heads against each other.

"You did?"

"Yes."

"What was it like? Did it hurt? I bet it was romantic."

Karla laughed sadly as she thought back to the experience and Deena tightened her grip on the elbow. "It was at his dad's garage. He seemed happy." They sat quietly for a moment as Karla felt tears welling up. "I guess that's all that matters," she added forlornly.

"You don't make it sound so good," Deena said as she dabbed at Karla's eyes with her shirtsleeve.

"I always thought it would be different…beautiful. Afterward, I felt dirty, like all of sudden I was a slut, someone easy."

"Why would you feel that way? You and Jesse have dated for almost seven months now."

"I know…" She looked at Deena and smiled but it was pained. "He said he loved me."

"Before or after?" asked Deena.

"After, so I think he means it," giggled Karla, but the anxiety quickly returned. "Deena, I'm scared."

"Scared of what?"

"I know he's really going to UNLV."

"That's great…isn't it?"

"Yeah, wonderful," replied Karla sarcastically, "and what do you think he'll do there?"

Deena looked at Karla quizzically. "Uh, play football?"

"And find somebody else. I don't want to lose him, Deena."

Deena grabbed Karla's hands and pulled her tight into a hug. "You're not going to lose him. He loves you, he told you that. You two were made for each other, you're right for each other. You have something that is supposed to last."

"You really think so?"

"I know so."

"I love him so much."

Karla felt a sob coming from her abdomen and though she tried to control it, it stubbornly came out. Deena pulled her tighter as she silently shook in fear of a future no longer certain.

"It'll be all right," Deena said softly. "He loves you."

Chapter 2

In the early morning darkness, Karla tossed about in her bed. The clock-radio which showed it was only 5:26 a.m. still had more than an hour before the alarm would ring, yet she was wide awake. Her stomach made a gurgling sound and the saliva in her mouth became hot and thick. She ran to the bathroom, kneeling in front of the toilet just in time for a stream of vomit to shoot out of her mouth. She felt dizzy as she slowly stood and walked to the sink. The water was cold in her cupped hands and she rinsed her mouth and splashed more on her face.

The next morning it happened again, and again two days later. This was not normal because the sickness only lasted for a short time in the morning and then she would feel fine again. The fourth time it happened she grew afraid, knowing from her health class that this was possibly a sign. She crawled back into her bed fearfully. If what she thought was causing this sickness was true, she knew her life would be altered dramatically.

After school on the fifth day since the mystery sickness had begun, she drove from Boise to Meridian and found a small supermarket that had a drug store in it. She walked in nervously and glanced around her to make sure no one was looking and headed to the pharmacy. On the shelf, she found the item she had come for. For a moment, she thought of putting it in her pocket and walking out but because of the fear of being caught, she decided against it. She slipped over to the teller that had the smallest line and handed it to her quickly so nobody would see. The teller, a woman was in her late 30s, glanced quizzically at the teenager in front of her. Karla nervously reached into her handbag and pulled out a five-dollar bill and handed it to her. The teller made a change and handed it to her as she quickly grabbed the item and stuffed it into her handbag.

"Good luck, honey," the teller said softly as Karla turned to leave, "good news, hopefully."

Karla looked back nervously and silently wondered if the woman had once been her, then quickly left. She didn't want to know but at the same time needed to have the answer. She ran into the bathroom as soon as she got home and clicked the locked on the door, pulled out the item, and quickly read the directions. It seemed easy enough so she followed it word for word and waited for what seemed like an eternity.

Two minutes later she had her answer. At first, she sat quietly on the toilet seat and read the directions again to make sure what she was seeing was correct. Slowly the enormity of it crept up on her until suddenly she understood and her body began to quiver violently as she struggled to stifle the sobs. She heard the front door open and knew her mother was home and panic began to overtake her.

"Karla?"

She couldn't answer.

"Karla, are you home?" her mother called again.

"I'm in the bathroom, Mom, I'll be out soon." She wondered if her voice was giving her away. She read the directions one more time and again it told her the awful truth. She was scared, alone. She knew if she stayed in the bathroom much longer her mother would suspect something was amiss. She flushed the toiled, wrapped the pregnancy test in toilet paper, and stuffed it back in the box and hid it in her handbag. She made sure no signs of the kit remained and then ran to her room and lay down on the bed. She had to think but was unsure if that was possible now.

*

Karla quickly glanced up and down the busy hallway. Voices and clanging lockers signaled the beginning of another day as students prepared for the first classes of the day. She slowly closed her locker and made her way to Mr. Jensen's Geography class. In class, she stared into space as he droned about landscapes of the Midwest and did not hear him call on her. A classmate nudged her to bring her out of her thoughts of doom.

"Ms. Thompson, can you please tell me the answer to number four?" he asked again. She glanced at her paper and realized that in her turmoil she had forgotten to complete the assignment. She mumbled but he quickly stopped and scolded her for coming unprepared. That was the last she heard as she again became lost in her silent fear.

The rest of the morning was much like the first period although no other teachers called upon her. As lunch neared, she stared at the clock that would not seem to move until the bell finally rang. She sprang quickly from her seat and walked as fast as she could back to her locker to put her books away and then raced to the cafeteria. Deena surprised her from behind and turned her toward her with a laughing smile until she realized that Karla was going through some kind of crisis.

"What's wrong?" she asked quietly.

"I have to talk to you, but not here."

"Let's get something to eat first…I'm starved."

"Deena, it's important," Karla whispered.

"What's wrong?" she asked, fearing the worst.

"I think I'm pregnant."

Deena stared at her in disbelief. It just wasn't possible. It couldn't be, not Karla of all people. "Oh God," she murmured. "Are you sure? How do you know?"

"I'm late and now I'm throwing up in the morning. Deena…I've never been late!"

"Maybe you're just stressed…Oh, Karla, you can't be pregnant," she said painfully.

"Yesterday I went to Meridian and bought a pregnancy test and, well, the wrong color showed up," Karla said quietly as her lower lip trembled. "Can you take me to the clinic on 53rd Street?"

"That's across town," protested Deena, "there's one closer we could go to."

"I know Deena," Karla replied irritably as she stared at her with raised eyebrows.

"Oh yeah, sorry about that, I can take you after school. I have tests in my next two classes so I can't really skip. Meet me at my locker after the last bell and we'll go."

"Deena, you can't tell anyone. Promise me you won't."

"I won't," she replied solemnly. "We'll go right after school. I promise." Deena looked at her friend who had a fearful look. "It's going to be all right," she lied as she grabbed and hugged her.

Karla nodded but she didn't believe it either.

After school, the two girls met at Deena's locker and they drove, without speaking, to the Free Clinic on 53rd Street. The office was small and sterile but it somehow felt dirty. Karla and Deena sat nervously in the waiting room, joined by women who were older and had a look that implied they were beaten down by life. Karla was finally called and she asked the receptionist if Deena could join her. The receptionist seemed as sterile as the building but she nodded toward Deena and motioned that she could join Karla.

A Physician's Assistant came in and took Karla's vitals and then drew some blood. A short time later another woman entered and gave her the news she was dreading to hear. The woman, who had graying hair and seemed to have no real personality, told her she was a counselor and gave her a business card and invited the two of them into her small office. Deena followed Karla and the two girls sat on a worn couch as the counselor coldly spoke of the limited options Karla had.

"Are you going to tell Jesse?" Deena asked as they stopped at a red light, breaking the silence that had lasted since they had left the clinic.

"I don't know," replied Karla softly as she stared out the passenger window.

"What are you going to do?"

"I don't know…God! Why?" and Karla began to wail uncontrollably.

Deena pulled into a parking lot and pulled Karla close, gently stroking her hair as she also began to cry. When their tears finally subsided, they simply held each other so that neither would be alone. Both knew Karla was about to go through a journey that only she alone could go through and Deena silently mourned the loss of their innocence.

"You could get an abortion," Deena finally said.

"I don't have the money," Karla replied hopelessly. "I don't even know if I could go through with it if I did."

"Make Jesse pay! He did this!" They sat quietly for another minute and pondered the situation. "I thought you were on the pill," Deena said quietly. Karla remained silent. "Karla?" Still, she did not answer. "Karla?!" demanded Deena. "You are, aren't you?"

"I am," Karla finally replied. "But I forgot to take it for about a week."

"Forgot…really? Karla, you didn't do this on purpose did you?"

Karla was silent and looked down. Had she? She was no longer sure. "No," she said finally. "At least I don't think so…Oh, Deena, I don't know. I'm so afraid I'll lose him if he goes to UNLV." Deena groaned. "If I'm pregnant, he can still go there and play…can't he?"

Deena slowly hit her head on the steering wheel. "Oh, Karla, what have you done?"

*

Karla walked into the living room where Hank and Corrine sat watching television. She sat between them and tried to talk, but nothing came out. Her fear grew as she sat.

"What's up, daughter?" asked her dad.

"I'm, well, um—"

"Spit it out, sweetheart," he urged.

"It's just, well—"

29

"No, you can't have the car," he said and her mother giggled.

Karla realized that she couldn't tell them, at least not right now so she stood up and started to walk out the room.

"Dear, are you sure you're all right?" asked Corrine.

Karla looked at the two of them, attempted to speak, but then just smiled nodded. "I'm fine. I'm just tired."

"Get some rest, dear," her mother said as she left the room.

Karla went up to her bedroom and lay down, staring at her at the ceiling. She tried to stifle it but tears fell from her eyes again. She climbed under the covers and buried her head in her pillow, sobbing into it until her strength was spent and slowly faded to sleep.

*

"I have a secret but you have to swear not to tell," Deena whispered to Tasha Johnson who was sitting next to her in Geometry the next morning.

"Ooh…do tell."

"You have to promise first," replied Deena.

"Not a word, I promise."

Deena made sure no one else was listening. She had the biggest news in the school and keeping it to herself was proving to be an impossible task. She had to tell someone or she was sure she would simply burst. Tasha was trustworthy. Surely, she wouldn't tell anyone.

"Karla's pregnant."

"What?" Tasha grabbed Deena's hand and her face showed the shock of the news.

"I took her to the clinic yesterday. I was there!"

"Oh my God…does Jesse know?"

"I don't think so, not yet anyway."

"What is she going to do? I can't believe this. She's really pregnant?"

"She is. I told her to get an abortion but she says she doesn't have the money."

"She can't have it, she just can't," lamented Tasha. "You're really serious?"

Deena nodded. "Please don't tell anyone else. You promised. You just can't."

"I won't," Tasha assured her, "oh, poor Karla."

Two hours later in Social Studies, Mr. Mitchell droned about the Supreme Court and how the justices decide what cases will be heard. The bell rang and he hurriedly gave the next day's assignment. In the back of the room, two sophomore girls dutifully wrote it down and grabbed their books. As they were walking down the hallway, one whispered into the other's ear.

"Did you hear about Karla Thompson?"

Karla's self-consciousness grew as the afternoon wore on. Everywhere she went she felt classmates staring at her. She was sure that she was hearing whispers as she walked by and she wondered if she were imagining this or if her nightmare was now out in the open.

The sound of the bell ended the school day and Karla hurriedly walked to Deena's locker. She leaned against it until Deena appeared. She could see Karla's serious expression and immediately regretted her conversation with Tasha earlier this morning.

"You told someone this morning, didn't you?" accused Karla, silently praying that Deena hadn't yet knowing she probably had.

Deena looked at her uncomfortably as she fumbled with the combination that would open her locker.

"I thought you promised you wouldn't tell anyone!" Karla said angrily.

"I didn't," stammered Deena, finally getting her locker open.

"Well I didn't tell anyone and now people know!"

"I swear, Karla, I didn't say anything," but Deena was unable to look at her.

"Why are you lying to me? I know you did."

She was caught and she couldn't hide her guilt. "I'm sorry, I couldn't help it," she said softly as her eyes began to tear up. Karla could only glare. "I'm sorry, I'm so sorry."

"I trusted you," Karla spat angrily. "You were my best friend."

"Karla...I...I'm so sorry," Deena whispered uncomfortably.

"I hate you," Karla said as she stormed toward the door. She walked into the cold February air and ran to her car. She stared blankly at nothing in particular as the parking lot emptied. No matter what she did know she was marked. She would forever be the Hester Prynne while at Boise High School. There would always be stares and whispers and as she thought of this awful scenario she broke down. Finally, she composed herself and walked slowly toward her house. She was relieved to see that no one was home when she arrived and could only surmise what a mess she looked like.

In her bedroom, she grabbed the phone and dialed Jesse's number. It rang five times before she gave up and hung up the phone. Where could he be? Did he know? She had to tell him before anyone else did.

Two hours later her phone rang and she quickly answered. Jesse sensed that something was amiss. Her tone was short and he wondered what he had done to make her angry. She had seemed distant all day so he had hung out with the boys. Obviously, it must be her time of the month he thought to himself callously. Hearing her on the phone now convinced him that he was right.

"What's wrong?" he said irritably after having no luck getting a normal conversation going.

"Nothing," she replied curtly.

"Yes, there is. Just tell me," he coaxed her. "It can't be that bad."

She didn't say anything, and yes, it was that bad. It was enough to destroy them.

"The coach at UNLV called me again. He told me the Letter of Intent will be here next Wednesday."

"Great," she replied sullenly.

"You don't really sound like you mean it."

"Jesse, I just have a lot on my mind."

"Well, then tell me. Maybe I can help."

Her eyes became watery. He was a good boyfriend. He had a good heart and the news that she was carrying was going to shatter all his dreams. How could she tell him?

"C'mon, Karla, did I do something wrong? Just tell me."

"I'm, I'm…I'm just tired." On the line, she heard him exhale the way he always did when he was becoming frustrated.

"Fine," he groused. "I'll talk to you later. Frankly, you're shitty company right now."

"Jesse—"

"Forget it," he replied just before the line went dead. She slowly hung up the phone and lay back on her bed. She should have told him, she knew that. Why had she been so afraid?

She knew the answer to that also.

*

Jesse grabbed the phone from his mother. He was still breathing from shoveling the snow off of the sidewalk and driveway from the surprise three inches that had fallen earlier in the day.

"You've got a serious problem, buddy," his friend, Allen, told him.

Jesse's heart stopped and he fearfully thought of the scholarship offer, petrified that he had done something to lose it. "What are you talking about?" He quickly sat on a kitchen chair, his heart sinking.

Allen quickly informed him of the hot rumor blazing around the school like an out of control fire. Jesse sat silently, dumbfounded at the news. He was dizzy, frightened. It couldn't be true. Karla surely would have told him, wouldn't she? Maybe it was true but it wasn't his. Maybe she had cheated on him. God, if only he could be so lucky.

After the bombshell, he ran to his room and paced. He collapsed on his bed, praying that this news simply wasn't true. They had only done it a couple of times and he was sure he had pulled out in time. Besides, she was on the pill. There was no way she could be pregnant he reasoned to himself. He decided he would call her and find out once and for all. But it couldn't be true; otherwise, she would have told him.

"Are you pregnant?" he demanded as she came on the line.

"Yes," she replied meekly as she broke down in tears. They were silent except Karla's sniffling as she fought to control herself so that her parents would not come into her room.

"Oh God," he moaned as the enormity hit him and his tears began to fall. "Do you know what this means? I thought you were on the pill." She could only whimper in the agony of the dilemma. "Karla, I could lose everything! Everything I've spent my whole life working for."

"What about me?" she finally managed to croak out through her sobs. "Do you think I wanted this to happen?"

"This isn't about you!" he exploded. "You don't have a scholarship out there waiting for you. I'm supposed to sign the letter of intent next week."

"This is about us," she replied defiantly. "This affects me just as much as you!"

"You're just a girl," he replied angrily. "I've worked my whole life so I could get that scholarship. God, I'm ruined. Don't you understand? You've ruined me!"

Maybe he was right. Maybe she had. Maybe she had skipped taking the pill so that she would get pregnant and he wouldn't be able to go to UNLV. "I'm so sorry," she replied meekly.

"Sorry? Shit Karla, sorry?" his voice thundered through the receiver. "I gotta go, I need to think…I'll talk to you later."

"I love you," she said anxiously, hoping it would fix everything. But in truth, she was now convinced that it was all her fault.

He didn't care. He took the phone away from his ear, looked at it for a moment incredulously, and slammed it down. His mind was spinning, his world suddenly so out of control. He had to think, there had to be a way to save the scholarship.

He began pacing again, unsure of what he could do. He felt like a trapped animal with no way to get away from the dangers that were coming his way. He was terrified, more afraid than he could ever remember being and he couldn't stop the tears that continued to fall from his burning eyes. He sat on his bed and stared at the floor. His future was slipping away and he was powerless to stop it.

The phone rang and he quickly grabbed it. "It's true," Jesse said quietly to Allen.

"I was afraid of that," his friend answered sadly.

"What am I going to do?" Jess asked in desperation.

"I don't know," Allen replied. "Will she get an abortion?"

"I don't know, I didn't ask."

"Shit, well ask then dumbass."

"I will," Jesse said as a slight sense of hope returned. They remained silent for a minute, each in their own thoughts. One sat in fear while the other was thankful he was not facing the repercussions of the other.

"You need to talk to coach," Allen finally said, breaking the silence.

"I don't want him to know," said Jesse. "I don't want anyone to know."

"He's going to know, it's only a matter of time. Hell, Jesse, everyone else knows…he may know already anyway."

"Maybe," he murmured.

"No maybes, Jesse, you need to talk to him or you can kiss your scholarship goodbye."

"What do you think he'll say?" asked Jesse.

"I don't think he'll be happy," replied Allen, "but if anyone can help you it's him."

"You're probably right," agreed Jesse.

"Call him, now."

"OK," Jesse said quietly. He would talk to his coach but it would have to wait until tomorrow. He hung up the phone and crawled under the covers of his bed. Slowly he faded off to sleep, but the rest would not a fitful one.

*

Jesse walked into Mr. Taylor's classroom who taught Biology and Earth Science. He was better known as the enthusiastic football coach who had led the Braves out of numerous losing seasons. This year's team had won the Southern Idaho Conference title and earned a berth in the state championship game. Mr. Taylor was short and squat with powerful shoulders and legs the size of tree trunks. He had a full beard and he wore his blonde hair just past his collar. Popular with the students, he was known to be a fairly easy grader and he loved to flirt with the girls and joke with the guys. Everyone knew that Mr.

Taylor was here for football and that he harbored hopes of moving up into the college ranks at some point, preferably soon.

"You don't have many good choices, son," Coach Taylor told Jesse after listening gravely to the news.

"I know," Jesse replied with eyes downcast.

"I can't tell you what to do, I can only tell you what will probably happen."

"OK," replied Jesse nervously.

"If you stay with the girl and have the baby, you're going to lose your scholarship. I wish I could tell you something different, but that is what will happen."

"But don't they have married housing?" asked Jesse hopefully.

"Jesse, she's a junior in high school. Unless she's going to school there, they'll never pay for you, her and a baby. It's just not going to happen, son."

"So, what do I do?" asked Jesse desperately.

"You should have kept your damn peter in your pants, boy," he replied sternly. "I told you, there aren't a lot of good choices available to you."

"What if I went to Boise State?"

"You'd have to be a walk-on, son. Everybody only has so many scholarships available. You have made it clear that you are going to UNLV so BSU has moved on. There's nothing available right now. You put all your eggs into the UNLV basket."

Jesse was silent. It was slipping away and all he could do was stare blankly at the chalkboard behind Mr. Taylor.

"What if she gets an abortion?"

"I can't tell you what to do, but that would probably solve your problem, wouldn't it?"

Jesse nodded as he glanced toward his coach, averting eye contact.

"Thanks, coach," he said as he slowly stood up.

"Good luck, son," replied Mr. Taylor as he went back to the paper he was grading.

Jesse slowly walked down the hallway to his locker. He had to find Karla, talk some sense into her. Surely, she would understand that they were both too young to have a child. The abortion thing was the thing to do and somehow, he had to convince her of this. His future depended on it.

After school, he rushed to Karla's locker. He hadn't talked to her all day and when he arrived, she gave him a look with cold eyes.

"I have to talk to you," he said. "It's important."

She put her books in her locker and reluctantly followed him to his car. "I talked to coach today," he stated matter-of-factly after they had settled in.

"Why did you do that?" she demanded. She looked hurt and angry and he wondered why she was being like this.

"I needed to find out if I could keep my scholarship. He told me that if we have the baby there's no way UNLV will give it to me. But he said that if you got an abortion everything would be fine."

"That's easy for him to say. Look, Jesse, this is about more than a stupid scholarship. This is something real that is inside of me. I don't want to get an abortion, and even if I did, I don't have the money to do it."

"It wouldn't cost anything at the Free Clinic," he protested, growing hot under the collar.

"It would cost at least $200 there, more if I went to a regular doctor. Are you really that naive?" she scolded.

"Maybe we could go in together and pay for it. Karla, we don't need this in our life right now and you know it."

"No, you don't need it in your life. You don't care about mine at all. This is all about you. I'm the one going through this. It's me everyone is staring at, me that they are whispering about. No matter where I go, people stop talking and look away from me until I leave. Your friends act like I've done something horribly wrong. I got pregnant, Jesse. I got pregnant from you. You did this to me so quit telling me how this is affecting your life."

"Karla, please. I know it affects you and I'm sorry if I seem selfish. But there is a way out of this and that is through abortion. I'll be there for you, I promise. I'll get the money somehow. Once we get this behind us everything will be normal again."

"Don't you understand, Jesse? Nothing is ever going to be normal again! I'm sorry, but I can't kill what I have inside of me. I can't do an abortion; I won't do it."

"Think about it, will you, Karla, please?"

"Maybe you should, maybe you should stop thinking like a boy and start thinking like a father. Whether you like it or not you're going to be one. You need to start acting like it."

"Karla…" but she didn't hear him as she climbed out of the car and into the cool air.

Jesse watched her walk away as another bout of panic overtook him. She walked away with tears that she was quickly growing tired of falling down her cheeks. Though abortion would be the easy way out, it wasn't right and that would mean that she would now be ostracized. Jesse didn't care about her and she felt used and betrayed by the boy that she had once dreamed of making a glorious life with.

That evening Karla gathered her parents around the kitchen table and broke the news to them. They reacted as she thought they would but after going through the past few days it was a relief to get it out. Hank harangued her about being careless as Corrine cried in anguish that her baby was now having a baby. Karla numbly waited for it to end and quietly went to her room as the storm began to subside.

Her father remained furious, trying to figure out a way to handle this horrible scandal that the damn jock had brought to his household. He grabbed the phone and dialed the Rayburn phone number. As Jesse's dad answered, he roared his venom to his counterpart on the other end of the line.

"You're all-American son just got my daughter pregnant. She's ruined and I'm going to ruin you and your family."

"What? Who is this? What is this about," George replied, confused by what he was hearing.

"My daughter's life is ruined because of your stupid, fucking son!" roared Hank and then he slammed the phone down.

"Jesse, get your ass down here," bellowed George as he hung up the phone.

"What is it?" Laura asked, alarmed.

"That was Hank Thompson. He says Jesse got Karla pregnant."

"Oh my God," Laura said as she cupped her mouth with both hands.

Jesse walked into the kitchen and George demanded to know if it was true. Jesse tentatively admitted it was so. Both George and Laura began alternately yelling and crying as Jesse cowered in the corner. He finally escaped into his room and wondered frantically how everything had gotten so out of control.

"You need to marry her," he heard his father's voice say about an hour after the riot in the kitchen. "You need to do what's right."

"But I'll lose everything," Jesse protested.

"You're probably right," George replied sadly and he sat beside Jesse on the bed and put his arm around his son. "But that doesn't change the fact that you have new responsibilities now. You need to marry her and make an honest woman of her."

"But, Dad—" Jesse said desperately as his eyes teared up.

"I didn't raise you to run out on responsibility," George replied resolutely. "You know I'm right. This is what you have to do." Jesse began to sob and George pulled him closer. Outside, Laura slid down the wall and began to cry silently. She was helpless to help her baby and soon he would be on his own.

Jesse stood nervously at the front door of the house that had become so familiar to him but this time he was afraid to knock. It had been two hours since his dad had spoken to him and he had been here at Karla's front door for at least ten minutes. Summoning all the courage he could muster he finally managed to ring the doorbell. He thought of running but there was nowhere to go. He heard heavy footsteps coming toward the door and his heart pounded as his breathing constricted. The door opened and standing in front of him was Hank with a look of hatred.

"Get off my property or I'll kill you," he said menacingly.

"Please, sir, I have to talk to Karla."

"You've done enough. Get out of here or I'll kill you—"

"But, sir—"

"Dad," Karla said sharply behind him.

"Go back to your room, Karla," George demanded though his eyes remained fixed on Jesse.

"No, dad."

"Please, sir," pleaded Jesse. "I won't be long."

George looked at him with hatred but finally moved aside to allow the sullen boy to pass through. Jesse averted the eyes that were boring through him and followed Karla upstairs to her room.

"Look, Karla," Jesse finally said, breaking the awkward silence between them. "If you want the baby, I'm not going to have you go through this alone."

"What about your precious scholarship?" she asked coldly.

"I'll probably lose it, but I don't care," he replied unconvincingly.

"Really?" she asked, wanting desperately to believe him.

"I love you," he said quietly. "I want to marry you."

"Marry me?"

"Yes, the baby's mine too you know," he replied with a sad smile.

"We're too young," she said as she looked toward the window and into the darkness of the evening.

"No, we're not, we're old enough to have a baby, aren't we? We'll figure it out."

"Really?" she asked softly.

"Yes, our baby needs both a mom and a dad. So, marry me, Karla, just say yes."

"I love you, Jesse," she said as she put her arms around his neck.

"I love you too," he replied, wishing desperately that his heart felt the same as the words his mouth had just uttered. But they didn't. He didn't love her. The truth was he abhorred her at this moment.

*

After school, Jesse called Scott Tyler, the recruiter from UNLV, who listened sympathetically but at the same time grabbed his list of quarterbacks that he had been recruiting. Scott told the anxious recruit that UNLV still wanted him and that they would probably still offer him a scholarship but then made it clear that there would be no additional money for a wife and child.

Jesse began to protest but Scott stopped him. "Jesse, you have to understand that our interest is in you only. To be honest with you this is very concerning because if you have a wife and child, on top of your coursework and the time you will have to put into football…well, son, it may be too much. In fact, the more I think about it the more I think it might be better if we go separate ways, Jesse," Scott said without emotion. "I'll let the coaching staff know that you are no longer an option for us."

As Jesse pleaded for him to reconsider, the recruiter wished him luck and then hung up the phone. Jesse felt dizzy. He called Mr. Tyler back but there was no answer. He thought of calling Karla and ending their relationship but instead, he sat, unable to move or think and the realization that it was over began to settle in. It was gone and there was nothing he could do to change it. He knew of only one person who might be able to help him and he called Coach Taylor.

"I told you this would probably happen," the coach said on hearing the news.

"There's got to be something you can do…Please, coach, I'm begging you."

"Jesse, college is a different animal. Livelihoods are on the line each and every game. You are a wildcard at best right now; nobody's going to want to touch you. You could be the reason somebody loses a job just because your wife is mad at you or your kid gets sick and your head isn't in the game like it should be."

"Coach, you've seen what I can do. I can help someone. Surely you know someone who is willing to take a chance on me. Please coach…"

"Look," the coach finally said. "No promises. I'll make some calls for you but I don't want you to get your hopes up. You're a good kid, but frankly, you fucked it up pretty bad, son."

"I know, coach, I know. Please help me, please…"

"I'll try, but I'm not optimistic."

Jesse hated Karla right now. Hated her more than anyone he had ever known.

*

She felt as though she had nowhere left to turn. Her parents talked about her getting an abortion and the more they spoke of it the more determined she became not to. Her supposed fiancé barely spoke to her since there was no football scholarship and she was sure that at some point soon he would be backing out of the marriage. Her friends had deserted her now that there was a bump in her stomach and the pregnancy was real. It was as if the pregnancy was a horrible, viral disease and she needed to be quarantined away from them.

The school was awful and getting worse. The stares were no longer hidden, the whispers no longer quiet. She was a pariah and alone among the hundreds that walked the halls every day. She slowly began to realize that the only answer was to drop out of school. Maybe once the baby was born, she would be able to go back but that probably would not happen either. On the day she went to the office and filled out the papers ending her enrollment she tried to be brave but it was only a façade that everyone could see through. As she walked through the front doors, she knew that her self-imposed exile was going to be permanent.

Home was no better. Her parents now shunned her and the house that had once been full of life and laughter was now eerily quiet. Mother and Father rarely spoke to her or each other for that matter. Each blamed the other for the pregnancy and her for the scandal they were now enmeshed in.

She was no longer wanted by anyone.

Chapter 3

The remainder of the school year was void of the joy and glory that Jesse imagined his senior year would be. Instead of looking forward to college and football, graduation meant the death of dreams that once had been in his grasp. When the big day arrived, Jesse marched to the pomp and circumstance befitting such an occasion but he hurt as the principal proudly pointed out the many scholarships that this graduating class had earned, but the name of the recipients was void of the one who had come so close. As the valedictorian stood in front of her class and spoke of the wonderful days of high school and bright futures that lay ahead, he felt the hopelessness of what was never to be.

With summer's arrival, Jesse spent most of his time in the private prison of his bedroom. He had no desire to be with friends for all they would talk about was the excitement of the coming year as they embarked on the new path their lives would be taking them. He sat in his room and waited for the inevitable that was quickly coming up. Soon, he would be married, and not long after that, he would be a father.

As June came to an end, he and Karla went to the Ada County Courthouse to make their union official. Waiting for them at the door were Allen and Deena. Deena had begged for Karla's forgiveness, realizing quickly the destruction she had caused by telling just one person the secret that Karla had confided to her. Since then Deena had become the only person that Karla could truly count on. Never again did she divulge the pain that Karla shared with her and their friendship had become tighter than it had when times were simpler.

They walked into the old brick and brimstone building and made their way to the office of the honorable Walter B. Hadley, Justice of the Peace. His office smelled of the years of the building and they anxiously waited as his secretary informed him that his 3:00 appointment had arrived. Jesse felt some relief with the arrival of his mom and dad. Judge Hadley walked out of his office and greeted them warmly but saw the large bump in Karla's midsection and he silently pictured a marriage that would end soon after it had begun. Still, his job was not to provide counseling, only to make their union official in the eyes of the State of Idaho. He quickly went through the proceedings and at 3:35 pm Jesse and Karla became man and wife.

Outside the courthouse, the six of them put on a brave front. Instead of excited chatter, there was the only awkward silence, no one really knowing what to say. After a few minutes of small banter, George and Laura gave the newlyweds a quick hug and then left them alone with Allen and Deena.

"I can't believe you two are really married now," Allen said to Jesse as they ate a banana split at the local Dairy Queen that served as the reception.

"Well, you were a witness," Jesse said as he laughed sadly.

"What are you going to do now?"

Jesse looked at Karla and she glanced toward him and smiled, but her eyes were void of joy. "I'll work with my dad," he finally said. "He's giving me a job at the garage."

"No football?"

"No offers. The coach was right. Once it was evident I would be marrying Karla the schools couldn't run away fast enough."

"Wow," Allen said. "I feel bad for you."

"It'll be fine," Jesse said optimistically. "I got a kid coming and that's going to be better than playing football." But Allen knew Jesse was only trying to convince himself.

"I just can't imagine what you're—"

"Shut up, Allen, OK? Everything will work out."

They sat silently, fiddling at their food but not really having any appetite.

"Come on you two," Karla finally said as she looked at Allen and Deena. "We're happy. It'll be fine. We got married, we didn't die."

They chuckled but gloom continued to hang over them. After finishing the desserts Deena and Allen went their separate ways and the newlyweds drove quietly to Jesse's house. Jesse noticed the house seemed smaller now that Karla was living here too.

"I'm sorry your parents didn't show up," Laura said to Karla as they cleaned the evening dishes.

"It wasn't unexpected, Mrs. Rayburn," Karla replied.

Laura smiled. "Karla, I'm your mother-in-law now, please call me Laura, not Mrs. Rayburn." Karla and Laura laughed and hugged each other. They had become close in the past month. Laura had been there for her because of the remorse she felt for her son being responsible for doing this to her. Karla's parents had made life unbearable at home and she had spent the past month spending as much time as possible with the Rayburn's.

Early the next morning instead of heading to the exotic honeymoon they had dreamed about in better days, Jesse was in his car driving to the University

District to his dad's garage. He quickly settled into the routine at the garage but as the summer wore on, he realized that this was probably not going to work.

*

August brought another football season again Jesse's resentment toward his new wife grew. Karla continued to grow in girth and Jesse found her uncomfortable to be around. She was moody and bloated and he began to find things to do so he wouldn't be forced to be around her.

Friday became Jesse's night for himself. He simply quit coming home in the evening after work and would instead drive to the high school to watch BHS play and recount his glory to anyone who would hang around to listen. After the game, it was to a sports pub by Boise State and a few drinks and more stories. There was always someone drunk that would agree to buy him a few if he recounted his greatest moments.

On the last Friday of September, Jesse came home from the pub and saw that the family car was gone. He saw a note on the door telling him to get to the hospital. He was tired and thought about going to bed instead but realized that it wouldn't be worth the bitching and moaning he would hear. As he drove to the hospital, he thought of a thousand other places he would rather be.

"Where were you?" his mother cried as Jesse walked into the waiting room of the obstetrics section of the hospital.

"I went to the game," Jesse snapped.

"You're not a kid anymore. We had to give Karla a ride here," his dad snapped in exasperation. "The damn game ended at 9:30. Where have been for the past two hours?"

"I got a beer," retorted Jesse, no longer caring what anybody thought about him. "Come on, I'm here now, aren't I? Are we going to argue all night?"

"It's just time for you to grow up," his mother said softly. "Now go in there and be with your wife."

"What? Go in there?" Jesse exclaimed.

"Damn it, Jesse, what did you think the birthing classes were for?" demanded his father.

"I didn't go, they were stupid…"

"You're being stupid and disrespectful. I won't have it," replied his father as he angrily moved toward him.

"Both of you stop it," Laura demanded as she stepped in between the two men. "Jesse, you need to go in there and be with your wife."

Just then the doctor came out of the birthing room. He was smiling but it quickly disappeared when he saw the tension.

"Is this the father?" he asked.

"Yes sir," Jesse replied tentatively.

"Would you like to see your new daughter?"

Jesse froze. Even when Karla was pregnant it had never seemed real. Now the child had arrived and he didn't know what to do or say. He was a father now and he was afraid.

"Come with me," the doctor urged. "If you are the father, you need to be in there."

Jesse followed him through the door and nervously put on the scrubs and entered the birthing room. He stared from the door and saw Karla was holding the child against her chest. He was afraid because it was real and he was not ready. Karla looked peaceful as she smiled toward Jesse. He tried to smile back but could only nod. Karla called for him and he walked in with slow, unsteady steps toward her and the child.

The nurse carefully took the bundle from the mother and placed it gently in Jesse's arms. She was bald and her skin pinkish. She was sleeping and her face made a scrunched look. He noticed the head was oblong and silently wondered if this were some sort of birth defect.

"Isn't she beautiful?" Karla asked. Jesse looked up, unable to speak. Karla again smiled joyfully and put out her hand for him to come closer.

"Have you thought of a name?" asked the nurse.

Jesse glanced toward Karla. "We've picked Rebecca," Karla answered. "Rebecca Laura Rayburn." Jesse looked at Karla and again attempted to smile, but his face remained passive. Karla smiled again. "Do you like the name?" Jesse nodded. "I love you," she said.

He tried to answer, but he was void of words. He looked again at the child in his arms, trying to muster up feelings of joy but remained empty instead. He realized they meant nothing to him and it bothered him that it did not bother him.

*

Jesse walked into his father's office at the garage wondering what he had done this time. George sat at the dusty desk with grease-stained papers and took off his reading glasses and rubbed his temples. The place was closed for the day and only Jesse and his dad remained.

"You're a damn disappointment," his father finally said, his voice slowly rising.

"Oh God," Jesse replied irritably, "Again?"

"You're never home. Rebecca's your daughter, you're a dad now," he said as he glared. "You don't help around the house. You spend no time with your wife and daughter and quite frankly you're not worth a damn here." Jesse paced around the small office, the same he realized that had sent him into his own private hell.

"What's your problem, old man? You're always on my ass. I'm sorry I'm such a huge disappointment."

"Oh, stop the woe is me, Jesse," George bellowed. "It's time to grow up, accept your responsibility as a husband and father."

"What makes you think I don't, just because I don't do it like you? Times are different, Dad."

"You can do the little things. Be home at night, get to work on time, be respectful. Damn it, Jesse, just stop fighting everything. You'll find things to be a lot simpler."

"Jesus Dad, I'm doing the best I can—"

"No, you're not, and quit using the Lord's name in vain for Christ's sake. Damn it…Do you see what you're doing to me? You refuse to take any responsibility for anything. It's always blamed, blame, blame—"

"Maybe I'm just tired of being ragged on all the time by you!" Jesse roared back. "I did what you told me to do…'Marry her, son, be responsible,' remember that? Well, I did that. I gave up everything to be the responsible one, old man, but it's never good enough for you. You bitch at me, Mom bitches at me, Karla… I'm sick of it."

George could only look at his son incredulously. "You are so self-centered," he finally said sadly. "It's all about you. Do you think your mom and I planned for another family to move into the house when you graduated? We thought that you'd go to college, be the star football player and have a wonderful life. Well, life doesn't always work the way we think it's going to and you move on, make the best of it."

"Whatever."

"Your attitude, it's just shitty all the time. It never ends. I keep thinking you're going to snap out of it but instead it continually gets worse. I don't understand it. You weren't raised that way."

"Fuck you!" Jesse exploded, his face turning red in rage. "I've had it. Karla and I don't need you and you can have your precious house back!"

"Don't talk to me like that or you'll be working for someone else!" George threatened.

"Maybe they'll treat me like a man instead of a kid. I don't need this," Jesse thundered as he ripped the garage shirt off.

"Careful, son!" warned George.

"Fuck you I said! I quit. We'll be out of the house by tomorrow, old man," Jesse hissed as he stomped toward the door. "You can kiss my ass." George watched his son run from the garage and jump into his car. Smoke rose as the tires squealed and he sped out of the lot and toward town. George sadly shook his head as the car disappeared into the distance.

The next day Jesse found a cheap trailer for rent and quickly moved Karla and Rebecca and their meager belongings. The trailer was old and small. It smelled like old dust and had cobwebs in the corners. The counters and carpets were stained and the one-bedroom barely fit their bed so Rebecca's small crib set in the living room.

Karla lasted one week before she took matters into her own hands. She found information at the Health and Welfare Office on subsidized housing and met with a representative of Housing and Urban Development. Two days later the family moved into a small but clean apartment on the east side of town.

Jesse's hunt for a new job wasn't proving fruitful and after two weeks he gave up. On Fridays he went to the football game and closed the bars after. BHS wasn't nearly the team they had been with Jesse leading the way and secretly he reveled in this. The more the Braves lost the bigger celebrity he became at the pub. He listened with sympathy to the locals who lamented about the fall of the team since the best quarterback in school history was no longer there.

After an evening of being bought all the beer he could drink by his growing legion of worshippers Jesse stumbled through the front door of the apartment. Grabbing one of Rebecca's Sippy cups, he drank some water to protect against a hangover and stumbled into the bedroom, collapsing onto the bed.

"Jesse, I can't do this alone," she said to him, her back against him.

"Shut up," he groused. "I'm doing the best I can. I didn't ask for this, you know."

"I didn't ask for this either. I need your help, I need you to be a dad," she said as she turned toward him and sat up.

"What you mean you didn't ask for it," he said, slurring his words. "You did this on purpose, I know you did. I should be playing at UNLV but you ruined it for me."

Karla switched on the light that sat on the small nightstand next to the bed and glared at Jesse. She had heard it over and over, the same old song and dance and she was tired of being his excuse for failure. "Why can't you be like you use to be?" she demanded.

"Everything's gone," he yelled back at her and the baby began to wail from the angry sounds emanating from the bedroom. "Ah shit…I don't need this.

I'm going." Jesse jumped out of bed and pulled on his pants as Karla went to the crib and gently lifted the crying child, rocking her back and forth to calm her.

"Jesse, please don't go…we need to talk about this," Karla begged as he opened the front door. He looked back at her and shook his head in disgust and then walked out. Karla hugged Rebecca tightly and rocked back and forth until the child was asleep again. She couldn't sleep and she watched the clock as the time changed intermittently. He wasn't worth her tears anymore. That was why she was so angry when they began to fall slowly out of her eyes.

*

Jesse was quickly running out of money and there were no jobs that interested him when he did take the time to look. Rent was due in the next couple of days and he didn't have enough. He realized his only choice was to go back to the old man. He dreaded seeing him again and thought of turning around as he headed to the University District toward the garage. In front of him, he saw Bronco Stadium and decided to pull into the parking lot to build up his courage. He climbed the steps of the stadium and found a seat in the upper section of the northwest corner as the team went through drills on the turf below.

As he watched the players perform below, he finally felt relief from the tension that was gnawing at him. He noticed how much bigger and faster they were than those he had played against in high school. The quarterback wasn't very accurate with his passes and he realized that if he had walked on, he may have been able to start as a freshman. Again, and again, the quarterback overthrew receivers causing the coach below to vent his anger toward the player and Jesse smirked. He could have played at this level…no, he could have starred at this level. But slowly reality set back in and he realized it was gone forever and he reluctantly walked down the stadium steps and back into his life.

The Mustang pulled into his dad's parking lot. Slowly he walked into the garage. George intently worked on an engine block and glanced at Jesse out of the corner of his eye. Neither spoke until George gave some quick instructions to the kid who had replaced him and then he slowly walked into his office, his son silently following behind.

"Dad, I need help," Jesse said as he entered the office. "Can I come back?"

George sat behind the desk with the clutter and oil-stained papers on top of it and looked at his son. The boy was a man now, he thought, but he continued to act like a foul-mouthed, petulant child. "Little tougher than you thought huh?" the old man replied.

"We're getting by," Jesse lied. "I just need a little help until we get on our feet."

"Word on the grapevine is that your wife did all the work to get you a decent place to live. You found a piece of the shit trailer I heard. You sat on your ass and she went out and found a nice subsidized apartment, at least that's the word," George leaned back in his chair and stared into his son's downcast eyes. "I can't help you, son. It won't work because you refuse to learn. We tried, but it didn't work out."

Jesse wanted to choke his father, throw him to the ground, and beat him senseless, but he couldn't because in truth the old man scared him and both knew it. "God, can't you help me?" he said, finally looking at the older man. "I'm begging you, that's what you want, isn't it? You know how hard this is for me."

"You haven't changed. I'm not bringing you back. I'll float you a loan though, get you through the month so you can get on your feet. How much do you need?" Jesse glared at his father. He didn't want the old man's money, but he didn't have any of his own either. "Here's $200. That should get you through," said George as he put the money in his son's hand. "Clean yourself up and make an effort, son. You've got a family now, time to grow up." George walked out of the office and back toward the engine block he had been working on with the new kid.

In the office, Jesse seethed. "You can shove it up to your ass, old man!" he shouted after him. "I'll make it, I'll show you!" Jesse looked at the money in his hand. The two one-hundred-dollar bills went into his pocket and he stormed out of the garage. He would show the old man…right after he got a beer.

*

Jesse hated working out in the cold, but at least it was a job. The house being built was nearly complete and soon the carpets would be laid, windows put in and ceilings plastered. Jesse laid the wire down where the sidewalk would be. The concrete truck would be arriving soon and he was behind. In the distance, the truck turned the corner and began lumbering up the road toward the house that was being built.

"You got the wire laid yet?" yelled the foreman to Jesse. "Truck's coming."

Jesse laid the last couple of feet and stamped it down underneath the boards and gave a thumb's up to the foreman just as the truck arrived. He helped with the concrete work, using a shovel to spread the mud and as he did, he felt the muscles in his arms, chest, and shoulder begin to strain. His once chiseled body was becoming fat and out of shape but he pressed on, not wanting to be ribbed by the veterans who kept calling him 'superstar.' As the truck pulled away, Jesse furiously shoveled the mud while other workers used trowels to smooth the cement. At the end of the day, Jesse slumped against one of the walls of the house and drank water out of the canister he had brought. He was sweaty and now that he wasn't working, he felt the crispness of the December day.

"Need to talk to you," the foreman said, standing over Jesse.

"Yes, sir?"

"Gotta let you go, kid."

"Did I do something wrong?" Jesse asked, surprised.

"Nah, the building's about done and I only need a skeleton crew to finish. You're the bottom man on the totem pole. Won't be much else to do until spring but you can come back then, we'll probably have something for you. You're not a bad worker…a little slow, but getting better."

Jesse nodded and slowly stood up as the foreman went back to the architecture plans. Jesse walked dejectedly toward his car, started the engine, and headed to the closest bar. He was out of work again and wasn't in the mood to deal with Karla or the child. Tonight, he would find solace in the mug. Who knows, he thought to himself, maybe I'll get lucky tonight.

Two weeks later Jesse stopped by Ron's Car Care Center, his dad's chief competitor. Within the hour he was wearing coveralls that had Ron's logo on the chest and was among the working again. It didn't take him long to realize that Ron only wanted him as ammunition against his father. He was nothing more than a grunt, cleaning the garage, taking tools to the mechanics, and doing simple janitorial duties. He wanted to walk out, tell the asshole what he could do with himself but he needed the money so he kept his mouth shut. In his spare time, he looked at the want ads, hoping that something would stand out, but everything he was interested in needed more than just a high school diploma.

At home, he stewed over his latest plight. One evening, while leaning against the kitchen counter eating another concoction that Karla called dinner, Jesse finally blew. "You did this to me you bitch," he said coldly to her as he pushed his plate away. "You've cost me everything and now you want to act like everything is fine…well, it's not."

Karla's face remained impassive as she grabbed his plate. Jesse pulled it out of her hand and flung it at the wall and the remnants slowly slid down the light-yellow plaster and onto the carpet. Rebecca, startled, began to wail. Karla glared at him as she picked the child up stormed out of the room.

"Don't walk away from me you whore!" Jesse roared. "Our life sucks and it's your fault!"

"I did this, really?" cried Karla. "Why is this always my fault?"

"Because I should have had more, I don't know what I ever saw in you! You use to be beautiful but now you're just fat and lazy!"

Karla's eyes welled up and her cheeks flushed as Rebecca screamed at the chaos around her. "Just stop it, Jesse," she pleaded.

"No, truth hurts don't it bitch. I hate you and I don't need the stupid fucking kid always crying!"

"Jesse…" but she could get no more out as she began to sob at the invective words.

"Ah shit," he said. "Here we go again. I'm leaving!"

"Where are you going?"

"Somewhere where there isn't a fat, ugly crying bitch," he said as he slammed the door behind him. Karla sat in the rocking chair trying to console Rebecca. She wondered who this monster was that she had once loved. He was lost and she was no longer sure she wanted to find him.

*

The snow flurries fell on the cold January evening and Jesse sat in the sports pub with Allen, Tommy, and Jamie who were back from school for their winter break. The days were long for Jesse at the garage but the evenings made up for it as the four friends reminisced about past exploits. Eventually, the talk turned to college experiences and Jesse uncomfortably realized how much he was missing.

His friends told him how great college life was and he thought back to the day he had watched Boise State practice. The quarterback was terrible and he knew that he could come in and get playing time right away. The more he thought of it and listened to his friends the more he yearned to give it a try. As he listened to the stories from his friends made, he realized that he hated Karla and Rebecca.

Eventually, the boys began to flirt with the girls but Jesse had no luck because everyone knew he was married and had a child. Each night Jesse went home around midnight and Karla and Rebecca would be asleep. Early in the morning before they awoke, he headed to work and after he repeated the previous evening.

In early February he drove to the University and went into the admissions office. The cute counselor with the bubbly personality gave him information about the school and explained the financial aid process between their innocent flirting. That evening he surprised Karla and stayed home, studying the information he had received from the girl he couldn't get out of his mind.

"What do you have there?" Karla asked softly.

"I think I'm going to apply to BSU, walk on to the football team."

Karla breathed a sigh and began to walk away.

"What?" he asked in frustration.

"Jesse," she said slowly. "We can't. We don't have the money. We don't have any money. BSU is expensive, how are you going to pay for it?"

"I'll get financial aid," he replied irritably.

"That will pay for you, but what about Rebecca and me?"

"What about you?" he countered. "Maybe you could get a job for a change."

"And who would watch Rebecca?"

"We could take her to daycare. Drop her off with my parents…I don't know. There has to be something we can do."

"Jesse, daycare costs money. Even if I got a job it wouldn't pay for daycare. And our parents don't want anything to do with us or haven't you noticed. My parents have disowned me and you've alienated us from yours."

Jesse began to pace around the living room. He could feel himself becoming more agitated and felt trapped in a world that she would not let him escape.

"Just once why can't you be supportive?" he asked in a rising tone.

"We have a child now. She has needs—"

"It's always about her!" he screamed. "I've had it…there's just no talking to you. You just don't get, do you? I need this, don't you understand?"

"For once, just once, you need to realize that with Rebecca it's no longer about your needs or mine," she replied, her anger finally coming to the surface. "That's what being a parent is about. Do you think this is what I wanted or needed? But it doesn't matter, it's about Rebecca!"

"Ah hell, there's no talking to you," he said as he slumped down on the couch.

"Jesse, please listen—"

"I'll be back later," he said as he stood and walked toward the door.

"Fine, run out again!" she screamed at him as the door closed.

She ran to the window and watched him get into his car and rev the engine. Rebecca whimpered in the background but Karla did not move from the window. She only thought of how she wanted to run away also.

Several hours later Karla heard the Mustang pull up in the parking lot and she got up from the bed and went into the living room. It was time to stand up to him. He had been lost long enough and it was time for her to fight for their survival. She heard him walking up the stairs and fiddled with the door as he tried to put his keys into the lock. After a few moments, the door opened and he stumbled in and giggled when he saw her.

"You're drunk," she said from the darkened living room.

"So what," he replied.

"Jesse, I need you…Rebecca needs you."

"Don't start," he snapped.

"I will," she said, her courage growing. "It's time for you to grow up."

He casually walked up to her and she looked up at him defiantly. She was not going to back down from him, not this time. Suddenly, his hand slammed against her cheek and she fell back on the floor.

"Jesse!" she screamed in terror. He laughed and stood above her where she cowered. Behind him, he did not hear Rebecca crying. He bent down and slapped Karla again and then again as she tried to ward off the assault in terror.

"You've ruined everything for me, bitch! I don't need either one of you dragging me down anymore, you understand?" he said menacingly as he stared into Karla's terrified eyes.

Karla's sobs and the baby's howls from the bedroom reverberated around the small apartment. Jesse stood up and laughed. "Don't wait up for my dear," he sneered as he opened the door and went back out into the night.

Karla remained in the corner, terrified by what had just happened. He had been an ass for a long time but he had never been physical with her. He was now dangerous and she had to get help. She ran to the bedroom, grabbed some clothes, and threw them into a bag. She pulled her screaming daughter out of the crib and sprinted to her car, praying that it would have enough gas in it to start.

She turned the key and the engine sputtered but then caught. She sped toward the Rayburn's house. The car was on fumes as it pulled onto the driveway and she grabbed the bag and Rebecca and ran to the door, desperately pushing the doorbell and praying that they would answer.

George groggily answered the door and looked at the two outside who was still in tears. "Please don't close the door," Karla begged. "We need help."

Laura joined her husband at the door.

"I'm not helping Jesse anymore," George replied resolutely. "He has to grow up."

"I'm not asking you to help him; it's Rebecca and me…" Karla pleaded.

"What happened to your face?" Laura asked,

Karla couldn't contain the sobs and dropped to her knees.

"Oh God," Laura murmured as she suddenly realized what her son had done.

"Please…" the sobbing mother begged with the wailing child.

"I'm sorry, but you two need to work it out. Go home Karla," George replied as he slowly closed the door.

"Oh God, please help us," Karla screamed.

George turned off the porch light and Karla slowly stood, trying to comfort her screaming daughter. As she walked back to the car, she wondered if it would start. It surprised her that it did and she began to drive slowly. A block from the apartment the car began to cough and lurch and she turned to the edge of the road just as it cut out completely.

Chapter 4

Jesse no longer had any desire to go home and only went because it provided him a place to sleep at night. He rarely spoke to Karla and Rebecca was always in bed when he did. If the child was up in the morning, he would ignore her tentative advances toward him. He had become a stranger in his own home and he found that this suited him fine.

After work, he headed off to Jack's Lounge, his favorite hangout. It was there that he began to socialize with some guys who were sympathetic to his plight and always kind enough to buy all the beer he could drink.

Abner Davis was tall and lanky. He had brown hair in a mullet that was spiked on top around his skinny face. He was outgoing and easy to carry on a conversation with. A year older than Jesse; he had been a bench sitter for the basketball team at Capital High School. Robby Van Delear was short and skinny, very quiet with narrow piercing eyes that would nervously look around the bar searching for an unknown enemy. He was Jesse's age but had dropped out of high school at sixteen. Always joining them was Alex Montano. Alex had been a champion wrestler in high school and his body was still firm and chiseled. He was gregarious with a sharp angular face and perfect black hair. When the enviable fight broke out in the bar, Alex was involved and would be raining fists upon the poor sucker who had dared to square up with him.

Jesse enjoyed being with them and as the friendship grew, they began to talk about his money woes and the effect it was having at home. One night as Jesse complained for the umpteenth time, they stopped him. Abner told him about a new enterprise the three had entered into and the initial success they were enjoying. In fact, it was so successful they were ready to add a fourth partner. Jesse listened intently as the enterprise was described to him and it quickly became apparent to him that what they were doing wasn't legal.

"Dude, you need to come to join us," Abner told him. "I can help you make some real green."

"I'm doing all right," Jesse replied coyly.

"Sure, you are man," Alex chimed in sarcastically.

"Look, man, you need to join up with us," Abner insisted. "How much money you get from your job at Ron's?"

"I make a maybe a thousand a month," and the three looked at each other and began to chuckle.

"We're getting by…" Jesse protested, now feeling self-conscious.

"You like your job?" asked Robby quietly.

"Fuck no. Ron's an asshole. He's just using me to piss off my dad. I'm just a fuckin' gopher," Jesse replied bitterly.

"You come with us and you'll be your own boss," replied Abner.

"Look, I got a pretty good idea of what you do," replied Jesse. "It's cool, I don't have a problem with it but I'm not into that. With my luck, I'd end up in jail anyway."

"Maybe dude, maybe not. I want to show you something."

"Show me what?" asked Jesse.

"Come out to my car," replied Alex.

"All right, but I don't think I'm interested. I'm just being honest."

"That's cool dude, but just come out."

They walked out into the parking lot and went to the trunk of Alex's '69 Ford Fairlane. The car was midnight blue and had big tires and chrome wheels. The panel down the side was black and outlined with white. The interior had smooth white leather seats and the panel shimmered from the lights in the parking lot.

"Nice wheels," Jesse said quietly. "When did you get this?"

"Last month…a lot better than the old Rambler I had before. Say, is that old beater over there yours?"

"Fuck you," Jesse responded, embarrassed at how bad the Mustang looked.

"It's cool, dude," laughed Alex as he opened the trunk. "Take a look at this." He grabbed a briefcase as Robby nervously looked around to make sure no one was nearby and clicked it open.

"Holy shit, how much is there?" exclaimed Jesse looking at the neatly stacked twenty-dollar bills.

"Ten grands, dude," Abner smirked. "That's just this week's take. Two weeks ago, it was a thousand. People like the weed, dude."

"I guess so," murmured Jesse.

"How much you making a month?" asked Robby.

"Thousand maybe."

"Ten K a week is better," Alex offered, "don't you think?"

"Yeah, it is," agreed with Jesse. "Look, I'll give it some thought. I'm not saying yes, but I'm not saying no neither."

"Cool. Keep this quiet dude," smiled Abner as he handed Jesse a small folded piece of paper. "If you want to get a hold of me, I'm at this number."

"I will," replied Jesse. "I'll let you know soon."

"Cool," replied Abner. "But you only have a short window. We have to get somebody quick."

Jesse nodded and walked to his car. He had some serious thinking to do and not much time to do it. The money looked so good, and it was easy. Those guys weren't Einstein's by any stretch of the imagination, but they were loaded and they were inviting him in. The only downside was jail, but if he made enough quickly, he could get out and pursue his football dream.

The next morning, he overslept and only woke up because the damn kid starting climbing on the bed. He gruffly pushed her out of his way and she started whimpering as he went into the bathroom. Karla came into the bedroom and grabbed Rebecca and quickly left, afraid that he would hit her again, or worse, Rebecca.

He took a shower and drove to Ron's, who was waiting for him at the entrance of the garage.

"Now I understand why your old man fired you. You're just south of worthless, kid."

"Good to see you too," replied Jesse.

"I'm letting you go. You've been late to work for the last time you little piss ant. Get out of here."

"I was planning on quitting anyway. Got a better offer last night," retorted Jesse as he turned and walked back to his car.

Jesse pulled up to a phone booth at the Circle K. He put a dime in the slot and dialed the number on the crumpled paper. Abner answered on the second ring and Jesse let him know that he was in. Abner invited him over and Jesse quickly wrote the address. In ten minutes, Jesse was walking through the front door and into the makeshift office at a rundown apartment complex on the east side of town.

"Hey QB, come in," shouted Abner excitedly. "Glad you're in."

"Thanks, bud," replied Jesse as he looked around the worn room.

"You ready to start?"

"Yeah, I need money."

"Here's a signing bonus," laughed Abner as he threw Jesse an envelope with ten 100-dollar bills. "I have the perfect area for you."

"Where?" asked Jesse.

"Boise High School, dude."

"I can't," protested Jesse.

"No man, you're perfect. People know you there."

"Exactly."

"Dude, you'll make a killing."

"But—"

"You like that cash in your hand?" asked Robby coldly who had quietly walked in behind Jesse. "You're not the quarterback here. I am."

"Maybe this isn't for me," Jesse replied nervously.

"That's fine, I was against bringing you in any way," Robby said in a controlled tone.

"Come on Robby, give him a chance," replied Abner. "Our boy got himself fired today."

"Sounds like you need us, Jesse," Robby said with a steely glare. Jesse could feel the guy's eyes penetrating through him and it made the hair on the back of his neck stand up, but he was right, his options had run out. If he wanted some cash, he was going to have to push at his old school. There was no other choice.

"Fine," he replied meekly.

"Go make some sales dude," Abner replied happily. "Split is 80-20."

"Wait a minute," protested Jesse. "Little lopsided isn't it? I'm the one putting my ass on the line."

"Overhead dude," replied Abner. "We supply, you sell. That's how it works. Relax; you'll be rolling in it really quick if you make sales. Then you can get your own crew and do the same with them."

Jesse nodded. Maybe they weren't taking advantage of him after all.

"Welcome aboard, dude," smiled Abner.

Abner stood up and put his hand out and Jesse tentatively took it. When he did, Abner pulled him close and Robby came up behind and stuck a .38 against the back of his head. "Don't fuck with us on money and I'll make you rich," Abner said as his smile disappeared. "If you do fuck with us, we'll kill you."

Jesse's eyes widened with fright. He had never felt a gun against him and pins ran up and down his spine. He nodded and felt the pressure of the gun barrel recede from his head. He knew he had entered into something that probably would not end well but already there was no escape.

*

Karla looked around the bedroom and sighed. He was such a slob. Why couldn't he help out, even just a little? She picked up his pants that were lying crinkled on the floor and a small bundle with a large rubber band around it fell out of the pocket. She bent down and grabbed it. It was money, lots of it. She took the bundle into the kitchen and put it in the sugar bowl. Where had Jesse gotten this?

He walked into the apartment and collapsed on the couch, turned on the television, and ignored the child that had come up to him hoping for some attention. In the kitchen, Karla boiled some water on the stove and nervously thought of the money that was in the sugar bowl. She had to know but was afraid to ask him but finally built enough courage to confront him and grabbed the rolled-up money from the bowl.

"Where did this come from?" she asked, her tone accusatory. He ignored her. "Work?" she asked again but he continued watching the television as if she weren't there. "Jesse," she demanded one more time.

"I saved it. I'm working," he finally replied. "Why can't you just get off my back?"

"Jesse, I know you got fired from Ron's! I called there today and they told me you're no longer working there."

"Maybe I got another job," he replied in irritation.

"Where?"

"Fuck off!"

"Where's the money coming from Jesse..." she angrily asked again.

"That's not your worry."

"Jesse, I've got to know where you're getting this money."

"Jesus, fuck off you leaching bitch!" he yelled as he sprang suddenly from the couch.

"I don't want drugs in this house," she said as she quickly backed away from him.

"Where'd that come from?" he demanded.

"I'm not stupid," she replied angrily. "You don't have a job but you have all this money!" He grabbed the roll of money out of her hand and she fearfully watched him as the door slammed behind him. He jumped in his car and quickly drove toward Boise High School, cursing her as he approached his destination.

Jesse had quickly built up a strong clientele of high school students by his alma mater and the money was flowing freely. After a day of sales, he would meet with Robby and get his take for the day and then head over to an old house to wind down. The walls were peeling paint and the windows were so filthy it was impossible to see through them. It had a small overgrown yard yet the grass was yellow from lack of water and the trees were maroon and decaying. Inside were a couch and two bean-bag chairs. The two inhabitants were guys he had worked with at Ron's and they had become regular customers for him. Jesse always had a couple of beers and then the three puffed on the discolored bong that they used to get high from the marijuana that Jesse provided, free of cost.

Jesse only went home now when he needed clothes or had nowhere else to sleep. He hated going to the apartment. It was always the same old story; a fight with Karla, the crying kid and soon thereafter he would be storming out anyway.

*

Rent was quickly coming due and Karla drove through town looking for Jesse to get the money from him. She checked out his usual hangouts but he wasn't there. She drove by a couple of new lounges that she had heard about and still had no luck. Finally, she tried a pub that was about three blocks from the apartment.

She walked into the dimly lit lounge and waited for her eyes to adjust. As they did, she saw Jesse sitting at the bar next to an older woman; he was slurring his speech and his eyes were slits from the pot he had just smoked in the restroom. The woman was also stoned and had her arms around him and was gently nibbling at his ear and he turned and kissed her on the lips as her hand slid down to his crotch.

Karla froze, quietly staring at the two of them. They had no idea that she was watching them and after a few more moments she crept out the front door. Inside her car, she cried bitterly as she returned to the apartment. At home, Karla quickly sent the neighbor who was watching Rebecca home and went into the bedroom. She was at her wit's end. She pulled a suitcase out from under the bed and quickly filled it with Jesse's clothing. Once full she grabbed two garbage bags from the kitchen and stuffed the rest of his belongings into it and set it outside of the door. She then grabbed a chair from the kitchen and lodged it against the doorknob so that the lying cheater wouldn't be able to get in.

The sun was just beginning to come up when Jesse's car lurched into the parking lot. He staggered out and began to walk up the steps toward the apartment when he saw the suitcase and two bags. He stopped momentarily, a smile on his lips quickly turning into sardonic laughter. He grabbed his belongings and struggled down the steps with the load while trying to keep his balance that was affected by the drink and drugs from the previous night. He threw the clothes into the backseat and thought of breaking in and leaving a few marks on the bitch, but then realized how tired he was so he started the car and squealed the wheels as he left. The old slut from the night before would let him sleep there.

*

Corrine heard the phone ring and she hurriedly put her robe on and ran to the living room. It was 6:30 in the morning and she wondered who could be calling at this hour.

"Mom, please don't hang up," she heard Karla beg as she put the phone to her ear.

"What is it, Karla?" Corrine asked groggily.

"I kicked Jesse out." Corrine was silent, unsure of how to respond. "Oh Mom, everything is falling apart—" Karla whimpered into the phone.

"Surprise, surprise," replied Corrine without feeling.

"Please, Mom—"

"Oh, stop it, Karla," scolded Corrine. "This was your choice. Your father and I begged you not to go through with the baby and this sham of a marriage, but no, you wouldn't listen."

"Mom—"

"Now that you see what we knew you don't like the consequences. You were too young to have a child and to get married, but you did and now you have to deal with the results," she told her daughter sharply.

"Mom, I think he's selling drugs and I saw him cheating on me last night."

"Oh, Karla…You thought that everything was going to be just like a fairytale. It's not! Grow up. You're both kids and now you have a child. You have to be responsible for the decisions you made, even if they turn out to be bad."

"Please Mom—" begged Karla.

"I'm sorry, Karla, you're just going to have to handle this yourself," Corrine replied as she hung up the phone.

Karla took the phone away from her ear and wondered what to do, where to turn. She and Rebecca were alone, unwanted. She crawled under the covers of her bed, scared. She tried to think, come up with a solution, but there was nothing for her and Rebecca and she knew it.

Rebecca, as children are miraculously able to do, sensed that things were amiss. She whimpered in her room and occasionally asked when Daddy was coming home. Karla didn't know what to tell her. She didn't want to lie but the truth was that Daddy may never be home again. The whimpering grew incessant and eventually turned into crying and screaming. Only sleep could bring relief for Karla, but it was only temporary before the horrible cycle began anew. She felt helpless. She was alone, no money, nobody to turn to. Rent was coming due and if it wasn't paid, she and Rebecca would be in the streets. This terrified her and thoughts began creeping in of ending her misery. She thought of running a hot bath and cutting her wrists but she was afraid that pain would be involved. She then considered taking a bottle of pills and lying down on her bed to go to sleep, never to wake up. But she loved her daughter and the thought that Jesse would get her terrified her. She had to get help, and somehow, she had to convince her parents to provide it.

She and Rebecca drove to her parent's home. She didn't know what she was going to say or how she would convince them, she just knew she had to try. She was fearful as she pulled into the familiar driveway. It seemed to be an eternity to her as they stood and she silently prayed that the door would open. As she waited anxiously, she thought of ways to try to convince them to help them.

"What are you doing here?" her dad asked when he finally answered the door.

"We need help," Karla said with all the courage she could muster.

"I can give you some money—"

"No Dad, we need a place to stay."

"Absolutely not," he said as he began to close the door.

"Please dad," she begged as she put her foot between the door and the frame. "I can't do this alone anymore." He opened the door and looked at her, remembering her as a child and how he had always wanted to protect her, but that child was now gone and at the door was someone who had made horrible mistakes and was now learning the price of them.

"I'm sorry, Karla," he said sadly. "You chose your path and now you have to figure out a way to make it work. Your mother and I can't bail you out every time things get rough."

Karla looked desperately at her dad. "I don't have anyone else I can turn to. If you won't do it for me, at least do it for Rebecca."

"Your mother and I raised you and obviously didn't do a very good job of it," he replied. "Why would we want to do it again?" Karla couldn't believe what he was saying. They were done with her and had no interest in Rebecca. The words stung, taking her breath away. He slowly closed the door, leaving her and the child alone on the porch, locked out of their lives. She slowly walked back to her dilapidated car and gently put the child in her seat and then settled into hers. She numbly started the car and silently drove back to the apartment. Inside she collapsed on the couch and Rebecca looked at her in concern too young to know why. The trembling child climbed up on her mother and gently laid her head against her shoulder and Karla slowly stroked her fine hair. Rebecca soon fell asleep and Karla gently took her to her crib, covered the child with a blanket, and quietly closed the door.

There only remained one option. She had to bring the monster back. He was the only one who could keep them off the streets. After a number of calls, she finally located where he was staying. Her friend next door agreed to watch the sleeping child and she jumped in her car ready to do whatever it took to bring him back. She tried to convince herself that things would be different this time but she knew she was only fooling herself. She remembered how things had once been but that boy had been engulfed by the selfish monster that had no feelings for either her or Rebecca. She found the house and a greasy man with glassy eyes who reeked of pot took her to Jesse's room where he was laying on his bed and drinking a beer.

"It's time to come home," she said resolutely.

"Really?" he said incredulously. "I believe it was you that had my bags packed and sitting outside our home. What makes you think I want to come back to the two of you?"

"Maybe I was wrong," she replied quietly, hating herself for begging this bastard back. "I miss you and love you."

"So," he replied cruelly. "I don't feel the same way."

"I know you still love us," she replied with her eyes downcast.

"There you go again…you always have to bring HER into it."

"She is our daughter," replied Karla with a flash of anger.

"I'm not sure she's even mine," retorted Jesse.

"You know she is," Karla said softly. "Please Jesse. I just want to start over. I promise it will be better this time. I'll change, I promise."

"No, you won't," he said as he took the last chug of beer from the can.

"I promise I will, I just miss you. Please."

"I'm tired of all the bitching," he replied but his tone had changed and she sensed that he was softening. "If I come back you don't nag me about who I'm seeing or what I'm doing."

"I promise," she murmured.

"And don't ask me about my business," he warned. "If you do, I'm gone for good."

"I won't. I just want us to be a family again."

"I'll be home when I get home, now leave me alone," he said.

She turned and walked out of the room. She had done what she had to and she hated herself for it.

*

Sales remained brisk and Jesse knew his notoriety was increasing and his bank account growing. Things were also better at home as Karla no longer gave him any demands and kept Rebecca away from him. His only responsibility was to make sure the bills were paid. In return, Karla gave him her body whenever he wanted it and allow him to do as he pleased. She had become just another slut in his list of wenches that he used to take care of his physical needs.

With more money coming in so quickly he began to resent that Robby and the gang continued to take so much of it. It was him that was increasing sales and opening new markets to the stupid kids at the schools. He had brought in the two junior high schools that fed into BHS and had also opened up the Borah schools. If he reasoned with Abner, surely he could convince Robby and Alex to give him a bigger cut. If not, maybe it was time for him to go out on his own.

He met Abner who was nursing a beer and writing some numbers on a napkin in the back of Jack's Lounge. Jesse tried to make himself look intimidating but Abner only smirked when he saw the fool walking toward him. "I need a bigger cut," Jesse demanded as he slid into the booth.

"I don't think so," he replied coldly, the smile no longer there. "You're making pretty good green right now."

"I've made you a ton of money. You told me I'd move up and be making more. When's it happening bud? I want more."

"I don't give a shit what you want," Abner replied in a steely voice.

"Listen dude, cut me in more or maybe I strike out on my own."

"Are you trying to threaten me Mr. Superstar?"

The two stared coldly at each other but then Jesse began to crack. Abner's eyes were vacant of feeling and Jesse realized he was capable of the same things that he knew Robby would do to him.

"I just want a bigger cut," Jesse said meekly.

"You work for me and do as I say. I'm taking good care of you. I gave you a job when you had nothing and the thanks I get are you threatening me?"

"I'm not threatening you, Abner," replied Jesse, scared but still determined to make more. "If I don't get a bigger cut, I have to weigh my options though. It's just business."

Abner took out his gun and set it on the table and leaned toward Jesse. The message was unmistakable.

"There's no I in team, dude. You try to go somewhere else and accidents could happen. So, the question I guess is do you want to live or die?"

"Alright already, it's cool dude," Jesse said softly. "Why don't you just put that away?"

Abner lifted the gun and cocked it, holding it so that no one at the bar would see it except for Jesse.

"You thought I'd be soft didn't you dude. You thought that Robby was the only one who plays rough. Get your ass up and let's go to the alley motherfucker. I'll show you how soft I am."

"Come on, Abner, you're the boss. It's cool."

"You still don't seem to get it. You work for me, bitch." He said quietly as his eyes pierced through Jesse. "I own you. Remember when I told you I would kill you if you fucked with me? Well, you're fucking with me right now."

"I'm not." Jesse croaked, "I'm sorry, just calm down."

"Fuck you…I own you, now say it."

"You own me," Jesse replied fearfully.

"Damn straight, now say it again." Jesse did as he was told and Abner put the gun back in his waist.

"Don't forget that," he said menacingly. "Now get your ass back to work. If there is any change in the money coming in, I'm going to assume you're fucking with me. What do you think will happen then?"

Jesse sat silently, scared to move, afraid to talk.

"Answer me, bitch!"

"You'll kill me."

"Good, we understand each other. Now get your ass to work."

Jesse quickly got out of the booth. They were serious and he knew that he needed to get under the radar because he had made himself a target. He had known that Robby was cold-blooded but finding out that Abner was also shocked him and he realized that Alex probably is no different.

*

Jesse tried to start his car, but it wouldn't turn. It had been acting up lately and now it was dead. He had sales to make so he grabbed the weed and put it under his sweatshirt and ran to Karla's car, opened the trunk, and put it under debris that had built up. He quickly drove within a block of the high school and did not notice the blue Monte Carlo following him. He parked and waited to work some customers when suddenly four black and whites swarmed around the car followed by the Monte Carlo. Eight cops jumped out with guns drawn and demanded him to step out of the car with his hands up. Jesse saw he had no escape. He fearfully opened the door and stepped gingerly out and was immediately tackled and cuffed behind his back.

"We've been watching you for a while dumbass," the plainclothesman from the Monte Carlo told him after reading his rights. "We have a warrant to check your car."

The weed was quickly found in the trunk and Jesse was thrown into the back seat of one of the squad cars. His mind spun and he wondered how much time he faced. He had never been to jail before and the thought of going made him tremble. After being booked on possession with intent to distribute charges, Jesse called Karla and told her where he kept his stash of money. She found it and two hours later Jesse was free again. Outside of the jail, he told her not to wait up for him and she began to protest but he ignored her as he climbed into his car that she had managed to get started. She watched helplessly as he sped away. Soon he was at Jack's updating Abner and downing Tequila to settle his nerves.

Abner quickly got him a lawyer and soon Jesse was in an immaculate office with old law books adorning it discussing his case. The lawyer, William Riley, was young and hungry and saw real potential in representing drug pushers. He noticed some problems for the prosecution immediately because the police had acted like Keystone Cops and that the warrant was for Jesse's car, not Karla's.

Three days later the lawyer and Jesse stood in front of the judge. Not only had the cops served the warrant on the wrong car, but they had acted hastily and not waited for Jesse to sell, thus they had no probable cause to open the trunk which yielded the weed which made the case. The assistant district attorney protested but the case of Idaho vs. Jesse Rayburn was history. Jesse cockily walked out of the courtroom, sneering at the cops who had busted him. Outside Jesse thanked Mr. Riley and soon he was heading to Alex's apartment to celebrate the victory.

"Dude, I can't believe you're out. I thought you were toast," Alex said as Jesse walked into his uptown apartment.

"Pigs fucked up, the warrant was for my car, not Karla's. They had to drop the case."

"Gotta love the bacon," laughed Alex.

"I hear that," replied Jesse. "You got any weed?"

"Not for free."

"C'mon man, I just got out. Float me some weed. I'm good for it."

"What are you going to do now?" asked Alex. "You're marked."

"I don't think so," Jesse said as he took a puff off the marijuana cigarette. "They got bigger fish to fry. You, Abner, and Robby for instance. I'm just a bit player, you guys are the bosses." Jesse let the smoke out of his mouth slowly and settled back in the leather couch he was sitting in. "This is good, nice, and smooth."

"You tell the cops anything?" asked Alex, realizing that Jesse was probably right.

"Nah, I wasn't in there long enough. I wouldn't worry about it too much, Alex, we're not talking about very smart cops here."

"Got some cash?" asked Alex.

"A little, but I need to make some sales quick. This is really good shit," Jesse said admiringly.

"Quality dude, it's from Columbia. We're expanding."

"I'm tired dude," replied Jesse, the weight now gone from the scare. "I want to find a real bed."

"Go to your pad then," replied Alex as he took a deep hit of the new weed.

"Nah, I don't want to deal with my whores," he replied as he laid his head back against the sofa.

"Your ruthless man…Karla looks really good. Your old lady still has a nice ass, even after having a kid."

"She's got a big ass," retorted Jesse. "You want her? You gotta take the kid too."

"Damn," laughed Alex. "Go lie down dude, you're definitely stoned now."

But Jesse was already asleep.

Chapter 5

Jesse sucked on the glass pipe as he held a lighter underneath the bulb that held the plastic-like rock of cocaine. He had heard about it, but this was better than he imagined.

"I like this shit," he slurred.

"Yeah," replied Alex, "twice the high as a weed."

"Where'd you get it?" asked Jesse.

"We're selling it downtown."

Jesse glared at Alex. They were already selling the shit without him? He was instantly pissed, sure that Abner and Robby were screwing him again. "How come they haven't given me any?" he demanded.

"You're at a school, dude. Serious-time if you're caught selling rock by a school," replied Alex irritably. He was growing tired of Jesse's entitled attitude.

"You making good dough with it?"

"Damn straight," replied Alex. "They love it downtown. Suits buy it all the time and nobody goes into an uptown night club without it. Splits better too, 60-40 with our contacts and we're scoring 25% percent higher in gross according to Robby. I swear the little fucker should be an accountant."

"Are you shitting me? I'm getting fucked again. I should be selling this shit," protested Jesse.

"Why," demanded Alex. "You're doing fine, dude. Somebody's got to supply the kiddies."

"I don't want to do just OK; I want some serious cash. That's what you promised, remember?"

"Fuck Jesse, I see why Ab and Robby don't want to be around you. You're always bitching. You're lucky I'm easier going but I'm getting tired of your whining. You're still the new guy and we've already had to bail you out of jail once."

"I bailed myself out, fucker," Jesse retorted.

"You're still hot," replied Alex, "especially if they see you downtown. At least at the schools, you can keep making bank and stay out of sight."

"Fuck that," yelled Jesse. The rock was giving him the courage he didn't know he had. "I'm tired of being everybody's bitch."

"Calm down dumbass," Alex ordered. "Put in your time and don't get busted and then you'll be the kingpin you want to be."

"Fuck you, Alex! I've put my time in and—"

"You're always bitching," interrupted Alex as he violently shoved Jesse against the living room wall. "You're not in high school anymore! I'm tired of listening to you bitch."

"Fuck you!" Jesse shouted as he pushed Alex back. Alex grabbed him and threw him down on the floor and kicked him in the stomach.

"No, fuck you. Just get out of here. I'm sick of you!"

"Fine," said Jesse as he grabbed the side of the couch to pull himself up.

"Leave the pipe, bitch," barked Alex as he grabbed it from Jesse's hand. "And don't come back!"

Jesse jumped in his car and roared out of the parking lot. The high was unbelievable and he felt indestructible as he drove. Those bastards were using him and he knew that at some point he would have to take them out for him to get what he had been promised. They thought he was easy, controllable. He would show them. They would pay and the empire would become his.

He pulled up to his apartment and ran up the stairs two at a time. Inside Karla and Rebecca were sitting at the table eating lunch and were startled by his entrance.

"Where have you been?" she asked. "I thought you were going to be home last night…"

Jesse's rage continued building. He felt superhuman. This high was better than anything he had ever felt and he loved how it was making him feel and the courage it was giving him. He glared at Karla; his eyes ablaze as she asked again.

"Shut the fuck up bitch," he replied menacingly.

"Don't talk to me like that in front of Rebecca," she scolded.

"I'll talk to you any way I want," he replied through gritted teeth. God, he loved the high he was feeling.

"If you're going to be like that then just go." She cowered as he approached her.

"Bitch, this is my house," he said as she suddenly felt the sting of the back of his hand whack against her jaw and she felt blood trickle out of the side of her mouth.

"What are you doing," she cried as Rebecca screamed in fear. "You're high again, aren't you?"

"Don't ask my business you fucking cunt," he said in a low growl as he slapped her again.

"Jesse!" she screamed, terrified of this monster disguised as her husband.

"Shut up!" he laughed as he grabbed her by her hair and pulled her to her feet.

Rebecca screamed and tried desperately to get out of her high chair. Karla felt lightheaded as he walked her into the kitchen and threw her roughly on the floor. He began to kick her and she went into a fetal position, putting both hands over her head to protect against the blows. She could feel herself losing consciousness and just as she was about out Jesse stopped and walked toward the frightened child who could not stop screaming.

"Jesus shut the fuck up you little shit," he said as he grabbed her and started shaking the child. "Shut up!" Rebecca screamed in fear and pain as he slapped the child and then did it again. Karla's survival instincts took over and despite the pain, she scrambled to her feet and grabbed an iron skillet. Jesse heard her behind him and quickly turned and blocked her attempt to hit him with it. He tried to hit her but lost his balance and fell back against the wall. Karla charged him again, determined to keep him away from Rebecca and he struggled to regain his balance and grabbed the skillet that she swung at him. He grabbed her by the hair with his free hand and pulled her toward him. As she came flying forward, she desperately brought her knee up in his groin. The shot was stunning and hit just right. He let go over her hair as he dropped to his knees. He was breathless and he looked up just as she wildly swung the skillet.

The iron hit him squarely in the temple and he immediately went black and fell forward onto the floor, his hands trapped underneath him where he had been grabbing his crotch. Karla grabbed the terrified child and clutched her tight against her chest as she ran to the bedroom. She grabbed available clothes and threw them into a bag. In the kitchen, Jesse began to stir and Karla put Rebecca down and told her to hide underneath the bed and not to make a sound. The child did as tell and Karla ran back to the kitchen with the skillet in her hand.

Jesse was slowly writhing on the floor and his eyes remained closed as he groaned. Karla prepared to hit him again as he rolled to his back. His glazed eyes slowly opened and looked at her and he mumbled incoherently as she raised the skillet. His eyes then closed again and his head fell to the side and Karla realized that he was out cold. She ran back into the bedroom and grabbed a few more items and then zipped up the bag and frantically called for Rebecca to come out from under the bed.

They ran down the steps to her car. She turned the key but the car only coughed, not quite catching. She tried again and it still wouldn't start.

Suddenly Rebecca screamed in terror and Karla saw him standing at the front door looking down at them. She turned the engine again with no luck. Jesse smiled wickedly and began to come down the steps. She turned the key again and still the engine refused to catch. Jesse stopped, still sneering and mouthed 'I'll kill you' to her. Terrified beyond anything she had ever felt before, she frantically made sure all the doors were locked. He took another step then stopped.

"This is your lucky day, bitch!" he laughed, and then he turned back toward the apartment. He slammed the door with all his might behind him. Karla turned the key again and finally, the engine caught. She jammed it into reverse and the wheels squealed as the rubber tried to grip the ground from the spinning tires. They caught and the car sped out of the apartment complex. She was too frightened to look back, afraid that he still would be there.

There was no going back with him again. This was no longer about her; it was about Rebecca. He had taken his hatred of them to a place she never imagined he would go. He would kill them if they went back, maybe not immediately, but eventually, he would kill them. She turned onto her parent's street and sped to their house. This time they would have to deal with the situation. Even if they didn't take her back, she would not leave without them taking Rebecca.

She and Rebecca ran to the door and Karla pounded on it furiously while looking behind her to make sure that Jesse was not coming. Still no answer so she pounded again as Rebecca clung with all her little might to her leg. Finally, she heard footsteps coming to the door and her mother tentatively opened it.

"Karla?" she said, surprised and concerned by the crying of the two that stood before her on the porch. "Oh Karla, we've told you…you can't come in." Karla pushed past her and pulled the crying child behind her into the house. In the kitchen, Hank heard the commotion in the hallway and ran to see what was happening. His daughter was clutching Rebecca and Corrine looked at him fearfully. Something serious had obviously happened because she had never seen Karla like this.

"Karla, we've gone through this!" he said sharply. "You can't stay here. I won't have your lifestyle at my house." Karla kneeled onto the floor and dropped her head hopelessly. She was hysterical, shaking as she sobbed and the child clung desperately to her neck also screaming in fear amid the madness surrounding her. "Karla, you need to go now!" he yelled as he grabbed her by the arm and tried to pull her up to her feet.

"Dad…" she wailed, "Jesse has lost his mind…he tried to—"

"I don't care," he said as he again pulled against her arm.

"Hank!"

He stopped when he heard Corrine's voice. She pushed him away and pulled Karla and Rebecca tightly against her. She glared at him and he slowly backed away while she gently stroked Karla's hair. "What has happened, honey?" she asked as Karla fought to regain her composure.

"He…hit me and Rebecca…" she said in a broken voice. Though no longer hysterical she continued to cry from the fear of him.

"Oh honey…" and she softly rubbed her daughter's taunt back.

"I have nowhere to turn," Karla moaned.

"Honey, you need to go to the police. We can't help you, but they can."

"Please, Mom—"

"I'm sorry honey, but your father and I can't become a part of what you've gotten yourself into," she said in a gentle yet firm voice. Karla could feel her strength returning and her resolve solidified. Maybe she couldn't stay, maybe her mother was right and the police could help. But right now, this was about Rebecca and whether they liked it or not the child was going to stay with them.

"You have to keep Rebecca," she said firmly. "I'm not safe and neither is she. Maybe I am responsible for my problems, but she isn't. I'll leave, but she stays."

"You really are scared aren't you," her mother said softly.

"Yes," replied Karla as she looked deeply into her mother's eyes. "I think he was trying to kill us."

"Then you shouldn't have gotten into the drugs!" her father gruffly interrupted. "I suppose you're going to blame your mother and me for that, but there is a big difference between having an occasional marijuana cigarette and being a junkie!"

"You think I use drugs?" asked Karla incredulously.

"Everybody knows it. Jesse got busted with drugs in your car, didn't he? You had to have known and condoned it. It breaks your mother's heart."

She handed Rebecca to her mother and stood up and glared at her father. "I've never used drugs in my life!"

"Right; and I suppose Jesse doesn't either."

"Why do you think we're here?" she snapped at him. "Jesse's hooked. He's a pusher and always high. He told me he was going to kill me when we were trying to get away! I'll leave, but Rebecca stays!"

"You really don't use them?" asked Corrine.

"Of course, not…I'm trying to be a good parent for my child, just like the two of you were for me. Maybe you did smoke every once in a while, and I don't agree with it, but you were always there for me, always, until Rebecca. I don't understand why you felt you had to disown me and my daughter, but you did. Well, you can continue to disown me if you want, but you will keep

Rebecca for now because she is not safe with me. If Jesse hurts me, he will hurt Rebecca. I won't let that happen. She stays here."

She bent down and gave Rebecca a tender kiss and then walked slowly to the door. Rebecca began to cry in panic and her wailing caused Karla's eyes to tear up and chin to tremble. As she turned the knob, Corrine glared at Hank.

"Karla, wait…" he murmured. She stopped and turned but he was quiet, unable to speak. She was his daughter, but she had let them down so badly he couldn't let go of his anger. She turned back toward the open door and began to step out. "You two can stay for the night," he heard himself say, "but only tonight. Tomorrow you'll have to find another place to stay."

Karla began whimpering, tears again falling but this time in relief. For now, she and Rebecca were safe. Now she would have some time to figure out a place the two of them could go. Corrine held Rebecca and grabbed her daughter, again pulling her tight. She looked at her husband who stood in silence. He felt chilled from her glare and he knew that the united front was now broken.

*

Rebecca slept soundly on the floor beside the bed that had once been her mother's. Karla quietly read a book that she had grabbed from her bookshelf while gently rocking in the chair next to the bed. The child sighed sweetly in her sleep and Karla looked down on her and for the moment enjoyed the tranquility of being back where there were good memories.

Corrine knocked lightly on the door and peaked in to see if her daughter was awake. Karla nodded with a slight smile and she quietly walked in, not wanting to awaken the sleeping child. She sat on the edge of the bed and the two mothers watched the child sleep.

"Kind of like old times," Corrine said softly as she looked at Karla.

"Not really," replied Karla sadly.

"I know. I miss you. But then I get angry."

"So do I, I feel disowned, alone," the daughter replied, then she looked lovingly at her daughter sleeping on the floor. "But I'm not sorry I kept her."

"She looks like you did at that age," Corrine remarked. She could feel the love for her granddaughter growing inside of her as Karla smiled, bending down and gently caressing the child's angelic face.

"Mom, why won't you let her be a part of your life?" asked Karla, the hurt in her eyes unmistakable. "If you want to stay angry at me that's your choice, but she's your granddaughter. She's a part of you because she came from me and I came from you."

"She's beautiful," replied Corrine as her eyes teared up in shame. "It's time we talked…tell me everything."

"About what?" asked Karla, but she knew.

"What has led you here begging us to let you stay?"

Karla looked at her mother and exhaled. She didn't know if she was ready to tell her everything but she knew that she must. "Are you sure?"

"Don't be afraid…you're safe tonight. Tell me everything," her mother implored. Karla began to weep quietly, the nightmare of the past few years coming back to her. She sat next to her mother and Corrine pulled her close and they rocked back and forth as Karla opened up about Jesse's descent into Hell.

"She was such a good girl," Hank said to Corrine after she had tucked her daughter into bed. "A father's dream, how could she have gone so astray?"

"Maybe she didn't," Corrine said sadly. "Maybe we did."

"No, we didn't," he protested. "We didn't get into the drug business. We didn't get ourselves pregnant. We sure as hell didn't hook up with a damn loser."

"Didn't we Hank?" asked Corrine. "I believe we both used marijuana and I don't believe we were married when Karla was conceived. I also seem to remember that you and my father didn't always get along so well either, especially before we were married. But neither your parents nor mine refused to help us when we needed it. We did."

"That was different; we loved each other and were going to get married anyway."

"Stop it, Hank," she scolded him. "We abandoned her in her time of need. We quit being parents when it became complicated."

"No, we didn't," but he was beginning to realize that maybe they had.

"We quit on her, turned her out. When she needed us the most, we just washed our hands of her." She stood up and grabbed the family album and sat next to him as she opened the worn pages. "Look at these pictures. That same girl is right down the hall from us. She made a mistake but she didn't run from it…shirk her responsibilities. She faced them. We were great parents when everything was easy, and she was an easy child. But then things got hard we just pushed her over the cliff and washed our hands of her. She came to us for help not once, but a number of times, and we would have nothing to do with her. Don't you understand honey? She continued to give us chances to be her parents and we just kept pushing her away."

"But—"

"Look at these pictures Hank. Go into her room. You have a daughter and granddaughter in there that need you. We're supposed to give them unconditional love, that's what parents do. We're getting another chance, darling. Do you really want to throw that away? It's probably our last chance."

He looked at his wife and his eyes became watery. Her words were making him understand how badly he had let his daughter down. He thought of his own father. The old man had been cold all of his life, but he had been there even though it seemed so he could always tell told him what a disappointment he was. He now realized that the old man was probably right about him. He was a disappointment. His most important responsibility had been to care for his daughter and instead he had thrown her out on her own when she needed him the most.

He slowly stood up and Corrine grabbed his hand and led him to his daughter's room. They quietly opened the door. He looked at the silhouettes of his daughter and her child that he realized he didn't know. They were beautiful, lying peacefully and facing each other as she had once done with him when she was that age. Corrine was right, he could not let this last chance slip away. He would become the father he always should have been. He looked at her and he felt proud of the strength she must have to be able to survive what she had gone through. His pride quickly was smothered by the shame of letting her down, not protecting her when he had been given the chance. He would not let it happen again.

They walked out of the room and quietly closed the door. He looked sorrowfully at his wife and she looked lovingly back at him. She was such a wise woman. It was one of her many beauties. He was thankful that she was still with him after all these years. As he looked into her eyes, he began to weep.

*

Karla finished putting the breakfast dishes in the dishwasher and grabbed Rebecca's hand and their bag and quietly walked through the hallway toward the front door. It was still quiet from the early morning hour and she did not want to wake her parents who had allowed her to stay last night. She would go to the police and file a report and then find a shelter for them to stay until she could figure out a more long-termed plan. As she reached the door, she heard a creak on the stairs behind her.

"Where are you going?" her father asked.

"You said we have to leave today," she responded.

"I was wrong," he said as he came down the stairs. "Can you forgive me?"

"I love you, Daddy," she said and she went to him and hugged him tightly. "I always have. I'm so sorry for everything…"

He kissed her on the forehead and then did the same with Rebecca. She could see he wanted to hold his granddaughter and the joy of this caused her to weep softly as she handed her to him. He hugged the little girl tightly as he looked affectionately at the daughter he had tried so hard to lose.

"No baby girl," he said softly to her. "I'm sorry. You're the only one that has acted like a parent. I just acted like an old fool. This is your home as long as you want it to be and it will always be."

They hugged tightly, reunited, and as a family once again.

Chapter 6

Jesse saw the student from Boise State he was supposed to meet had just walked in. It was late afternoon and he took the last swig of the whiskey on the rocks in front of him and put a dollar on the bar. He glanced at the kid who was trying to be nonchalant and gave him a slight nod and walked toward the men's room.

Jesse had finally moved out of the school zone selling weed. Alex had gone to bat for him with Abner and Robby and for the past month, his new territory had been the University District selling both crack and powder cocaine to the rich snobs at the college. The money was great and the sales were easy. The snobs partied every night and he made more just on the weekends than he ever had selling weed to the high school brats.

He took a piss in a yellowish urinal in the empty bathroom and soon the kid walked in nervously, looking around to see if there was anyone in the stalls.

"How much?" Jesse asked as he shook his penis to get the last remnants of urine out of his bladder.

"A half," the boy replied nervously.

"Big night huh? That's going to run you 50."

"I only have 40 dollars," the kid said.

"Not going to get a half then, are you. Here's a quarter. I'll take 25."

The kid reached into his pocket and pulled out a worn twenty-dollar bill and five ones and handed it to Jesse who gave him a small bag with white powder in it. The kid put it in his pocket and nodded to Jesse as he walked out. Jesse looked in the dirty mirror with dried watermarks and stared for a moment, not liking what was looking back at him. He shrugged and turned on the faucet and waited for the water to warm and then splashed some on his face. He was tired because of the bimbo he had done it with earlier in the morning and he needed to wake up.

Sitting at the bar again he ordered another whiskey on the rocks and nursed it. There was a newspaper next to him so he grabbed it and started reading the sports page. Inside was a story of the next great quarterback to come out of Boise. The hotshot was a senior at Borah High School and at the rate he was going he would probably break all the records of the once-great Jesse Rayburn. As he read, he thought about what could have been had the whore just aborted the damn kid. He would have been in the NFL by now he was sure.

He hated the kid most of all. She represented everything that had been taken away from him. The little shit had been demanding, always wanting attention and bawling when she didn't get it. He was glad the two of them were out of his life now. His dreams of glory, long ago ended, now were replaced by bimbos, coke, and punks who got their shots because daddy paid their way. He had earned his the hard way. Given up everything to reach it and when he had finally grabbed it the fucking kid and whore had ripped it from him.

As much as he hated them, he hated his old man more. The bastard had insisted that he 'do the right thing.' That had worked out well for him. So, well that now he was sitting in a downtown bar drinking whiskey and waiting for the next customer who wanted the white powder up their nose. Do the right thing he thought bitterly. If the fucker had really cared about him, he would have told Jesse that the right thing was to go to UNLV, graduate, and play in the NFL. Then he could have taken care of the bitch and baby.

The only thing he had going for himself now was the money he was making. The powder and rock pocketed him about three grand a week. He had a nice car, the mustang being replaced because of the little accident he had one night after a little too much partying, but he liked the Charger he had gotten to replace it and he loved the hum of the engine on the open road.

The place was starting to pick up and he walked back into the bathroom again. There were a couple of patrons at the urinals so he went into a stall and sat down, pulling out a small vile about an inch long. He gently shook some coke out onto the top of his hand and snorted the powder into each nostril. This stuff was smooth. He reached into his pocket and pulled out ten bags. He probably had about a gram, maybe a gram and a half. If he could sell it all it would be a nice night. He pulled his pants down and sat back on the toilet. He heard the door open and through the crack saw it was an undercover he recognized. He dropped the bags behind the toilet and sat quietly, waiting for the bacon to leave.

"I heard you might have some coke," he heard him say.

"Not me," replied Jesse.

"C'mon man, I got fifty dollars and I need a half."

"You have the wrong guy," Jesse replied, realizing his night was over.

"But they told me—"

"Dude, let me shit in peace. I'm not a dealer and I don't have any coke. Somebody gave you the wrong information."

The undercover realized that there would be no bust so he walked out, trying to sound like a typical customer but actually sounding like a cop trying to sound like something he wasn't. Jesse laughed after the door closed and then settled back on the toilet. A couple of minutes later he walked out and finished his whiskey before heading out the door.

The buzz was kicking in and Jesse gunned the Charger as it sped down the freeway toward his new pad in Meridian. The sun was just going behind the mountain and the light was an orange hue that shown through the clouds. He loved this time of the day because it always brought him back to football. Those were the days when he was the king, the best there ever was. But eventually, those thoughts would fade and the bitterness of all that was lost returned.

Suddenly he swerved to the side of the road and quickly felt his empty pockets. How could he have been so stupid? He had left the coke behind the toilet. Damn, that was at least $800 in merchandise. How would he explain that to Robby? Robby was the threat. He could handle Abner and Alex, but Robby was scary. He had no feelings and it was all about making money. Word on the street was that Robby ran the show and had ordered a couple of killings of dumb-shits that tried to invade his territory. Robby would not take kindly to lost merchandise. He had to get it back.

He turned around at the next exit. In ten minutes, he was back at the bar but now there was a line waiting to go in. Jesse parked the car and ran as fast as he could to the line. He couldn't wait to get in so he ran to the front amid the protests of the college students who were already in line.

"Where do you think you're going?" asked the new bouncer that Jesse didn't recognize.

"I need to get inside. I left something."

"I don't think so," replied the newbie cockily. "You want to go in, get in line just like everyone else."

"Look, dude, I just gotta go in for a minute." Jesse protested as he tried to push past him. "I just got to get something I left."

"Sure bud," the bouncer said as he grabbed him and pulled him back, "in line."

"Why you hasslin' me?" demanded Jesse. "I come here all the time. I was just here an hour ago."

"There's no hassle here, just get in line."

"I told you I have to get something. It'll take thirty seconds."

"I'm not going to tell you again," the bouncer said in a menacing voice.

"Fuck you!"

"You need to go now, bud!"

Jesse was nose to nose with the bouncer and for the first time noticed how big the guy was. He looked menacing with his crew-cut hair and his arms were bigger than Jesse had ever seen.

"Last chance bud," the bouncer snapped.

Jesse glared at him and again attempted to get by him. The bouncer was quicker though and grabbed Jesse by the back of the neck and arm and turned him toward the street. They began walking quickly and Jesse felt the ache from the strength of the guy's hands that pinched against his skin. He could feel all the eyes watching him be humiliated and he was helpless to stop it. When they reached the curve, the bouncer threw him down on the ground and pointed at him in a threatening manner. Jesse looked up and knew it was no use. He stood up as the bouncer walked back and briefly thought of tackling him but knew that if he did that he'd be banned from the place and easy money would be lost. He dusted himself off and walked toward his car.

He turned into an alley where he had parked it against a dumpster and reached for his keys. Just then he felt a sharp pain on the top of his head and he fell in a heap. He felt boots kicking him in the stomach and rolled into the fetal position. He glanced up and saw two men over him and one bent down going through his pockets. He wanted to grab him, but he couldn't move. The guy bending down rifled through his pockets and grabbed the vial of cocaine. He then grabbed the wallet and pulled out the cash.

"Where his keys?" asked the larger attacker.

"I got them," answered the guy going through his pockets and he tossed them to him.

"Got a bag back here, must be a drug dealer, he's got a lot of cash."

"Grab it, let's gets out of here," and they began running down the alley.

Jesse rolled to his knees and supported himself against his car, pulling himself up.

"You guys are dead!" he yelled at them as they sprinted away. "You hear me? Dead!"

He found the keys still in the trunk door and slowly closed the lid after pulling them out. Limping, he made his way to the driver's door and painfully stuck the key in and unlocked the door. He slid into the seat and started the engine. The car lurched forward and soon he was on the freeway.

He had to think. He had lost a gram of cocaine and now a thousand dollars had been taken out of his trunk. Robby would not be happy and he wasn't sure if Abner and Alex could save him.

*

It had taken some time but Karla finally felt safe at night. No more worries when Jesse would be coming home, wondering what mood he was in or the smell of other women he had emanating off of him. Rebecca was sleeping through the night now, no longer shrieking in terror from the cruelties of a drug-induced father. Karla had forgotten what peace in the evening was like and relished the security her parents now provided.

The days were calm as she and Rebecca recovered from the torment of the past. Karla helped her mother around the house and tended to her child who was always smiling now. The two mothers talked throughout the days, re-establishing the connection that had once been severed as they tended to the necessities of running a home now filled with the joyful sounds of a child once again. Corrine relished having her daughter back and joy would fill her heart as the granddaughter would laughingly hug her for no reason, much like Karla had done so many years earlier.

Hank eagerly looked forward to walking into the house in the evening to the sound of the patter of the little girl's feet, straining to get to her new-found grandfather as fast as she could. He loved her with all his heart and she could feel it despite her age. She knew this man was kind and made her feel safe in his arms, unlike the father she had tried to win over but had insisted on shunning her instead.

Hank sat at the dinner table playfully poking Rebecca in her chest as the child squealed in delight. In the kitchen, Corrine pulled dinner out of the oven as Karla sliced some cherry tomatoes for the garden salad she had quickly put together, the aroma of the food filtering into the dining room. "Have you thought about the future," Hank called out to Karla as she put the finishing touches on the salad and Corrine grabbed a large spoon and stuck it in the brownish liquidized hamburger and potato dish. "What do you want to do?"

"I have a child now," Karla replied as she placed the salad on the table. "I'm pretty limited."

"Honey, we can help. We want to help," he replied as Rebecca again roared in laughter at the poking finger.

"But there isn't really much I can do," she said as she sat down, her mother gingerly placing the hot dish on an oven mitt so it wouldn't leave a mark on the table. "I don't have a diploma."

"Why don't you think about it some?" he replied as he winked toward his wife. "You have your whole life ahead of you."

"That's right," Corrine said as she put the brownish mixture onto the plates and handed them out to her daughter and husband. "Give yourself a chance, darling. We're here for you. I know we're a little late, but we do so want to help."

"Well…I will," Karla smiled. "I love both of you."

"We love you too," replied Corrine, grabbing her daughter's hand and slightly squeezing it. "A lot of people love you and want to help. Let us, OK?"

Karla nodded and smiled. Her life was taking another turn, but this time it seemed to be going in a direction that had hope, purpose, and most importantly, security for Rebecca. Above all, Rebecca's needs must be met, and if that meant she accept help from others to put herself in a position to provide for her, she would.

*

The dull light from the television shown in the darkening room as the sunset behind the mountains that guard the city in the canyon. The child quietly picked up another toy and gently placed it upon the grandfather who was sleeping on the recliner while the Braves baseball game on the Superstation played silently in front of him. Corrine watched her as she knitted and the child carefully grabbed a stuffed mouse and waddled back to her grandfather.

After the last toy was carefully placed on sleeping man the child jumped up on the couch and climbed upon her grandmother, insisting on receiving the necessary attention for the work she had just finished. Corrine looked toward where the child's outstretched finger pointed to and quietly told her what a wonderful job she had done. Rebecca, so proud of herself, locked her little arms around her neck and squeezed with all her might, and Corrine lovingly rubbed the child's back, whispering praise for the enterprising child. Karla watched from the corner of the room and mentally took a picture in her mind. It was as she always imagined it would be, if only for a moment. At last, she felt excited about the new day that tomorrow would bring.

The next evening as Karla and Corrine cleaned the pot that the lentil soup, they had made that night the phone rang in the hallway. Corrine called for Hank to pick it up but he and Rebecca were already outside in the back checking the raspberry bush he was so proud of. On the third ring, Corrine gave up on her husband and quickly picked up the phone as Karla finished scrubbing the pot. A few moments later, Corrine came back into the kitchen and handed Karla a towel.

"It's for you dear," she said, her face impassive.

"Who is it?"

"I think you should take it."

"It's not Jesse is it?" asked Karla, her face showing concern that the nightmare may begin anew.

"No," replied Corrine, "but this is a call you need to take."

Karla walked into the hallway and picked up the phone and she noticed that she was slightly shaking. Her mother walked up behind her and gently rubbed her neck for support.

"Hello," Karla said softly, afraid.

"Hi Karla, this is Laura Rayburn."

Karla glared at her mother. Why had she allowed this woman to call her? It was her son who had nearly destroyed her and she had done nothing, NOTHING!

"Please don't hang up," Laura pleaded. Her shame was overwhelming and she knew there was no reason for her daughter-in-law to speak to her, she could only silently pray that she would give her a chance. Karla sensed the desperation Laura was feeling, she had felt it herself when they had turned her and Rebecca away when they had needed help and she wanted to remain angry because of the hurt this woman had allowed, but she was different and she felt herself softening. Corrine continued to softly rub her neck and silently nodded encouragement to her.

"Karla, George and I…" she said hopefully into the phone. "We…we want to see Rebecca. I know we probably don't deserve too…please." Karla was unable to speak. She was angry but at the same time, she wasn't. She wanted to lash out yet at last the parents seemed to finally understand the importance of letting Rebecca be a part of their lives. Though she was thankful for this her pride still wanted to punish Laura and George. These conflicts confused her. It was something she had never felt before and as it built, she felt her eyes redden and fill with tears.

"I know we haven't been there for the two of you," Laura said haltingly through her own tears. "We're so ashamed—"

Suddenly Karla's anger and the confusion of her feelings evaporated and a feeling of tranquility overcame her. "Mrs. Rayburn," she interrupted barely above a whisper. "It doesn't matter how I feel about you. Rebecca is your granddaughter. She deserves to know and love her grandparents…and be loved back."

In her den, Laura broke down in sobs. They came from the shame she felt yet the unbridled joy that was surging through her. She was not deserving, yet she was being given another chance, allowed to be a part of the child's life by the very person she and her husband had thrown out of their lives because of the sins of the son.

"I'm so sorry Karla, I'm so sorry," she stammered nearly incoherently. "Thank you so much…"

"Tell me when you'd like to see her…"

"I'm so sorry," Laura cried into the phone. "Thank you so much…"

Karla gently hung up the phone and hugged her mother. "I love you so much, honey," Corrine whispered into Karla's ear. "I'm so proud of you." She gently kissed her daughter on the forehead as the backdoor opened and the laughter of the child filled the house.

*

Karla enrolled in a GED class offered by the University and began to feel a liberation she had not felt since before the pregnancy. The coursework was not difficult for her and she found the hours at the school provided freedom from the burdens that had for so long made her feel as though she were trapped in a cage, alone yet gawked at by onlookers much like the animals in the local zoo. She felt hope again, not just for her but for Rebecca as well.

She attempted the GED testing. She knew the material that she was being tested on, but the doubts that had been built up by the way Jesse had treated her for so long filled her with fear after she had completed the final test. Maybe he was right, maybe she was worthless and dumb and ugly and all the other horrible things that he had told her she was. As she waited for the scores to come back, she trembled at the thought that he could be right. If he was, what kind of life would Rebecca have?

Soon she heard the news that she had craved to hear. She had passed, was now a certified high school graduate. She had proved him wrong, not that he would care or even know. But it didn't matter, she had done it and through this success, she knew that she no longer needed him. The certification had finally freed her from the chains he had placed her in and she could leave now, free of the hell that he had so deliberately placed her and Rebecca in.

Within an hour she was at her parent's lawyer who was providing the number to an excellent divorce specialist. It was time to be the person she had dreamed of being when times were simpler and hope arose with the sun every day. He was the enemy; his world was one of darkness, decay, and abuse. She was stronger than him and she felt free as she signed the papers the lawyer put in front of her to represent her and Rebecca in the divorce that would be the last link between his world and her newfound light.

The divorce proceeded quickly and soon the formality of going to court to officially end the marriage was set. She never heard from him and he deliberately skipped the proceedings. At last, the judge grew tired of waiting for the respondent to respond and on a clear spring morning, Karla sat in the courtroom with her counsel patiently waiting for her emancipation.

The judge came into his courtroom and looked disapprovingly at the empty respondent's table. The papers were all in order except for the absence of

Jesse's signature. He had waited long enough, given the scoundrel countless opportunities to respond. With a flick of his pen, he ordered a default judgment and ended the marriage, giving full custody of the child to the plaintiff who sat at the table with her counsel with a relieved look of not victory, but of a nightmare finally ending.

Karla was eager to live again. She had a sense of confidence in herself that for so long had been dormant. She could do things that before she had been afraid to even think about. She dreamed; an act that for so long she hadn't dared attempt because of the pain of knowing that it was beyond the realm of possibility. No longer would she allow anyone or anything to break her down to the state she had been with the monster.

With hope brought courage and she began making plans for building a secure future for herself and Rebecca. She had survived the starless night and each new day brought wondrous opportunity. She wasn't afraid of the work and sacrifice she would have to make because it had been earned through her tenacity. She was in control of her own destiny. She would need more schooling, but now she went into it with the belief that anything was possible.

She applied to the University, determined to get a degree because it would open the doors needed to create the life for her and her daughter that had been forfeited for so long. The child was not the reason for the difficulties of the past, but the fortitude for the mother to forge headlong into a future of hope.

*

The manila envelope was taped to the door. He didn't have to open it for he knew what was inside. The bitch had done it, she had found some crooked robe to give her what she wanted and now he was single again. He walked into the apartment and went to the refrigerator and pulled out a can of beer. Popping the top, he found a used glass and ran it under the water, rinsing out the remnants of the last beer he had who knew when. He poured the golden liquid into the wet glass and continued to debate whether or not he should open the envelope.

Why bother, he was a busy man and hadn't had time to go to the court to let them know what kind of a leaching bitch she had been. He didn't care what the judgment was. The fact was she wasn't going to get a dime from him. She didn't want him anymore? Fine, fend for yourself then he thought to himself.

But something strange began happening to him. It pissed him off initially but he couldn't shake it. He began remembering her back in better days, before the pregnancy, the marriage, and all the subsequent crap that had followed. He remembered seeing her the first time in high school. She was so cute then, so bubbly. She had a personality that you just wanted to be around. It was infectious, titillating in ways. And God, she was so gorgeous, even then. Her blonde hair perfectly feathered out to the side, her skin soft on her high cheekbones, and the eyes, the blueness as deep as a mountain lake. You looked in them and you saw yourself at your best.

He remembered the first date, the giggling at the movie as they cuddled together during the scary parts of the dumb horror flick they had chosen. After the movie she had scooted next to him as they cruised the drag, letting everyone know that they were now a couple. She had worshipped him and he had admired her. It had once been so perfect but now it was gone and it was her fault. The bitch had taken one last thing from him, she had taken herself and now he was denied of everything.

He heard a knock on the door which took him out of past days. He stood up, flung the envelope toward the garbage, and opened the door where the landlord and another man stood waiting. "Mr. Rayburn, we're here to inspect your apartment," he said as Jesse remembered the note that this day would become.

"I didn't hear anything about this," he lied.

"Maybe you should read your lease sometime, or the letters we send to you, or the notes that we place on your door," the manager replied smugly.

"Whatever."

The two men breezed past Jesse and began to look around the filthy apartment. As the landlord spoke, the other wrote on a form he was carrying. They quickly went from room to room and Jesse lay down on his couch, waiting for the inevitable 'clean up this mess' from the balding landlord who obviously thought his shit didn't stink.

"Mr. Rayburn, have you been using illegal drugs in here?" Baldy asked.

"No."

"There appears to be some damage now that has happened since you began renting."

"I think it's time for you to go," Jesse hissed. He didn't have to take it from this asshole and his little friend. This was his place; he hadn't burned it down. So, it was a little messy, what was the big deal?

"There have also been reports of loud parties," the landlord replied, ignoring Jesse's suggestion. "We've heard and seen people coming by this apartment at all hours of the day and night. Is there a chance you may be doing a little dealing?"

"That would be illegal, wouldn't it?" Jesse murmured without looking toward the landlord.

"Yes, it would, but that's not my main concern," replied the landlord, still ignoring Jesse's attitude. "My concern is that it would violate the terms of your lease."

"Wouldn't want that to happen, dude," Jesse smirked.

"Do you think this is fun and games Mr. Rayburn?" asked the landlord, his voice suddenly becoming low and cold.

"No, sir."

"This apartment has damage and is filthy. It smells of marijuana, there are numerous reports of complaints," he said, now glaring threateningly toward the tenant. "You are in a very precarious situation, Mr. Rayburn." He walked over to the kitchen and peeked in again, letting his words settle. "I would suggest that looking for a new place of residence might be a positive step for you." He stood over the couch and smiled at Jesse. Jesse tried to pay no heed to him but he noticed that though the man was older, he was powerfully built. His black spectacle added to the intimidation he emanated toward him and he felt vulnerable. Finally, the landlord turned toward the door. As he walked out, Jesse summoned the courage that had escaped him while Baldy had stood over him and he flipped the aggressor off. He found comfort in his protest, but only momentarily.

He threw his clothes that he wanted into a black garbage bag and found his stash of cash. He took a quick look around the apartment and tossed the key into the trash. He hated this place anyway so it wouldn't be any loss leaving it. He walked out the door and tossed the black bag into the back seat of the Charger, revved the engine and drove away from the dump. As he sped toward town, he silently cursed himself, he had left a six-pack in the refrigerator. Dumb, he thought to himself, real dumb.

He found a rundown hotel on the old section of town and paid cash for a month with the stash of money that was supposed to go to Robby. Fuck him, he thought to himself. I'll make it back soon enough and the little prick won't even know. He scored two deals on the way to his room and realized that he may have stumbled into a gold mine. He quickly went back out into the streets and made some quick green before heading to his regular haunts.

At night he listened to the sounds of the old place and he felt as though it was creeping into his head. The only way he could deal with it was to smoke some crack that he should be selling. The feeling was no longer immediate and he realized that more of the blow was going to him instead of the streets where the profits were. He knew that sooner or later the boys would figure this out and would want their money.

During the day he always saw someone following him and it began to drive him crazy because he didn't know if it was bacon or one of Robby's grinders.

He remembered having to beg Robby not to off him when his money had been stolen at the night club. Fortunately, the little prick had given him a second chance because he had given such a good description of the attackers. Within three days a story had come out in the paper about two bodies being found in a trash bin behind Borah High School. Authorities had worried that there was a drug war coming on but after the autopsies on the victim, it had been established that it was just some random murder.

Robby now controlled the business. Abner was still his right-hand man but Alex had mysteriously disappeared. Neither talked about the lost partner anymore and everyone working for them knew not to ask. Word on the street was that Alex had decided to wrest control from Robby, thinking that he would be an easy mark. It hadn't worked out and no one knew if Alex was dead and buried somewhere or if he had realized his danger and took off for greener pastures south.

What everyone did know was that Robby was now the undeniable king of Boise and he was not a man to be messed with. Jesse knew that his friendship with Alex had placed him in a bad light and then being robbed had further eroded his standing. Every day brought new fears that Robby was going to 'make a change' and the paranoia within Jesse grew.

Out of the corner of his eye, he saw the glint of her golden hair and immediately recognized her. She looked good, better than he could ever remember seeing her look. Her ass was tight again, tits big and firm, and no spare tire. Best of all, there was no sign of the child. He wanted that woman, wanted her back with him where she belonged.

"Karla, come over here, baby," he cooed as he came up behind her.

"Jesse!" she said, surprised to be seeing him and even more stunned by how he looked. He had aged dramatically. His eye sockets had deep rings around them and he was so skinny. His hair was long and unkempt and his clothes were filthy. He had to keep pulling up his worn jeans and the t-shirt had a big hole in the back. "Leave me alone," she said nervously as she quickened her pace to get away from him.

"C'mon bitch, you're still my wife!" he said as he grabbed her.

"We've divorced Jesse," she said angrily as she tried to pull her arm away from his grip. "Maybe if you weren't stoned all the time—"

"Shut up whore," he mumbled. "Why'd you do that to me?" He pulled her tightly to him and wrapped his other arm around her. His breath smelled of old smoke and alcohol and Karla felt herself becoming nauseous.

"Let go of me," she said, the feelings of the old terror overtaking her again.

"Shut up!" he laughed as he grabbed her by the jaw with a luring grin.

"Let go," she cried as she tried to push him away from her.

"I'm not going to hurt you, baby," he insisted.

"I don't like how you're talking to my daughter, asshole," Jesse suddenly froze, unsure how to proceed when all of a sudden, he felt ripped from her and thrown roughly onto the hot sidewalk. Hank jammed his knee into Jesse's chest and he felt the air escape.

"She's my wife," he protested, his voice shaky. "Let me go, old man before you get hurt." But it only elicited a laugh from the father and he put his hand around Jesse's throat and slowly started to squeeze, enjoying the sight of him wheezing to get a breath and trying to pull the hand away.

"I think I'll be alright," Hank said sarcastically. "You take a look at yourself lately? Lost some weight I see, looking a little drawn." He loosened his grip on the neck and slowly stood up, glowering at the shell that was now Jesse. "Stay away from my daughter or I'll kill you."

He watched them walk away and felt the heat of embarrassment that the old man had caused him. If he had his piece the two would be dead right now, but he didn't and all he could do was watch. He slowly stood up and went back to his corner. He still had sales to make, still had to bring in some dough to keep Robby off his back. He didn't think about what was lost, he didn't think at all anymore.

That night he stumbled up to his room, everything blurry from the beer and blow. There was someone by his door, standing there watching him make his way toward him. Suddenly Jesse realized that Robby had decided to get him so he turned and began running down the hall. In his haste, he quickly realized that his legs weren't working as they should be and he ran into the wall. The man chasing him quickly tackled him and gruffly grabbed his hand and placed an envelope in it.

"You've been served," he said and then he got up and walked to the staircase and began to descend down it. Jesse watched him and then struggled to get up. Safely inside his room he ripped open the envelope and peered at it, trying to shake the blurry vision and the spinning in his head. Finally, the words became clear. It was an order. He could no longer go within 1000 feet of his ex, daughter, or her family.

The bitch had gotten a restraining order. Fine, he thought, a thousand feet was close enough to shoot her. Then he passed out.

*

College exhilarated Karla, made her feel worthwhile. She found interests she hadn't known before, developed confidence in herself that had not shown before. She loved the challenge of it, the development of her mind which in turn caused her spirit to blossom toward all around her. She was no longer someone's wife or child. She had become her own entity.

Every day was a challenge for her. There were no days off or summers to refurbish the battery. In the mornings she cared for her daughter. Then it was off to school until the early afternoon. Once classes were done, she drove the short distance from the University to George's garage and took care of the books. After closing, she would return home and spend dinner with Rebecca and watch her until the child was bedded down, and then it would be three or four more hours of studying.

With the summer's classes, she was able to shave a year off and now that she was entering her final semester, she excitedly looked forward to the internship she needed to graduate. The internship was with a social work agency that concentrated on working with single mothers and she was bursting with ideas of how to provide services that would give them the help that she had so desperately needed in the not so distant past.

Rebecca continued to grow as children do and as time passed, she developed an unbreakable kinship with her grandparents. She loved being with her grandfather in the back yard as he would plant and tend. She became his special helper and they were nearly inseparable. Meanwhile, Karla's internship kept her away from home longer and longer until finally, it came to an end. All that was left was preparation for finals and creating the perfect resume.

The final exams were nerve-wracking and Karla was sure that everything she had learned in the past three years had mysteriously disappeared into thin air. She felt her heart thumping in her chest as she tried to concentrate on what the questions were asking and what the best answer would be. Somehow, she made it through the last question of the last exam, and now she could only wait to see if she had done what was needed.

Following the last exam, she drove to the agency she had interned at. They had invited her for an interview and she wondered why she had agreed to meet them at this time. She was a nervous wreck and emotionally exhausted but she knew she had to soldier on. She pulled into the parking lot and rushed inside, fixing her hair as she went.

She tried to hide her anxiety as she answered the questions the interviewers put forth. She was thankful that she knew them from the past three months of her internship but it did not lessen the pressure she felt to impress them. The questioning went on for thirty minutes and then she was asked to wait out with the receptionist for a few minutes.

The receptionist, Hillary, tried to calm Karla with some light chatting but sensed that Karla was distracted and soon left her alone. Karla braced for the worst and tried to convince herself that there would be other opportunities, but nagging doubts refused to dissipate.

Finally, what seemed like an eternity, the director invited Karla back into the conference room. As she walked in, she tried to read the faces of the interviewers but quickly gave up and sat, awaiting the verdict.

Ten minutes later she calmly walked out of the building to her car. She unlocked the door and slipped into the driver's side, started the car, and drove out of the parking lot. Ten minutes later she was sitting at a spot she had often gone to study. It was quiet and across from the University. The river was lower than usual but the sound of the water rushing against the rocks as it headed to some unknown destination calmed her. The sounds of it always brought a sense of joy to her. She watched it quietly as she sat back against an old oak tree and felt the soft, warm grass underneath her. She had survived and the realization of it brought an overwhelming joy that she had never experienced before. On Saturday she would graduate, she no longer feared the results of the exams.

On Monday she would become a professional social worker. She had done it. She had beaten him. She was truly in control of her destiny. She and Rebecca were safe. That had been through Hell and had somehow come out the other end. The two of them were stronger for it and the darkness no longer caused them fear.

*

"Jessie?"

"Yeah, who's this?" he said groggily into the phone that had awoken him from another drug-induced stupor.

"It's your father."

"What ya want, old man?" he stammered. "How the fuck you get my number?"

"I wanted to see if you hand any plans for this afternoon."

"Why?"

"Karla's graduating and I thought—"

"Are you fucking serious?" he roared as he suddenly sat up in the bed that was void of the blankets that now lay on the soiled floor.

"Well, I thought it would be nice if—"

"Karla and me not even married no more."

"I know son, but it would give you a chance to see your daughter."

"My daughter? What makes you think I want to see anyone at all? I a busy man…besides, you all ruined my life. That should be me graduation' today, not that lazy bitch."

"Son, stop it!" George could feel his ire growing and he was quickly regretting that he had made the call. "When are you going to grow up? You're killing yourself with those damn drugs and low life's you hang out with."

"What you know about it. You can go fuck yourself old man!"

"I just thought it would be nice for Karla. Show her some respect for what she has accomplished."

"Fuck all of ya!" he screamed into the phone before slamming it down on the hook. He hated them. They had ruined him and now the dumb ass was asking him to come to watch the bitch that had sent him here. Shit, had they all lost their marbles?

He lay back down on the bed and the girl who was nude next to him grabbed a sheet and pulled it over her bosom.

"Who was that?" she asked groggily.

"A fuckin' asshole," he said as he grabbed her breast.

*

Karla's parents smiled with pride as she walked across the stage to receive her diploma. George and Laura smiled also, but their pride in her was tinged with the pain of what their son had done to her and the path he had taken. Meanwhile, little Rebecca clapped with glee and pointed out to anyone near that the beautiful woman that was waving to them from the stage was her momma.

After the ceremony, the five of them went down to the stadium floor and hugged the graduate in the mass of humanity that had assembled. Rebecca insisted on being held by her mother and chattered excitedly about seeing her on the big stage and asking questions about the stage and what the diploma was and then telling her that lots of people were here and then insisting that she needed to go on the stage with her momma. They laughed joyfully at the child's wonderment and basked in the glow of Karla's success of truly beating odds that only the strongest willed would dare attempt.

"Hey Karla, congrats girl," screamed Jessica, a classmate who had also just graduated. Jessica had been Karla's study partner for the past two years and they had become close. Jessica was from rural Montana and had felt out of place when she had found Karla. She was overweight and had a pockmarked face but Karla had drawn out her personality which was bubbly when she was comfortable. "We're going out tonight to celebrate and we're hoping you could join us."

Karla smiled and looked at Jessica and four other graduates. "Come on out with us," they agreed.

"Thank you, guys," she said, still smiling. "But I can't…"

She had a new job to get ready for and she smiled at her daughter and kissed her on the cheek.

Chapter 7

Jesse downed the whiskey and walked to the bathroom. He was pleased no one else was in there and he went into the last stall and closed the door with the unmentionable graffiti scratched into the wall. Inside his pocket was a vial that held the purest cocaine he had snorted in a while and he pulled it out and put it to his nostrils and sucked the white powder up into his nasal passage. Immediately he felt the warm glow the good stuff always provided and he took another snort from his other nostril.

He walked to the sink and turned on the faucets full bore, the water splashed against the sink and the spray felt cool against the exposed skin of his arms. This was going to be a good night for him. Fuck Karla, let her graduate. He didn't care anymore but he was still flabbergasted that the old man had called and invited him to go witness the damn travesty.

He went back into the lounge and spotted some possible customers. They were three college guys. Obviously having one last big night before the summer break and they had the look of partiers. They were playing pool and Jesse knew that he had about an hour to make a sale to them or they would be gone for the evening. He went to his spot at the bar and ordered a double. When the barkeep brought it, he pulled a ten out of his pocket and told him to keep the change. The barkeeper put the change in his pocket and moved on to the next customer as Jesse took a sip and continued scoping the threem playing pool. After they finished the game they strolled to the bar and stood next to Jesse to order three more beers.

"You guys football fans?" Jesse said to the shorter one who was standing next to him.

"You talking to us?" he said, suddenly realizing that Jesse had said something.

"Yeah, you guys football fans?"

"Who isn't?" the shorter one shrugged.

"Know who I am?" asked Jesse, figuring that they must know that he was once a great quarterback for Boise High School.

"No, should we?"

"I'm Jesse Rayburn."

"Still doesn't ring a bell."

"I played…I was the best player in the state six years ago."

"What college you play for?" asked the second kid who was a little taller and had a couple of days' growth on his face.

"Didn't," replied Jesse, a little self-conscious now. "I played for Boise High School."

"High school glory…whatever," and the three of them start laughing and the barkeep smirked as he handed them their bottles of beer.

"No, I really was good," protested Jesse, no longer interested in selling some blow but now eager to defend his past exploits. "I was supposed to play for UNLV. I was supposed to but…"

"But you sucked," laughed the short guy next to him.

"What'd you say?" demanded Jesse.

"If you were so good you would have played for somebody," the short one taunted. "Looking at you I'd say you've done more talking than throwing, stud."

"You got a smart mouth, punk!"

"Look bud, maybe if you tell your story to enough drunks, you'll find somebody to worship your bullshit."

"Fuck you," growled Jesse, his hands clenching.

"Ooh, that was quick," said kid laughed.

"At least I played," Jesse murmured. "At least I was good once. What about you," he said as he jammed his bony finger into the short one's chest. "What'd you ever do?"

"I grew up, toker," he said as he pushed away Jesse's hand.

"Smart college boy, huh?"

"Smarter than you, toker."

Jesse suddenly threw a right hook and the boy ducked as the punch whizzed over where his head had once been. The short guy threw an uppercut as he stood back up and Jesse felt a sudden pain in his midsection. He desperately grabbed him and felt more punches land in his exposed kidney. At the door two bouncers quickly ran to the action that was happening at the bar and pulled the two men apart. The three college students quickly placed the blame on Jesse whom the bartender backed up and the bouncers began pulling Jesse toward the back door.

"Don't you know who I am?" yelled Jesse as he struggled against the two bouncers who were leading him ever closer to the exit.

"You need to go home dumb ass," the bigger bouncer replied angrily. "You're always starting trouble here. Just go home, Jesse."

"I'm Jesse Rayburn," he shouted toward the three college kids. "I was the best player in the state. I could have played in the pros."

"Go home and look at your trophies," the younger bouncer retorted as he opened the door and roughly threw him through it. Jesse landed with a thud in the alley and glared, shaking from embarrassment and anger. "No one gives a shit here," he heard the bouncer shout as the door slammed and he realized once and for all that no one really did care anymore.

*

Jesse drove the jet-black Trans Am he had bought himself just a week earlier down University Boulevard. He didn't know where he was going but the night breeze that entered through the open window as he drove made him feel better. Off to his left, he saw the stadium with the lights on and he wondered what was going on. He slowed his car down and saw people in the parking lot and then he remembered again.

Everyone looked so happy and proud and he felt the muscles of his neck tighten and jaw clench. It was the graduation, Karla's graduation. It was supposed to be his night but she had stolen this from him too. The thought of her getting a diploma made him angrier and for a moment, he considered plowing into the parking lot and taking as many out as he could. Instead, he kept driving, but now he knew where he was going. He sped through the yellow traffic light and his anger continued percolating. He quickly pulled up to the old hotel that had long since become his home and ran upstairs to his room. He tore through the old, scratched dresser, pulling out clothes until he found his .38 Special. Grabbing it, he stuck it in the waistband of his jeans and then dumped a box of bullets onto his dresser and put a handful into his pocket.

He raced back to the bar and parked where he had a good view of the door. People slowly moved in and out of the door but there was no sign of the three frat boys who had disrespected him. As he watched, he thought of the boys and how the smartass short one had taunted him and then smacked him for no reason. He reached into his pocket and pulled out the vile of coke and took two quick snorts and felt the familiar warmth descend through this body.

As he sat waiting, his thoughts turned to Karla and Rebecca. How old was the kid now? Five maybe, or was it six? Who cares? The two of them had ruined him and had put him here. He was in a life that he couldn't escape because of them. Instead of being what he was destined to be, he was just another mule for Robby.

Suddenly he saw two familiar faces walk out of the front door. It was two of the three guys who had trashed him and he thought about getting out and shooting them right there. But the one he wanted to be was missing. The short little smart ass was still in there and he was the one that was going to pay tonight. He watched the other two walk down the street and turn the corner and disappear from view. Sooner or later the little fuck would walk out and he'd be waiting. He'd show him the repercussions of having a smart mouth. Tonight, the little prick would pay.

*

The child screamed in glee as Laura brought out the celebratory cake. The white sheet cake was frosted with a graduate standing in the middle of a diploma with four candles surrounding it. Karla laughed at her daughter's antics and Hank bent down to light the candles. George and Corrine followed behind Laura and also began laughing as the child started to sing 'Happy Birthday' to her mother.

"I don't think it's my birthday yet darling," Karla cooed to the child as she finished her rendition. "Would you like to help me blow them out?" The child excitedly joined her mother as they bent down and blew, extinguishing the flames from the candles and then Rebecca clapped her hands happily. The family sat on the porch and ate the cake as the child raced around the yard and then would occasionally come back to the mother and enjoy another bite of the frosting that Karla scraped off.

As the night grew dark, Rebecca finally began to tire and soon was sitting on her mother's lap as she rocked slowly back and forth on the rickety rocking chair that was now weather-worn from years of service. The adults talked quietly among themselves as Karla stared lovingly at the sleeping child. She excused herself and took Rebecca into her room and gently pulled her shoes off and placed her under the covers of her bed. Tonight, Rebecca would sleep in her special dress.

As she walked back out to the porch, Hank and Corrine began picking up dishes and taking them into the kitchen. Meanwhile, George and Laura gently grabbed Karla and walked toward the front door.

"George and I are just so proud of you," Laura said, smiling lovingly into Karla's eyes. "You're such a wonderful woman and mother." Karla smiled as she wrapped her arm around Laura's elbow. "We're so thankful you have allowed George and I to be a part of your and Rebecca's life, especially after…" and she fell silent, the shame quickly moving to the surface. Laura felt her eyes begin to mist and Karla grabbed her hand and gently squeezed it. Corrine quietly walked out of the kitchen and gently rubbed her shoulders knowing the pain she must be going through. She had felt it many times herself.

"I'm sorry…I'm just so sorry, Karla. I wish Jesse would…" she fell silent, her lip quivering in the anguish she was feeling. "I'm sorry."

George tried to control his emotions but he couldn't any longer. His eyes, which had been sad for so long finally filled with tears, and though he succeeded in stifling the sob, the tears fell freely from his eyes. "He used to be such a good boy," he stammered. "I'm so sorry Karla…"

Corrine kissed her husband on the cheek as Hank joined them at the doorway. Karla looked at the pained couple and could feel the hurt they were feeling. "Now George," Laura said softly. "We need to stop." She looked at Karla and smiled at her despite her pained expression of guilt. "This is Karla's day."

Karla grabbed the two of them and hugged them tightly and then she kissed each tenderly on the cheek. They were good people and they had been wonderful to her for the past three years. "I'm so thankful for everything you've done for Rebecca and me," she said softly to them. "You know we both love you dearly."

"Oh Karla, you are so good to us," Laura replied, her voice breaking.

"We just so proud of you, you've become a daughter to us, the daughter we never had," George said softly. They walked quietly to the car. Karla realized that they would probably never be able to forgive themselves for the shame they felt, but she had let them know that she had forgiven them long ago. She watched them pull out of the driveway and waved as they drove away from the house and back to their own private shame and she felt a deep empathy and silently prayed that she would never suffer from that type of anguish over Rebecca.

*

The radio played softly as the car idled. Jesse stared at the door waiting for the target to emerge and the longer he watched the angrier he grew. He fingered the gun and checked the opened cylinder to make sure all five bullets were in. He wondered how many times he had checked it but at least it killed time while he waited for the little prick to come out of the bar.

The door opened again and Jesse smiled to himself. The mouthy little guy emerged and turned right, heading up the street. Jesse quickly turned off the engine and climbed out of the car as he placed the gun back in his waistband. He waited for his prey to move up the sidewalk a little and then he crossed the street and fell in behind him.

The kid stopped at the lounge at the end of the block and Jesse smiled. It would be perfect. The place was dimly lit and there weren't very many customers inside. He walked past the bar and jogged to the alley opening, slipping behind a garbage bin and took out his vial of coke. He lifted it to his nose and took a hard snort into his nostrils. He quickly took another in his other and relaxed for a moment to let the high calm his nerves.

At the corner, he quickly glanced around. It wasn't well lit on the streets and there were no crowds. He should have an easy time getting out and hoofing it to his car. He would make it quick, surprise everyone, and escape into the night. There were no longer any self-doubts about what he was going to do. This punk was going to die tonight.

He walked to the door of the bar and opened it. It was as he expected; dimly lit and only three customers at the bar. The kid was at the end of the bar nursing a beer and checking out the ass of an old lady who was talking to the barkeep. Jesse quietly walked over to a table behind him and sat down, checking out the escape routes and making sure that no one was expecting trouble.

The kid slowly walked down the bar and sat in a stool next to the woman. He watched him flirt for a moment and realized that the time was right. He quietly stood up and walked over toward the boy and woman. As he approached him, he pulled the gun out and covered it with both hands.

He was now right behind him and he reached out and tapped him on the back. The kid turned and as he faced him Jesse violently cold-cocked him with the gun, opening a two-inch gash on the kid's face as he crumpled to the ground. The woman screamed and quickly backed away while the two other onlookers and barkeeper stared in horror.

Jesse stood over him and aimed the pistol at his chest and pulled the trigger. The explosion caused everything to go into slow motion and the sounds in his ears sounded far off. The kid bounced slightly from the impact of the bullet hitting his chest. Jesse felt himself pulling the trigger again and saw the kid bounce. He then pulled it three more times as the screaming woman ran wildly away and the two men sitting at the bar flew behind it and ducked. Jesse pulled the trigger again and again, but there were no longer any bullets in the chamber and he finally realized that he had to get out.

He ran through the door and sprinted up the street toward his car, revved the engine and squealed the tires as Charger shot down the street. He needed to calm down or he would be spotted immediately. He drove toward the University and stopped on the empty bridge over the Boise River. No one was around so he rolled the window down and tossed the gun, listening for a splash from below. There was none but he realized that he wouldn't hear it because the river was running so fast.

He drove through town and then headed for the freeway. He drove without any idea of where he was going. He tried to think but his mind could only see the bouncing caused by the bullets going into the chest of the kid. He wouldn't be talking trash to anyone else. He had gotten what he deserved and Jesse felt a new power that he had never felt before although he was sorry, he hadn't put a bullet in the punk's head.

He suddenly understood why Robby was the way he was. Robby had killed in the past and Jesse now understood why he was no longer afraid of anyone. Everyone talks of killing, but few are able to go through with it. He now had this in common with Robby and he knew that it was going to change everything.

The coke slowly began to wear away and Jesse felt the enormity of what he had just done. Soon they would be looking for him and the odds were that they would find him. He had to find someplace to hide, to get his head straight, make a plan. He couldn't go back to his place because that would be the first place the cops would look. There was only one place and he quickly turned around and headed toward a destination he had not been to in years.

*

George and Laura pulled into their driveway and saw the silhouette of a man sitting on the steps that led to their backdoor. George pulled in slowly and recognized the face that stared into their headlights. He pulled up to the garage and cut the engine. "Jesse, what are you doing here?" he asked as he and Laura stepped out of the car.

"I'm in trouble," Jesse murmured, "big trouble."

"What is that all over you?" asked Laura as she came closer to her son.

"Blood," replied Jesse dryly.

"Oh my God," she said as she slumped down over him. "What have you done?"

"I killed a guy," replied Jesse in a matter-of-fact tone. He stood up and walked to the screen door and waited for his parents to open it. "He had it coming. He had a big mouth but he's not saying much now."

"Oh God," Laura said as she sat on the step and began rocking back and forth. George stood at the bottom of the steps and stared blankly at his son, trying to register what he had just been told. Surely it couldn't be true, not his boy. Surely, he hadn't done this. "Oh God," Laura said again with tears welling up in her eyes.

"It's not my fault," protested Jesse. "He had it coming."

George climbed the steps and opened the door. He had to get some water, something to clear the dizziness he was feeling. His heart was beating and he wasn't sure if he were feeling chest pains or if his heart was simply breaking.

He chugged a glass and refilled it, chugging it again as Jesse pulled out the kitchen chair and sat in it.

"Jesus son, you've finally done it. You've destroyed your life!" he bellowed as Laura continued to rock back and forth outside on the steps. Jesse sat silently and George sat down across from him, drinking a third cup as he tried to think of what to do.

"You need to call the police son," he finally said quietly. "Turn yourself in."

"Fuck that!" shouted Jesse and he stood and began to pace around the kitchen. "I'm not going to jail. Hell, they don't even know that I did it. I just need some cash from you so I can get out of town."

"Son, for once in your life you have to take some responsibility," George replied as he stood and grabbed Jesse. "This isn't something you can run from."

"I don't have to do shit!" thundered Jesse as he broke away from his dad. Laura slowly stood, tried to walk, but her legs gave away and she slumped again and buried her head in her hands.

"Jesse, you have to do it or I'll do it for you," George pleaded. "You've gone too far now."

"I am not going to jail," hissed Jesse. "The little shit had it coming."

Laura slowly stood again and finally made her legs work. She walked to the counter and slumped into a stool. She tried but she could not look at her son. He was gone and only this evil shell remained.

"Laura, call 9-1-1," George said softly. "Tell them Jesse is here."

"Mom, don't!" cried Jesse desperately. "I am not going to jail."

"Yes, you are son," she said sadly, finally able to look the grotesque figure that was once her little boy. "You'll probably go for a very long time."

"Mom!"

"Don't make it worse for yourself," she said softly.

"No!" he screamed and he ran out of the house. George and Laura looked at each other as they heard the slam of a car door and the squeal of the tires as it pulled hastily away from the house.

"Oh, George—"

"Call the police, Laura," he said quietly as he poured more water into his glass. The chest pains were gripping him but he had to be strong and he drank the water resolutely as Laura dialed the phone and put it to her ear.

Jesse sped toward Caldwell and found a motel on the west end of town that was by itself and appeared to be mostly empty. He checked himself in and quickly went to his room. Inside he opened a briefcase filled with money and cocaine and grabbed the white powder and spread it out on the top of the television.

The warmth felt good and it helped him to relax. His body was beginning to tire and he realized that he had not eaten yet today. He felt in his pocket and found some change and walked out to the vending machine and grabbed some chips and a Dr. Pepper. Back inside the room he devoured on the chips and watched television. By the time the news came on with the story of the shooting in downtown Boise he was asleep.

All he heard was the crash and when he looked up, he saw six revolvers in his face. He was quickly turned over and his wrists were cuffed tightly behind his back. The cuffs were cold and the tightness of them created painful red welt from his movements. They grabbed him harshly as one read him his rights and quickly took him out to the cruiser whose blue and red lights temporarily blinded him.

The car raced toward the courthouse where the jail was located and went behind the building to an area that had high walls. They pulled him out of the car and waited momentarily for the large steel door to automatically open. Everything had become a blur to him as they took his picture, fingerprinted him, and filled out the paperwork for the prisoner. The grogginess would not dissipate and he wondered if this were nothing more than a dream. He tried to snap himself awake but still, the cloud hung over him.

Three officers walked him down a hallway and he heard the clang of a door being opened. They jammed him face-first on the bed, took the cuffs off him, and then turned and walked out. Jesse heard the door slam shut and suddenly the grogginess evaporated and he became aware of where he was.

For the first time in years, Jesse's mind was clear, and that clarity brought a fear beyond anything he had ever imagined.

KUNA, ID
2018

Chapter 8

Jesse glanced toward the sharpness of the grinding lock of the stainless-steel door disengaging and rose from the white cement slab with the inch-thick mattress that had served as both a couch and bed since he had been sent here from the Idaho Maximum Security Institution in 2007. He picked up a box that had his meager belongings: a roll of toilet paper, a couple of Louie L'Amore novels, his toothbrush and toothpaste, and a worn black comb.

"You ready Jesse?" asked one of the two burly guards in the ash-gray shirt and pants with the shiny black military-style boots. On his hip was a taser and pepper spray and he wore a black baseball cap with ISCI stitched across the front of it on his head.

"I guess," he replied dryly.

"Big day for you," replied the other who dressed the same as his counterpart but was shorter in stature and closer in age to the convict.

"I've waited for this day a long time, Jim."

"Thirty years is a long time indeed," Jim smiled as he adjusted his cap.

"Yeah," replied the prisoner as he passed through the door and began walking toward the commons area with the box against his chest. He was now in his 50s and more than half of his life had been spent behind iron bars, cinderblock walls, and large metal doors. He had entered the old Idaho State Prison during its last years of operation, moved to the IMSI when the old prison had shut down and spent the last four years of his time here at the Idaho State Correctional Institution. He still stubbornly held some of his natural hair colors against an increasing number of grayish streaks that the anxieties of surviving in prison presented. His long angular arms retained much of the muscle of his youth as exercise had become a way to pass time to nowhere but his aging stomach now bulged out into a small pot just beyond his shrinking barrel of a chest. His face was wrinkled around the eyes which each carried a small bag. His hands, though still powerful, had brownish age spots, and his voice now raspy from his pack a day habit.

"Need me to carry that?" asked the younger, more burly guard.

"Nah, I don't have much." They stopped at a large door that led out of the module and waited for it as it slowly slid sideways.

"Well, let's go," the guard named Tom said as he gently nudged the prisoner forward. "Gotta get you checked out, Jesse." The convict glanced at him and his eyes softened for the first time in years.

The process went quicker than he had expected. Some papers to sign, an inventory to check and then he was given some jeans, a new button-up shirt, and some cheap tennis shoes. The clothes were crisp and he tried to remember the last time he had felt anything besides the coveralls he had worn for so long. He tightened the laces of the shoes and his feet began to cramp from the tightness and he smiled at the feeling because it was different than the looseness of the worn flip-flops that were standard wear in the prison.

Tom and he quietly walked to the entry of the prison and the guard reached toward Jesse and they gave each other a firm handshake. "I don't want you to come to back here Jesse, it's time you found a life of your own."

"I guess you're right Tom."

"Odds are that I'll see you again, but you've changed. I think you might have a chance out there."

"Thanks, Tom," he said as the guard gave him a pat on the back and then signaled for the door to be opened. They stood quietly as it slowly moved; sunlight from the outside seeping in, Jesse cupped his hands over his eyes. "Make sure they keep the dogs penned up," he joked half-seriously.

"Stay out of the perimeter and you should be all right. They are a nasty lot aren't they?"

"I haven't been able to win them over," Jesse mumbled as he walked out into the bright sunlight. He didn't look back as he heard the door start to slide shut and felt the warmth of the day which caused his neck to begin to sweat underneath the starched collar of the new shirt he was wearing. At the first gate, he looked at the dog in the perimeter who warned him with a low growl not to come his way. Jesse didn't wait for it to become fully opened before he passed through. He continued to the final gate which did not move until the gate behind him finished closing. At last, he heard the clank of metal and the click of the large lock and the last hurdle between prison and freedom began its slide. He waited until it was completely open and for a moment stood still, unsure what he was feeling.

At last, he walked through it and to the waiting taxi cab that was idling just a few feet away from him. He opened the door but then looked back at the cold facility he had just left behind. The gate moved slowly back to its shut position and Jesse listened for the clang of metal and the click of the lock. He was free now, on the other side of the heavy iron and concrete that had held him captive from the outside but as he crawled into the car he wondered if he was really was free or just entering a new prison.

*

As the cab cruised north on the old Meridian Road, Jesse stared stoically out the window. It had been twenty-nine years since he had last been a passenger in a motor vehicle outside of the prison and he felt some lightheadedness from the ride. His stomach churned and though the cabbie was only driving 50 miles per hour it felt three times that.

"Could you slow it down a little, it's been a while since I've been in a car," he said as he gazed out the window.

"No problem," the cabbie responded as he released the pressure of his foot off the pedal.

Jesse thought of the last time he had come through here. It was back in '89 when the old prison had been shuttered and the inmates had been relocated to Kuna. He remembered riding the prison bus, shackled at the ankles and wrists with a chain surrounding his waist attached to both. It had been a much more uncomfortable ride on his way to the maximum-security unit after serving at the old prison in Boise.

He remembered looking out the window of the bus back then and seeing nothing but undeveloped fields of dirt and sagebrush. The transfer had occurred in the heat of the summer and the bus he had ridden had no air conditioning or shocks for that matter. Each bump in the road sent a jolt through him and he was sure the driver had tried to hit each pothole along the way. He reminisced that the emptiness of the countryside was much like the way he felt inside, void of any hope of freedom and the silent anxiety of only time lying ahead of him.

"How long were you in?" asked the cabbie, hoping to start some sort of conversation.

"Long enough," replied Jesse without looking at the driver. Now hotels and malls and shops and office buildings littered the countryside. Cars zoomed by his window and past them, he could see people going here and there and all of them seemed to be in some sort of hurry. Everything was so much bigger now, faster than he remembered.

"Things have changed some, huh?"

"Some," he acknowledged.

"Must feel good to be out, huh?" asked the cab as he slowly increased the speed of the car, wanting to get the con to his destination as quickly as possible so he could get back to the airport and pick up fares that would tip. Jesse didn't

107

answer but instead continued to stare in silent fascination. "I said it must feel good to be out, huh?"

"I heard you," Jesse replied while trying not to sound irritated but the fact was that this guy was starting to wear on his nerves.

"Not a talker huh? That's OK. I'll leave you alone, bud."

Jesse felt the twinge in his stomach again as the car entered the freeway and again picked up speed. His hand tightened on the door handle and his other pressed against the seat. The cabbie sped toward Boise and finally slowed down as he entered the freeway exit ramp on Boise Avenue. The city had changed, gotten bigger and the people seemed to be everywhere. He wondered why they were in such a hurry and questioned whether maybe it was the same as before but because he had been gone so long, he had forgotten what being on the outside of the walls was like.

The car turned onto an older street in need of a new coat of asphalt and pulled in front of an old building with a painted sign that was chipped and peeling reading METRO HOTEL. The place had obviously been quite the sight once, but that was a long time ago. Now it looked like a flophouse and Jesse wasn't sure he wanted to get out of the cab anymore.

"Here you go, bud. The state has already paid the tab but I'll take a tip," said the cabbie.

"Maybe the next guy," replied Jesse as he opened the door and grabbed his box and a bag the prison had given him with a change of clothes. He looked at the drab building and for a moment had thought of dropping everything and running but there was no place to go and this was no longer the town he remembered.

"Cheapskate," the driver muttered as he pulled away from the curb. "I hate driving the cons."

Jesse again felt the painful twinge in his stomach and he realized that it had never been from the ride but fear of being out. Alone, he was now truly alone. No family, no friends, nothing. He felt lost, scared of the speed that the world was going, and began to wonder why he had wanted for so long to be released. He began to think that his reward for the last years of good behavior was not freedom but a release into an urban jungle that he was not prepared for or equipped to survive.

"Mr. Rayburn?"

Jesse turned toward the voice. It came from a small man with greasy hair and horned rim black glasses who was sweating on the forehead and had drenched his shirt under his pits.

"I guess that's me," Jesse answered tentatively.

"Let's get you moved in." He gently took the bag from Jesse's hand. "This all you have?"

Jesse nodded and obediently followed the man into the grayish brick building that stood three stories tall and towered over the other buildings of the used up block.

"I'm Carl, Carl Jackson," he said as they entered the lobby area of the old hotel that now served as a halfway house for recently released convicts. "I imagine you feel pretty overwhelmed right now. I saw that you had been incarcerated for thirty years." They walked up the stairs to the second floor and Carl took him to room 212. "Here we go," he said as he unlocked the door and walked in.

Jesse looked at the sparse room. It had a double bed that had obviously been used for years without a change of mattress. In the corner, a door led to the bathroom that held a standard toilet, sink, and a stand-up shower. Under the window by the bed was an old iron heater and Carl chuckled as he mentioned that it might clank every now and then. He pointed out that the old place now had electrical heating and pointed to the control on the wall. A small television sat on a scratched table and the room had a small kitchenette with an old oven and a microwave that sat on the miniature refrigerator that looked as old as Jesse felt.

"Here's your key, Mr. Rayburn," Carl said as he handed it to him on his way out of the room. "If you have any problems just come to the front desk and we'll fix it up for you." Jesse watched the door close and the quietness of the wood hitting wood surprised him. He had become used to the clanging of the metal doors and had forgotten that a door could be as quiet as this one was even with its squeak from the hinges.

He put his box on the bed and sat down on the worn mattress, pushing his hand against it and feeling the softness that the thickness of the mattress produced. Again, he thought about all he had forgotten while inside. Things were different out here, too quiet, and it was unsettling and it dawned on him that he was not at all prepared for this new world he had stepped into. He felt as though he were Rip Van Winkle and he wanted to go back to sleep and wake up back where his previous life had ended.

*

Jesse walked to the front desk and rang the small bell on the counter that brought Carl out through a door that led from his small office. When he saw it was Jesse, he motioned to him to stay for a moment and he disappeared back into the office and shortly after emerged with some papers in his hand.

"I was just about to call you, Mr. Rayburn. I have some paperwork I need you to fill out," he said as he led Jesse to a small table in the lobby. Jesse filled out the papers deliberately and handed them back to Carl after a few minutes who in turn handed Jesse a phone number.

"You need to call this number to get in touch with your parole officer. You can use the phone behind the front desk today but any calls after this will have to be from the payphone in the lobby."

Jesse followed Carl to the phone and dialed the number. The automated system of the answering service bewildered him and Carl took the receiver from him until he finally got an actual person on the line and handed the phone back to Jesse. He answered some quick questions and motioned to Carl for a pen and paper. He wrote down the address and the direct number of the probation office and then hung up.

"Am I close to Front Street?" he asked Carl.

"It's three or four blocks over. What time's your appointment with your parole officer?"

"3:00"

"Better get going, you have 45 minutes or so," and he gave Jesse directions to the Ada County Probation and Parole building. Jesse walked out of the building and noticed how vulnerable he felt once outside and on the street. He continually glanced around him as he walked until finally reaching Front Street. Again, he noticed the speed of the cars and the quickened pace of those around him and he tried to control the paranoia he felt growing inside of him.

Two blocks later he walked through a glass door with ADA COUNTY PROBATION AND PAROLE stenciled on it. He announced himself to a serious-looking deputy behind a thick glass who pointed towards a phone and he picked it up and waited. Jesse did as instructed and soon a voice on the receiver asked for his name and told him he would be met momentarily. Jesse hung up and found a seat on a gray, plastic chair across from a soda dispenser and waited nervously until a man in tan slacks and a brown shirt with a badge hanging around his neck asked him to follow. They silently walked through a set of doors toward a sterile office at the end of the hallway. The deputy pointed towards a chair and told him to have a seat as he walked around the desk.

"I'm Robert Jenkins," he said as he began thumbing through Jesse's folder. "I'm your parole officer. You got out earlier today I see."

"Yes sir," Jesse responded as he looked around the office that was spotless yet barren. He noticed there were no pictures of any family or friends and the metal desk was devoid of everything but a folder, a laptop computer, and a phone. Robert fingered through the folder and occasionally took his pen and jotted a note or two on the page he was looking at.

"That's a long stint you served," he said as he looked up from the folder. "Fortunately, you're still a relatively young man." Jesse nodded. He didn't feel young anymore but there wasn't anything to be gained by arguing. "I see you served 30 of a 35. That means that for the next five years you need to follow the terms of your parole or you'll be back inside. Do you understand this?"

"Yes."

"Let's go through the basics. Right now, you have a curfew of 9:00 pm. Obviously no drugs or alcohol; actually, let me make a copy of this so you can follow it." Robert walked out of the office and Jesse stared out the window. The day was sunny and again he became fixated on how fast everything and everyone was. Robert returned a couple of minutes later and handed Jesse the copy and pointed to where he was at on the page.

"All right, let's see. No alcohol or drugs. You will need to be at the halfway house for another month at least until you get your feet underneath you, then you'll be expected to get your own place and take care of yourself. You still understand everything?" asked Robert and Jesse nodded. "Good. We have a job for you at Logan's Lumberyard." He reached into his desk and pulled out a business card and wrote down the address and the phone number on the back. "You have to stay in-state and we will meet weekly for the next month but will eventually cut back to once month. Any questions so far?"

"No," replied Jesse as he accepted the card that Robert handed to him.

"Do you have any family nearby?"

"I don't think so," replied Jesse.

"That's either a yes or a no, Mr. Rayburn."

"I have a daughter but I don't know where she is. I haven't seen her since before I went to prison."

"I understand, how about your parents? Are they still alive?"

"Both have passed on," replied Jesse evenly.

"I'm sorry. Now, Mr. Rayburn, I'm not here to reform you. In theory, the prison system did that…" Jesse smirked despite himself. "Yes, well, as I was saying, my job is to make sure you integrate back into society without being a danger to yourself or others. I'm not your friend or confidant. If you follow your program of parole, everything will be fine. If not, it's my job to put you back into incarceration. Do you understand?"

Jesse nodded and wished the meeting would end.

"You will be subjected to random drug tests that can occur at any time. We don't give more than 24-hour notice and if you do not show up it is considered a positive test which will violate your parole, do you understand?" Jesse again nodded.

"Tomorrow you will start at your new job. Give the address I gave you to Carl Jackson at the halfway house and he'll get you to your job."

"All right," replied Jesse as Robert reached into his desk again and grabbed another one of his cards and he wrote a date and time on the back of it.

"That's all I have for now. I've set up our next appointment on the back of my card," he said as he handed the card to Jesse. "Call me if there is a problem."

Robert stood up and stretched out his hand to Jesse and the two men shook and then he led him back down the hall to the waiting room. As Jesse left the building, he stopped and looked to his left and right and then turned left and walked slowly, hoping that he was going the right direction.

*

He sat on the bed and stared out the window toward the setting sun that was slowly disappearing behind the mountains that appeared to be closer than they actually were. The light shone brightly through his window and he watched it slowly move across the room as the sun dipped further behind the hills until the last remnant of its rays slipped out of the window and a darkening shadow replaced it. He realized he had never watched the sunset before, not that he had many opportunities in the last thirty years. After he had left the old prison in '89 none of his cells had windows, just an eight by the eight-foot slab of painted brick and cement.

He was afraid of what the future held for him. All the people and the fast pace of everything made him paranoid, but the sunset that he had just watched provided him with an understanding at last of why he had so desperately wanted to be free for so long. The simple pleasure of seeing the sun dip behind a mountain, something taken for granted by so many, provided him with a true insight of what freedom actually was and for the short period he had watched this wonderment of nature he felt a peace within himself that he did not known existed and reveled in the enthrallment of something that was much bigger than him and felt a closeness to an outer being that before he had only pretended to know.

He walked to his door and toyed with the lock, locking and unlocking it; a simple procedure that for so long had been in somebody else's hand on the other side. He opened and slowly closed the door, repeating these four more times. On the fifth time, he stepped through the doorway because he could and looked down the hall and then stepped back into his room, not closing it but instead running his hand up and down the narrow length and feeling the brass dead latch, slowly pushing it in and out. He began to close the door again but

112

stopped and slowly opened it completely. Tonight, he would sleep with an open door. He did not care if that would make him unsafe. Tonight, he had a choice and if someone were to come in and do him harm, at least it would be because of the decision of a free man to spend at least one night of his life out in the open, not locked behind another door.

He slowly pulled what meager belongings he had out of his box and found places for each of them. He grabbed the bag with the new set of clothes provided by the prison and took them to the closet and carefully hung them from the wire hangers that were now bent and showed the years of usage they had put in. His bed was mussed from where he had been sitting and he carefully ironed out the wrinkles with his hand and fluffed the pillow he had pulled out from under the bedspread and covered it again and then he walked back to the door and admired his space.

He felt pangs of hunger and he decided to go downstairs to the kitchen and grab something to eat and realized that for the first time since going inside he was deciding for himself when he would eat. He closed the door and locked it with his key, checked it to make sure and proceeded down the steps, and saw a sign pointing toward the dining room and followed it. He saw some tables and a long bar with seats latched to the floor and sat down. A person unfamiliar to him from behind the bar told him what was being served and Jesse nodded and he disappeared into the kitchen and came back a minute later with a plate that had a toasted tuna fish sandwich and a bowl of cream of celery soup. Jesse asked for some coffee and a man with a white t-shirt and apron around his waist and his long hair in a hairnet grabbed a cup and filled it with the thick black fluid that barely changed color when Jesse put cream in it.

As he ate the sandwich, he thought about his parents. George had suffered a heart attack the night he had been arrested and had never been the same. Within a year he had sold the garage and lasted only a few more painful years before a massive heart attack hit him while sitting in a lawn chair by himself in his back yard. Laura had soldiered on after George's passing and Jesse remembered seeing her for the last time after he had put a dime into his sentence. A couple of months later he had received word that she had died from lung cancer from a smoking habit that had begun after her husband's death. He hadn't even known she smoked until they told her of her death. He remembered that he hadn't felt anything about them dying and in fact was still blaming them for calling the cops and putting them on his trail among their other failings.

Now he thought of what their life must have been like. He had been their pride and joy growing up and their nightmare after. He hadn't cared and treated them in such a horrible fashion but had only realized it in the last few years. He remembered clearly when it had finally dawned on him what he had done to them. He was in one of those supposed self-help groups run by prison missionaries or whatever they were and one had confronted him when he started complaining about the old man. The do-gooder had made him angry and he had stood up to walk out but this time the guy had followed him and signaled for the guards not to let him out of the room. He continued to push him and Jesse had threatened to beat him to death but still, the guy wouldn't back down and kept badgering him on what he had done to the old man and not vice versa. Finally, Jesse had just shut up and the man gently led him back to where the group was sitting and before he knew it he was telling them what he had done, things he had said and the anger he had felt for being made to 'do the right thing' that he was sure had led him here in the first place.

Since that time Jesse hadn't been able to shake the things out of his head that he had done to his folks and a strange pain had developed because they were gone now and there was no way to let them know that he now realized what a horse's ass he was. He desperately wanted to apologize and start over with them so he could find some way to make it up to them but they were gone now and it was too late. When they had died, they had left this world with the knowledge that their son hated them and that pained him because they hadn't deserved that. He couldn't fix the past he realized, but he could start over and maybe be half the guy he had once dreamed of being and he became determined to make the effort this time. He owed them at least that.

*

Jesse washed the remaining remnants of shaving cream off his face and put tiny pieces of toilet paper over the minute cuts that never seemed to stop bleeding. He walked to the closet and pulled out the new set of clothes and put them on quickly and left the room to get some breakfast. As he passed Carl, he suggested to Jesse good-naturedly to take the toilet paper pieces off his face and he embarrassedly smiled and rubbed his hand over his jaw to knock them off. In the dining room, he saw it was buffet style and walked over and grabbed a plate and put some eggs and a couple of pieces of bacon on it and grabbed some orange juice and sat down at an empty table.

The food wasn't great, but it did taste better than the crud they served behind the walls. He quickly ate the food and took his plate up to the side of the bar and put it in the dirty plate holder and walked out to the lobby to talk to Carl.

"My parole officer told me that you would be taking me to a job he has lined up for me," Jesse said.

"Yeah, I'll be leaving in about ten minutes. The van's outside. There are four of you going today. You're going to Lloyd's Lumberyard, aren't you?"

"Yeah," Jesse replied and then he went and sat down in a large, cushiony chair to wait. Ten minutes later he was in the van as it made its drop-offs and soon Carl pulled up to the lumberyard.

"Call this number when you're done tonight and I'll come to get you." Jesse nodded and stepped out of the van and felt the nerves in his stomach tighten. The van pulled away from the curb and Jesse anxiously took some deep breaths and then walked into the office where a middle-aged lady with colored red hair sat at a desk typing on a computer. She asked if she could help him without looking up from the screen in front of her and Jesse told her who he was and handed her the paperwork that Robert had given him the day before. She glanced up from the screen to look at the papers and then disappeared into the back. He walked to the chair by the door and sat down hoping that he wasn't showing how nervous he felt and she soon reappeared and went back to her work without saying anything to him.

A few minutes later a man came from the back and called his name. The man was also middle-aged with a balding head that was already sweating. He was large with a big stomach and thick hands and he wore a white button-up shirt and blue jeans with steel-toed boots on his feet. His voice was deep and he appeared to be in a hurry and somewhat irritated that whatever he had been doing was being interrupted. He led Jesse to his office which reminded him of his dad's. It was small and musty, dust overtaking everything but the top of the desk, which was cluttered with papers and invoices and a laptop with an oversize mouse plugged into it.

"Jesse, here's the deal," he said gruffly as he sat down in a wooden chair with rollers on the bottom that squeaked as they moved. "I'm Tom Mitchell but you call me Mr. Mitchell. I own this lumberyard, bought it from Mr. Lloyd back in '97 when he retired. He was a good man and he started this program where we give jobs to newly released convicts like you. I've never been crazy about it myself but I've kept it going in honor of him and I've been told that I'm supposed to give you a job. That means you're taking a spot from someone else, someone I would have interviewed, checked references, and hired."

"Yes sir," Jesse responded, feeling his anxiety raise.

"Personally, I haven't had much luck with you parolees but hey, I get free labor from it because the state pays for you as part of your entrance back into society. You have four weeks to prove you're worthy of keeping because then I have to pay you. If you're not worthy, I drop you. If anything is missing, I'm going to assume you're behind it. Don't steal from me, you understand?" The words sounded eerily familiar from more than a quarter-century before and he remembered how well that had ended up for him but he nodded.

"Good, let's get you to work then," he said and they walked out of the office and out toward a pile of boards where a tall man in a dusty baseball cap was barking at a couple of workers who he deemed to be moving too slowly.

"Todd," Mr. Mitchell shouted and the taller man barked some quick orders, spit some tobacco juice on the ground, and walked toward them. "This is Jesse Rayburn. The state has sent him to us. Let's see what he can do. Jesse, this is Todd Miller, he's my foreman. What he says is the law out here. He's your Todd," and with that, the proprietor turned and walked back toward his office.

"You ever work in a lumberyard before?"

"No sir," replied Jesse.

"Go over there," he said pointing to another pile of two by fours. "I want you to stack that load twelve across and twenty-four high on that trestle. Make sure they're even." Jesse started piling the boards as he had been told but soon, he felt winded and his arms began to tire and his back ached from bending over.

"You need to pick it up, convict. Looks like you've been lying around on the public's dime for too long. We have to work out here, now pick it up because I have more things you need to get done today," Miller sneered as he walked past him

Jesse nodded and tried to pick up his pace. For the rest of the day he put up with the razzing and kept trying to work faster to keep this guy off his back but no matter what he did the asshole always came back and was unhappy about something he had done.

He survived the day and leaned his head against the window of the van as it lumbered toward the halfway house. When it arrived, he slowly climbed the stairs to his room but it was painful as muscles that he had forgotten about now screamed from being awakened from their slumber. He was hungry but too tired to go back down so he lay on his bed and stared out the window.

He was out now, there were more freedoms than before but today had taught him something. Though he was no longer behind the walls and razor wire and the dogs patrolling the perimeter, nothing had really changed. He still had to answer to people that didn't give a shit about him. The bulls wore plain clothes now, but they were still in charge.

Chapter 9

The woman behind the mahogany desk finished the final notes of her previous visitor and looked down at her daily planner to see who was next. She had met with four clients already today but she still had a few minutes before the next one so she opened her side desk drawer and pulled out a small bag of carrots and carefully pulled one out and took a small bite of the textured nub.

Her office was tastefully decorated though not elaborate. The desk faced the wall away from the door and against another wall was a comfortable white sofa with firm cushions and tasteful small pillows on each end. In front of it was a glass living room table with three decorative clay jars filled with shined pebbles. Across from the couch was an antique rocking chair that had been refinished and now had an off-white pad on the seat. The carpet was a light salmon color while the walls, which were decorated with art-deco prints was the color of the pad that rested in the rocking chair. In the corner, she had a mahogany bookshelf that matched the desk and was filled with books written by psychologists and experts in their fields.

She glanced at her watch and saw that it was time to meet with the next appointment just as her phone buzzed to let her know that he was here and waiting. She grabbed another carrot out of the bag and grabbed the folder she had along with her notepad and walked out into the hallway toward the reception area. She handed the folder to the receptionist who in turn handed her another with information about this upcoming visitor and introduced the two.

"Good morning," she said to him as she stuck out her hand to shake his. "My name is Margaret Taylor."

"I'm Jesse," he said quietly, taking her hand that was soft in his. The woman led him down the hallway toward her office while offering small talk to try to alleviate his anxiety at the first meeting. She invited him to sit on the couch as they entered her office and she sat in her rocking chair and opened the folder, seeing a mug shot of the man sitting before her and realized that he looked familiar to her. She quickly scanned his folder and immediately recognized him from many years before and did her best to hide her surprise as she wondered how he had come to this point and then vaguely remembered the sensational stories of shooting from many years before.

He looked at her and she reminded him of someone from years earlier also but he couldn't place her. She was a pretty woman, not beautiful and though she was now entering middle age she still showed signs of what she must have looked like in her youth. She had fashionable black reading glasses that hung from beads over white button-up top and brown slacks with black high heels, not so high to be slutty, but about an inch which gave her a professional appearance. Her brunette hair with an occasional gray strand was shoulder length and her skin was tight though wrinkles had begun to develop around her eyes. She was neither overweight nor skinny and he noticed she had no ring on her left hand but did on her right and he realized that she had probably once been married but was no longer.

"So, you are Jesse Rayburn," she said in a friendly tone. "As I told you, my name is Margaret and I'm an LCSW which is a fancy way of telling you I'm a counselor. I have my own practice here but I also work for the State of Idaho to help people like you integrate back into society."

"People like me?" and he immediately felt a flush of anger and resentment toward her. She obviously felt she was better than him because she was educated, but as quickly as it came it went away for he knew she probably was.

"I'm sorry. Probably not the best wording I could have used. What I mean is that the State of Idaho contracts with me to work with recently released parolees who have been incarcerated for a significant period of time. My job is to help you make the transition back into society successful and help you deal with issues that could cause you problems in the future. I also want to help you recognize the triggers of those problems and how to deal with them before you do something that will cause you to become re-incarcerated. Does that make sense?"

Jesse nodded his head. He kind of liked her already. She didn't seem to have any agenda or pre-conceived notions about him other than the information she had in the folder that was sitting in her lap.

"So, you have been out for approximately ten days it looks like, is that correct?" she asked.

"Yes," he replied.

"And you are currently living in a halfway house at 621 Idaho Avenue, room 212?"

"I guess that's the address," replied Jesse, feeling self-conscious that he didn't know as he began to fidget with his fingers.

"Carl Jackson is the overseer of the house?"

"Yeah."

"And you've met with your parole officer I assume."

"I have."

"I have here that you are currently working at Lloyd's Lumberyard on 10328 Capital Boulevard. Tom Mitchell is your employer?" Jesse nodded but didn't speak. He didn't like the guy and figured that his employment would end as soon as the cheapskate would have to start paying him instead of the State.

"How are you doing at the halfway house, any problems?"

"It's fine."

"And your job?" she asked while still looking down at the papers in front of her.

"Same," he replied without any conviction in his voice as he began to nervously pat his fingers against his legs.

"I'm sorry if this is boring, Mr. Rayburn, but the state has paperwork so I find it best to get it out of the way as quickly as possible."

"That's fine, I understand. You can call me Jesse if you wish. My father was Mr. Rayburn. I've been called a lot of things, but not that recently."

She looked up from the paperwork and smiled and then it hit her. She knew who he was. She remembered him from a different time when the entire world was at his fingertips. As she remembered she felt sad for him, the loss of what could have been, and the scandal of her freshman year in high school of the star quarterback came rushing back into her mind.

"Do you remember me, Jesse?" she asked softly.

"What? I'm sorry, no, should I?"

"I remember you."

"Really, from where? Did you come to the prison or something?"

"We went to school together at Boise High School. I was a freshman when you were a senior."

"Really?" asked Jesse, "I can't seem to place you but I admit you seem familiar to me."

"Not surprising," she giggled. "I kind of hung back being a freshman, but I actually had a secret crush on you."

"Really—"

"Yes. I grew up in a football house I guess you could say. My dad played in college so Friday nights were always family night at the high school games. Anyway, I remember watching you play and I had a secret crush," she laughed and he doused in the friendliness of it, the non-threatening nature of the way she spoke to him and the thrill that after all these years somebody actually remembered him.

"That was a long time ago," he smiled and he saw that she was starting to blush for opening up to him.

"Longer than I care to remember, Jesse. You were quite the player I remember. I remember a time where you threw a touchdown pass at the end of the game which I think won a conference championship for us. That was very exciting."

"That was against Bishop Kelly," remarked Jesse, remembering the game like it was yesterday. That had been the zenith of his career, the night that UNLV had told him that they wanted him. "Yeah, that was a good night."

"I remember that you had a girlfriend back then that you had been going out with for some time. She was so pretty, a cheerleader, I think…Who was she?"

"I don't remember," replied Jesse darkly. The conversation had suddenly taken a turn toward an area in his life he didn't want to go. Margaret recognized this immediately and decided to push him a little, see where it led.

"I'm just trying to think of her name," she said innocently. "As I said she was very pretty and I'm sure you had been dating her for a long period of time." Jesse's face remained impassive and she could tell he was trying to check out. "She was my competition, you know," she pressed in a joking manner.

"I don't want to talk about her," he said quietly as he looked away from her and toward one of the fashionable art-deco prints on the wall.

"I'm sorry," Margaret said and she sat quietly for a minute waiting for Jesse to say something. He finally looked back toward her, the silence in the room beginning to drive him crazy.

"What's that got to do with this anyway?" he asked, the silence being more than he could handle. "I'm here because I was told to meet with you."

"I'm sorry Jesse, is it still all right for me to call you by your first name?" and Jesse nodded that it was. "That was rude of me. I was only trying to break the ice so to speak."

"It's alright," sighed Jesse, "just brings up bad memories."

"All right, let's get back to this paperwork so we can move on," she said as she looked back down at the papers on her lap. "So, I see you served thirty years for aggravated assault. Could you tell me what happened?"

"I got drunk and shot a guy."

"Jesse, I need a little more information. Could you give me some details of what led to the shooting?"

"It was a long time ago, I don't remember," he stated coldly.

"I think you do."

"I did my time."

"No, you've completed thirty years of your thirty-five-year sentence. You still have another five years of probation to get through before your sentence is complete. I want to help you get through that successfully. Now, could you please tell me more about that evening?"

He stared at her coldly, glaring into her eyes, and in the deep recesses of his mind, he was impressed that she didn't seem to scare easily.

"Why are you so angry, Jesse?"

"Who says I'm angry?"

"You do, with your eyes, your non-verbal cues, your body language, the tightening of your fists, the grinding of your teeth…would you like me to continue?"

"I don't know, you're the counselor, the LSCC, LWSC, or whatever you said," he replied.

"LCSW," she answered. "It stands for Licensed Certified Social Worker."

"Whatever. I'm sure all your questions can be answered by the file. Thirty years and all I am is a damn file."

"All right, let's see what your file says. Hmmm…" she looked at the file and began reading and let the silence grow knowing that it made him uncomfortable but he remained defiant and held his tongue. "I see you were involved in different groups while in prison. Can you tell me about them?"

"It's in the file," he replied condescendingly as he looked at the clock on her desk.

"I see you were in Alcoholics Anonymous, Anger Management, MRT, a bible study group…that's interesting."

"Beats being in a cell," he replied and she looked up with a slight smile as she now had a direction to go.

"So, did you gain any insight from being in these groups?"

"Insight?" he laughed.

"Did you learn anything?"

He didn't answer and he could feel his stomach being to knot. He wanted to leave and get some air to calm down. He didn't like being angry anymore and this woman was pushing some buttons that he had forgotten he had.

"Maybe you were just using these groups, running a con," she said as a brow rose slightly.

"Why do you say that?" he asked dryly, but he realized that maybe she had his number.

"Because you're not saying anything, was it a con Jesse? Were you just trying to fool the parole board maybe?"

He didn't answer. Maybe she was right; maybe all he had done in those groups was used them to impress the board to let him out. Then again, maybe she was just another do-gooder who thought she had all the answers but didn't know shit.

"You haven't told me that you learned anything yet so I ask again, were you just taking these groups to con the parole board? Show them how you were rehabilitated?"

Jesse stood up and glared at her and was amazed that she showed no outward signs of fear. "Can I go?" he asked in a menacing tone.

"You're not in prison anymore Jesse. You can leave whenever you wish." He began walking toward the door and reached out for the knob. "Before you leave Jesse, I want you to think about something."

"What?" he asked, not turning to face her.

"When I was a freshman and you were a senior, I was afraid to talk to you. I was awe-struck. I'm not that girl anymore. When you come back, and at some point, I hope you will, leave the prison attitude at the door. I'm here to help you but you have to help with this process. I've worked with a lot of convicts. Some successfully, others ended back in prison. Those that leave the attitude behind tend to make it. It's going to be up to you."

Jesse turned toward her and glared. He realized that what she had said was probably true but she was no different than anyone else. She was just another prison guard, just one dressed in nice clothes with a nice place to work, but in reality, nothing more than a bull. She stood up and walked toward him and he thought of walking out before she got to him but something made him stand there.

"Here's my card," she said as she reached out to him. "I hope you will eventually want to deal with the issues that you've carried with you for years and new ones you'll be experiencing. When you're ready, give me a call."

Jesse smirked and took the card from her and glanced at it. "I suppose anything's possible," he said and then he walked through the door and pulled it shut. "But I wouldn't hold my breath, counselor," he said under his breath.

Chapter 10

Jesse put the key in the knob and turned it and the door opened. He walked through the small hallway that led to the main room of the studio apartment in the old, former Catholic school that was now a subsidized apartment building for the downtrodden. It wasn't anything special, just a room with a small kitchen connected to it. On the left side of the small hallway that led into the main room was a closet with sliding doors. Across from it was the bathroom with a bathtub that had no curtain, a small sink with a mirror above it, and a nondescript toilet. In the main room, the floor was covered with a deep brown carpet with off white walls surrounding it. Around the corner was a simple kitchen with a sink in the corner and four scratched cabinets above it that led to the oven below them. Introducing the kitchen to the living room was an old fridge that made straining sounds at it attempted to retain the coolness necessary to keep the perishables from perishing.

Carl had informed Jesse last week that he needed to find a place to live because the state only paid for a month at the halfway house. He checked the want ads in the *Idaho Statesman* and inspected a couple of places but had settled on this because the rent was cheap and it was only a ten-minute walk to the lumberyard. In the living room was a small bed against the near wall and on the far side another closet and a couple of worn chairs that sat in front of it. In the kitchen sat a table with two rickety chairs. He put his bag on the bed and carried his box to the table and set it down. In the box was everything he had brought with him from prison and sitting on top of it was the lease he had just signed.

Though small it actually seemed quite big to Jesse. After a quarter of a century in an eight by eight-foot cell and a month in the halfway house, this was bigger than both combined. He had liked it the first time he had seen it, had a homey feel to it, a place that he could call his own and he had agreed to the $250.00 rent. The job was earning him a little over a thousand a month and thus far he had no bills which made him feel kind of wealthy. If he could keep the job, he'd be fine, but every day was a struggle and he was hoping that maybe something would pop up to take its place.

He hated the job. Not so much the job he realized but he hated Mitchell and the foreman Miller. Both were pricks, but the foreman was the biggest and really needed a good beating. Every day he took the abuse and did the best he could but each new morning he was finding it harder to go back. He had survived the first month and now he knew that his job was tenuous at best. Mitchell only wanted convicts because they were cheap labor to him. Jesse knew it was just a matter of time before he would be letting him go and getting himself another freebie for a month to do the shit work that needed to be done. Miller's job was to give Mitchell a reason to fire the con and he was good at it though he had not yet found the right button to push on Jesse to give the boss a reason to give him the heave-ho.

He survived for another week without any real incidents at work. Miller gave him more crap over being a convict, but he was getting his work done with time to spare and yesterday Mitchell had actually paid him a compliment. Maybe he would survive, at least long enough to put a little money aside for a rainy day. At night he worked on the apartment, moving the sparse furniture around, spending time at the supermarket, and finding things he needed to spiff up the place or build up his food reserve. He enjoyed this new feeling of independence, making decisions for himself, and he started to feel some optimism about his future. Even his parole officer was saying good things to him and seemed pleased with his progress in transitioning to the outside.

Three days after he met with Jenkins at the Ada County Probation and Parole office, he hit the snooze button of his new clock radio when it went off at six in the morning. When he looked again, it was 7:17 and he scrambled out of bed and pulled on his clothes. He burst from his apartment and ran as fast as he could to the lumberyard. He clocked in at 7:35, five minutes late, and mentally prepared himself for the taunts he knew would be spewing out of Miller's mouth.

"Where the hell you been, dipshit?" the foreman hollered at him as he came running out of the office.

"I'm sorry, I overslept," Jesse mumbled.

"Sure, you did. I think you were out partying last night's convict. You need to take your job seriously!"

"Yes sir, I'm sorry boss."

Todd glared at him and Jesse looked at the dusty ground to avoid the icy stare. "If you're going to act like a dipshit you can do dipshit work. Go over behind the warehouse and help clean up. Try not to screw that up, convict!"

"Yes sir," Jesse replied and he began running toward the warehouse. Miller watched him and took out his can of snuff and put a pinch between his cheek and gum. Convict wasn't going to last much longer and he knew that soon he would be breaking in another that the State of Idaho would send them. He smiled because he knew that soon he would be getting another bonus for getting rid of paid help.

Jesse joined Jeremy Jacobs who was raking refuse into a pile and quietly grabbed a rake and did the same. Jeremy was a college kid who was back for the summer and using the job to help make some money for next year's tuition. He was a short kid, sandy blonde hair that was cut short and was pretty quiet most of the time. When he saw Jesse coming towards him, he was a little intimidated, he knew Jesse was the guy just out of prison but he seemed pretty nice the few times they had run into each other. Still, he didn't want to make him mad and the guy didn't talk much so he kept his head down. They worked together quietly and for the next couple of hours raked the broken boards, cardboard, and wire on the ground into piles.

After finishing the last pile, Jeremy grabbed the wheelbarrow and a couple of shovels and the two started loading and taking it over to a burn pile set up at the edge of the lumberyard. They worked quietly and made good progress, Jesse loading the junk into the wheelbarrow, Jeremy raking to keep the piles tight. Jesse stuck the shovel into the refuse and threw it toward the wheelbarrow. As he did, Jeremy saw some cardboard and wire and stepped toward it to rake it into the pile. Suddenly he did he felt a hard shot across his jaw and crumpled to the ground, still conscious but seeing little white dots against a black backdrop.

"Jeremy! Jeremy! You alright kid? Jeremy, can you hear me?" Jesse cried as he leaned over him. Jeremy slowly opened his eyes and rubbed his jaw. He saw blood on his hands as he set up. "Jeremy…you OK kid?"

Todd saw the convict leaning over the kid and came charging over and threw Jesse away from Jeremy. "What the hell happened here?" he screamed.

"I accidentally hit him with the shovel when I was throwing this stuff into the wheelbarrow," Jesse replied as he stood up and dusted himself off.

"Accidently? Sure, it was. You're not man enough to face me down so you hit Jeremy huh?" screamed the foreman, pushing Jesse in the chest.

"That's not what happened!" protested Jesse as other men in the yard ran over to see what was going on.

"Sure, it didn't," Miller screamed into Jesse's face, "just an accident, kinda like when you shot that kid…yeah, that's right, I looked you up, convict."

"Boss, it was an accident," Jeremy said woozily, "I'm OK."

"Shut up Jeremy!" the foreman hissed. "You want a piece of me, convict? I fight back, you fucking pussy!"

Jesse did and it was taking everything he had not to beat the asshole to a pulp. Tom Mitchell came running from the office as he saw the growing crowd and heard the yelling in the yard. "What's going on here?" he demanded as he pushed his way through men to get to the center where he saw the bleeding kid and his foreman's nose to nose with the convict.

"Rayburn here hit Jeremy with the shovel, boss!"

"That true?" he asked, his eyes settling on Jesse.

"It was an accident, Mr. Mitchell."

"Jeremy, go get that looked at, there's a first aid kit in the office," the owner said and he directed a couple of guys to help Jeremy. "You hit him on purpose, Jesse?"

"Of course not, I was throwing the refuse into the wheelbarrow and wasn't paying attention. It was my fault but it wasn't on purpose," Jesse said, his eyes downcast.

"He was also late this morning, boss," sneered Miller.

"That true Jesse?"

"Yes sir, I overslept."

Mitchell's piercing eyes seem to stare straight through Jesse. He was quiet and Jesse stared back pleadingly at him. He hadn't done it on purpose, it was just an accident and he felt bad for the kid, but accidents did happen in lumberyards. This couldn't be the first time he thought to himself, it just couldn't be.

"Hasn't been smooth, has it," Mr. Mitchell finally said quietly.

"I'm doing all right," protested Jesse but his heart was sinking.

"Not really. Todd here tells me you're slow and now you're coming in late and people are getting hurt."

"I'll do better, Mr. Mitchell."

"I don't think so, son. I don't think this is the right place for you." Jesse could feel himself redden with embarrassment. Not only was the guy firing him, and he was doing it in front of everybody.

"Please, I'll do better."

"Nah, I gotta let you go. I'll contact your parole officer; let him know you need something different."

"Please Mr. Mitchell," pleaded Jesse.

"Good luck Jesse," he said. "Everybody gets back to work now; we have a schedule to keep." He motioned Jesse to follow him back to the office and began walking.

"See ya convict," smirked Miller as he walked off.

Jesse slowly trudged behind the owner toward the office. His mind was vacant of all thoughts and only a fury to beat the foreman remained.

*

126

Jesse stewed as he walked out of the lumberyard and crossed the street. So, this was how it was going to be he realized. No matter what happened, he was always going to be the convict and it was always going to be his fault when things went wrong. If it was like this on a job, imagine what it would be like every time a crime was committed. He was always going to be suspected. Each step he took on the cracked sidewalk only increased the anger already roaring inside of him. He had served his time; paid back the state for something he had done over a quarter-century ago. Why couldn't they just let him be, let him try to get some sort of life going, but no, this was how it was going to be and the injustice of it caused his blood to boil.

He should have beat that stupid little foreman senseless. Guy was such a joke. If he had been inside, he would have been somebody's mule. Chances are the little shit wouldn't survive a month on the inside. There were three ways to die on the inside, State taking your life, another inmate taking it, or the pansy-asses that weren't strong enough to survive. They usually found some way to stretch their neck and call it a day.

Then to his horror, he realized that maybe he was a pansy-ass. Just one shot, he could have laid him out and killed him before dumbass even knew he was dead. Instead, he had slinked behind Mitchell like a coward. He had allowed the bastard to embarrass him in front of everyone and then had just signed some papers and slipped out the front. Shit, truth be told, he truly was a pansy-ass out here on this side of the walls.

It wasn't working. He wasn't meant to be on the outside. He had been kicked out of his home and now he had to figure out a way to get back in. Shouldn't be too hard, hell, he was a convict and he had no place to hide. Cops would find him easy. He just had to figure out a way to get back to where he belonged, his true home. He was an institutionalized man now; he needed the prison. He couldn't believe he was thinking this, but it was true. That was home, it was what he understood. He had nothing out here, no friends, no help, and now no job. He had to figure out a way to get back.

If he was going to go back in, he wanted it to last and the only way to do that was to kill someone. He had the perfect person; the foreman was going to pay. It was time for him to die so he could live once again in a world he was familiar with. He didn't have a gun, but he didn't need one. The little prick was going to die by his hands. There would be no problem finding the evidence to send him back, hell, he'd probably turn himself in and confess. There wouldn't be any leniency either, just a convict who beat the parole system again and society's outrage would send him to rot away in the prison system. It was perfect because as he slowly decayed, he would enjoy the thoughts of Todd

Miller's last moments in his mind. They wouldn't be able to take that from him. He'd have those until the day they stuck the needle in him.

He began planning it in his mind. He would stake the little prick out, see where he lived. All he needed was some rope and a solid stick to turn the tourniquet and watch the life leave his eyes so that all he had when he was done was the dead man's stare. It would be easy and shouldn't take long to accomplish. If he played it right, he could be on his way back to the pen by the end of the week.

For the first time in a while, he smiled. He had a purpose again. As he walked, he came upon a tavern at the end of a block. The *Budweiser* sign flashed in the window and an old cardboard OPEN sign hung below it. He had nothing else to do so he walked through the door and walked up to the bar and sat in the stool. Today was a good day to get drunk and an early start was always better than a late. The bartender glanced at him and finished drying a shot glass and then walked over to him.

"I'll take a beer," Jesse said. It had been years since he had been in a tavern and ordered a drink. He wasn't sure what kinds there were anymore and felt a little embarrassed.

"Kind of early isn't it?" responded the barkeep.

"Not today it isn't."

"You got it, so what do you want, a draft or bottle?"

"I'll take a Bud on draft."

"Mug or a pint?" he asked.

"A mug will do," Jesse responded and the barkeeper grabbed a mug out of the open cooler and filled it. As he did, white particles started to form around the mug and Jesse's mouth starts watering.

"Here you go, buddy. Starting a tab?"

"Nah, here's a five, keep the change," Jesse responded as he threw the bill toward the barkeeper. "Thanks, bud," he responded and Jesse put the cold mug to his mouth and felt the chilled liquid go down his throat.

It was a typical tavern, tables with chairs in the dining area, a couple of booths in the back, and a little dance floor with a small stage to the side. It had old '70s paneling around the joint and posters of different beers hung on the walls. He was the only customer right now and the barkeeper who had a white apron around his waist continued drying shot glasses. Jesse took another sip of the cold brew and looked up at the flat-screen television that was in the corner. The sound was down and it was on the sports channel which was showing all the sports news from the evening before. He looked above the bar and saw Boise State memorabilia and a BSU football helmet signed by someone he didn't know sitting on the edge of a shelf under the television.

The beer was good. It was smooth and he realized that this was the first beer he had had since getting out. It seemed to have a calming effect on him and soon his mind wandered into his past and settled on the times he was in prison. He remembered the way that time stood still while he was on the inside. He grew older but everything always seemed to stay the same. At first, he had been a tough guy, not wanting anybody to take advantage of him until he had been beaten almost to death by a couple of fairies who wanted him to become their new ass. After time in the infirmary, he had been put in solitary for his own protection and to pass the time he had started taking some classes. He didn't really care about what he was learning about, only that it gave him something to do in the cage he was stuck in.

He remembered how much he hated Karla and Rebecca during the years while he was in there. They had cost him so much, been responsible for him being where he was at. Sure, he had done some drugs, but he was making money for them, keeping them fed and clothed but their only thanks were to leave him high and dry after he had done so much for them. Then he had met a prison minister who through the years had helped him change the way he thought. The minister made him talk about things he didn't want to think about, things that deep down he knew but refused to acknowledge. The guy had made him understand what being a man was about in a way that no one else ever had. He taught him about taking responsibility for what he had done, but more importantly, choosing to do the things he had done to put himself in there. He taught him what accountability was and how he needed to take it for his own sake so that he could move forward. It was funny he thought to himself, he had met with him for years and didn't even know his name. He had just always called him Chap, short for Chaplain. Chap had been a good guy, a no-bullshit type of personality who just shot it straight.

He took another sip of the beer and then another. There was only one more drink left and the barkeep looked at him.

"I'll have another," he said to him and then took the last swig out of the mug. He thought of Chap again, the things he had said to him over the years and he kept coming back to the responsible thing. Chap was right. It would feel good to kill the foreman, but that was what the old Jesse would do. Chap had this thing he called belief. He had believed in him and cajoled him to believe in himself. He wouldn't let him down. He was a different man. He wasn't going to fall into the old trap that had sent him to prison in the first place. He was better than that and he knew he had to get out of the quicksand he was sinking into. He had to get help.

The server poured him another mug of beer and Jesse put another five on the bar and nodded his appreciation. He took a sip out of the mug and left a dollar on the bar and put the rest of the change in his wallet and saw something sticking out of the wallet and as he closed it. It was a business card and he grabbed it and saw it was the card that Margaret had handed him. He looked at it while the bartender went into the back and brought some bottles of hard liquor out. He thought of calling her but wasn't sure whether to or not. It couldn't hurt he realized and he asked the barkeep where the phone was and he pointed over toward the restrooms. Jesse walked slowly toward where he had pointed but realized he didn't have any dimes so he turned around and traded a quarter for two dimes and a nickel.

It was time for him to make a change; he couldn't go on trying to do it by himself anymore. He needed help and at least she was somebody that had once thought he was something. Maybe she could get him through it, maybe not, but it was worth a phone call anyway.

He put a dime in the phone and was surprised when no dial tone came up. He clicked it a couple of times and then his eyes widened. The phone needed fifty cents. He looked around to make sure the bartender hadn't seen him make a damn fool of himself and quickly put two quarters in and dialed the number on the card. A woman's voice came on the line and he told her he needed to talk to Margaret. She asked for his number and he explained he didn't have a phone and he was at a payphone. She put him on hold for a minute and went back to Margaret who was meeting with another client. Jesse thought of hanging up. She probably wouldn't want to talk to him anyway after the way he had left their only meeting. There was something about her though he couldn't put his finger on it, she had something that made him stay on the line.

Margaret read the note her administrative assistant handed her and quickly set up another appointment for the person she was counseling and then pushed the blinking red light on her phone as the client left. "Margaret Taylor," she said professionally, but she knew who it was and her heartbeat quicker than normal. Ever since he had walked out she had secretly hoped he would call. She liked him though not in a romantic way, at least not yet, but she liked his quiet strength and she really believed that she could help him.

"This is Jesse Rayburn," he said, unsure what to say next.

"I'm glad to hear from you, Jesse."

"I'm, uh…" he didn't know what to say to her. He didn't know what he was feeling. All he knew is that he didn't like where he was now and he needed help to become something that Chap had seen in him.

"It's all right, Jesse, what can I do for you?" she asked and she hoped that he wouldn't suddenly hang up. She wanted to help him find his way but at the same time, she wanted to get to know him better, and then she realized that she was coming up on a very dangerous line and that she had better get control of herself.

"I thought about going back to prison," he said, and immediately it brought her back to what she was and what her job entailed.

"I'm listening," she said.

"I was going to kill a man, make sure they didn't let me out this time," his voice was low and serious and for a moment, she was afraid that maybe he had. "I didn't though," he said as she breathed a sigh of relief. "I think I finally realize that I'm tired of being in prison. I need help." She smiled. He was reaching out, asking for a life jacket.

"Let me help you, Jesse," she said with empathy.

"You'll let me try again even after the way the last one ended?"

"Of course."

"What do I do?"

"Where are you?" and he told her. "Why don't you come down right now, I'm free for the next two hours. Are you within walking distance? I think a walk might do you good."

"I will, thank you Margaret," he said quietly.

"I'll see you soon," she replied and she hung up the phone.

Jesse looked at the phone for a moment before hanging up. Was he ready for this, ready to actually trust that someone could actually help him? He knew that his way didn't work here. This wasn't a prison; it was something that could be good but he had to learn it just as he had learned prison life when he had gone in. He dropped off his bag at the apartment and then started walking toward the address that was on the card. He was afraid of what he would find, but for once was not in fear of taking the chance.

He thought of the job he had just been fired from and the foreman that he had wanted to kill so badly this morning. He was better than the guy and as he thought of this, he felt new, for it had been so long that he had considered himself better than someone. He realized the warmth of the light felt good and he quickened his pace toward Margaret's office.

Chapter 11

In the darkness of his room, he stared out the open window as the soft light of the dawn slowly overcame the dying shadows of the moonless night. The stillness was broken by the lonely chirp of a bird awakening from its slumber and he slowly sat up in his bed and threw off the sheet and placed his feet on the soft carpet of the floor. He stuck a cigarette in his mouth as he walked to the open window and sat on one of the rickety kitchen chairs that he had put in front of it. He put his feet on the window sill and crossed them and he let the clean air wrap itself around him and then lit the cigarette and took a long drag and slowly blew the smoke toward the dusty screen.

His mind wandered toward thoughts of Margaret as he stared out onto the concrete and asphalt of a street that had once been bustling but was now just filled with down-and-outers like himself. She wasn't such a bad dame he thought to himself. He tried to picture her in high school but could not place her, course it wasn't as if there were anything about her that would stand out. She wasn't considered a beauty by any stretch of the imagination, but she had a certain something about her, maybe it was her smile which gave a sort of handsomeness, though women didn't appreciate being called such. She was a doer though. He thought of how she had met him at her office after he had called her from the bar, providing a sense that somehow everything was going to be all right. It seemed almost maternalistic in nature, yet empty, without the warmness of the mother bringing the child to her bosom.

Shit, he wondered to himself, why the hell was he thinking like this? Maybe it had been because he had been without a woman for so long. He remembered when he was behind the walls, he had often fantasized about being out so that he could feel the softness of a woman's body against him, but now that he was out, he knew the chances were remote at best. He was an old man now, well past his prime and he knew that no woman gave him a second look, much less a first. Margaret was different though. She seemed to have some sort of interest in him. Hell, she had gotten him a job very quickly after the lumber yard fiasco. It wasn't the greatest job, just stacking boxes at a local soft drinks' distributor, but it paid fairly decently and people there left him alone to do his work. The best thing about the job was that the foreman didn't appear to give a shit that he was an old con, he just gave him his directions and left him alone until the job was done and then gave him another.

Margaret and he were meeting once a week now. She was no bullshit, told him how things were but listened to what he had to say. He knew that he was nothing more than just another client to her but when he was with her, he felt like he was with a friend, someone who really cared. She had a way of making him open up about things that he thought he had long put to bed. She made him go places that he had been away from for over a quarter of a century and then she would bring him back to his current reality. She wouldn't let him blame others or be the victim, always quick to point out that he had done a bang-up job victimizing others during his life. When he tried to state his case for doing the things he had done she never would let him minimize his culpability and reminded him that payback was meant to be a bitch. She was good at finding ways to keep him dangling on the hook so he would come back another week to pick up where they had left off. She was a talented broad. She was as she said; good at what she did for a living and she really didn't show any fear of him.

As weeks turned into months, she quit meeting him at her office. Instead, they now met at the Starbucks that was down from her office in the Capital District. He was more open when he was relaxed, more apt to contemplate on the conversations they were now having. She slowly led him back through his life, reminding him of the good times he had experienced to stop him from trying to victimize himself; forcing him to deal with the awful things he had done as he had descended into a hell of his own making.

As his trust in her grew she began to make his probe into a realm he wished to avoid. She prodded him to think about the lost relationship with Karla and Rebecca though he would struggle against it with all his might. He could not forgive them for everything he had lost. If Margaret could get him to talk about them it would quickly disintegrate into anger because of his deep-seated belief that his life would have been so much better had they not interfered with his goals and aspirations. She persisted and his anger slowly began to melt and in its place was the despair of a life nearly lost. This new realization led him to the regret of a wife and child deliberately lost from him forever.

He finally stood up from the old chair in front of the window and walked toward the bathroom and he thought back to his yesterday's meeting with Margaret. She had told him that it had been a real step for him and he wondered what that meant. He thought back to the session and realized that for the first time he had gone through a whole session without blaming the woman of his past. He had finally realized that he probably still loved Karla even though he knew there was no chance of ever being with her again. He remembered now, remembered word for word what had been said.

He turned on the shower and the little bathroom quickly filled with steam but he did not notice. Instead, his mind was back at the coffee shop, sipping on one of those new-fangled coffee concoctions that until he had gotten out from the prison had not even known existed.

"You know, I hated Karla and my daughter for a long time," he remembered saying to Margaret as he toyed with the Carmel Macchiato that she had ordered for him.

"Say your daughter's name," Margaret urged and he quietly did as told. "Was it justified?" she asked him thoughtfully.

"I thought so at the time," he reflected. "I felt like they took away my life. Took away what had always been my real love." He had stared into the brownish liquid in the white cup and had not been able to make eye contact and he realized that it was because for the first time he really felt guilty and he wasn't sure if he felt good about having this feeling or not.

"It was only a game," she had replied.

"Not to me it wasn't," he replied tersely. "Football was everything to me. It made my parents proud of me, I got my friends from it, made me the big man on campus." He looked at her and smiled sheepishly. "Got me noticed by girls, one of them being you I believe."

Margaret laughed softly and nodded her head. "Guilty," she giggled but quickly she turned serious again. "So, I think what you're telling me, or actually yourself is that it gave you your identity."

He grabbed his cup and took a sip. It was still hot and he felt a burn on the tip of his tongue that immediately became numb. She was on to something and as he realized what a true statement it was.

"Yeah," he agreed, "something like that." He thought for a moment and she did not interrupt him, sensing that he was about to go somewhere that he had not been to in a long time. "When Karla got pregnant, I saw it all slip away."

He wanted her to say something, but she only stared at him in silence yet willed him to continue exploring the path he was on. "I had always taken it for granted that football was what I was going to do with my life," he said finally to break the silence that unnerved him. "Then it was gone and I hated Karla for that." He was no longer looking at Margaret, but instead staring at the wall behind her and feeling himself drifting back to that time of hopelessness. "When the baby came, I hated her also because she was the reason it was gone. I felt those two were the reason that what should have been never was."

"Why is it so hard for you to say her name?" asked Margaret.

"Because she was the reason for all my failures," he said with downcast eyes.

"Do you still feel that way?"

"No…yes, I don't know. I guess it depends on the day. Right now, I guess I don't but who knows how I'll feel tomorrow?"

"Are you saying that because you think that is what I want to hear from you?" she asked point-blank. He was taken aback from her directness and felt his defenses rising but then saw that she was not trying to push a button or get him angry and he relaxed and thought deeply about whether or not he was just trying to tell her what she wanted to hear.

"No, I don't think so Margaret," he finally answered. "I've had a lot of time to think. Eventually, I guess everyone realizes that life just happens and it's not always going to be as a seventeen-year-old plan it. I now know I was my own worst enemy and that I grew to hate myself as much as I hated them. Karla dealt with it for a long time and then moved on with her life when it became unbearable with me. I guess I forgot the most fundamental lesson of football back then."

"What was that?"

"You have to adapt during the game. I was great at doing it when I was on the field but I never could adapt my life off the field and thus I've now thrown half of it away."

"That's pretty profound, Jesse," she said, her eyes interlocking with his. She realized that he had made a breakthrough and she felt a surge of energy, more like a volt, that comes with the excitement of seeing another gain a moment of clarity about their life. "Are you still hurt?" she asked.

"Not at the girls, only that I was too stupid to figure it out years ago. But now I've got another chance to try to create a life for myself here on the outside. Hopefully, I won't fuck it up."

The hour had gone so quickly and he remembered that he had wanted to ask her to stay a little longer, but he hadn't. She put a couple of dollars on the table and for just a moment the con in him thought of grabbing and pocketing them but instead, he just followed her to the door. She opened it for him and as he walked past her, she gently grabbed his elbow. "You're off to a good start," she had said.

He smiled, maybe he was but he still felt stuck in the quicksand, but at least he had a hold of a branch and the sinking had stopped, if only momentarily.

*

She picked up the phone on her desk and heard his now familiar voice.

"You got some time for me today?" Jesse asked and she was immediately concerned.

"What is it?" she asked. "Are you in some kind of trouble?"

"No, but I do need to see you. It's important," he replied. She realized that his voice sounded excited and she allowed herself to relax. She quickly gazed over her schedule book and saw that she was full for the rest of the day.

"Can we meet after five?" she asked. He told her they could and she quickly jotted it down on her planner. "I'll just meet you here then. You're sure everything is fine?" He again reassured her and hung up.

At five he walked into the reception room and sat on the overstuffed couch and grabbed a magazine. Shortly after finding an article that interested him about places to see in the Sun Valley region she walked out and nodded for him to come back to the office. He got up and noticed that getting out of the couch seemed much harder now than it had as a younger man and he followed her to the office and sat down in the chair he regularly sat in when they met here.

"You look chipper today," she remarked as he sat smiling at her.

"Do I?"

"Yes," she replied. "What's going on?" He continued to smile at her and her curiosity grew and she asked again.

"I got a goal," he finally replied proudly. "Something I haven't had since I was in high school. It just came to me out of the blue it seems like."

"That's wonderful, what is it?" He admired her face. She had a slight smile yet it was mixed with a questioning look and wonderment of what in the world he was hiding from her. "I'm hoping you called me to share it with me," she said, somewhat teasingly, but at the same time really wanting to know just what it was he was wanting to do.

"More than that, I want your help." She looked at him quizzically and he smiled back at her. What did he possibly have up his sleeve she wondered?

"Well tell me what it is and I'll see what I can do," she replied. His smile disappeared and in its place was a look of seriousness. She wondered if that was a look he once had in years past when he was the great quarterback that everyone wanted.

"Well, OK, here goes Margaret," he said solemnly as he leaned forward in the chair toward her. "I want to find Rebecca." Margaret sat back in her chair and realized that she had not hidden her surprise well. Jesse's face became impassive and he wondered if he had made a mistake telling her. He had really felt that he could trust this woman but it was occurring to him that again he was wrong in his assumption. She was going to be just like everyone else he had known. She was going to discourage him from doing it, telling him it wasn't the right thing to do. Why had he been so stupid to think that she would understand?

"I see," she said after a long pause. "Do you think that's a good idea?" There it was, right on cue. She wasn't any different than the others. He could feel his face turning crimson and his muscles tightening. He wanted to get up and walk out. Why had he been such a fool to think he could trust her. Trust had gotten him nothing but thirty in the can.

"Ah, never mind," he said stonily as he began to stand up from the chair. It had been nothing but a pipe dream and he was angry at himself now for putting himself in this situation when he should have known that it was only going to end up being a dead end.

"Jesse, tell me more," she said softly and he looked at her to see if she was really serious or if this was just another ruse. He saw her face and her eyes looking at him with empathy, a sincere interest that he hadn't noticed before and he wanted to trust her but he couldn't bring himself to do it. "Jesse, I didn't say I wouldn't help, but I have to know why you want to do this and what your plan is." He continued to stare at her and then finally sat back down in the chair.

"That's why I need your help, Margaret," he said as he tried to calm himself. When the calmness overtook him, he noticed that he was beginning to feel tired and realized that the anger no longer drove him, merely fatigued him instead. "I don't have a plan," he confessed. "I just know I want to find Rebecca. I want to find my daughter."

"When did you see her last?" she asked.

"God, it's been a long time," he acknowledged to her. He realized he couldn't remember when, but he did remember that she was crying. "It was before I went inside."

"So why now?" asked Margaret, gently probing Jesse to justify his need.

"She's my daughter," he said simply. He looked out the window and he felt his eyes begin to mist, a sensation that he had not experienced since the first night in prison. He thought back to that horrifying nightmare. He had tried to control it but instead, it had controlled him and he remembered the taunts from the other nearby inmates and the overwhelming fear of wondering how he was ever going to survive.

"I'm a different man now I would like to think. I realize she probably wants nothing to do with me but I just want to see my daughter, if only for a minute. I want to tell her I'm sorry. I need to let her know that I was wrong."

She handed him a tissue and slowly he felt an intense pain of loss that for so long he had kept bottled up in the deep recesses of what had been a wasted life. Rebecca gave him a chance to do something positive, even if it meant more heartache.

"You talk about closure…" he said through his tears. "There is no closure unless I let her know that I recognize what a loser I was and that I'm trying to be different now. I'm trying to be a man now." He dabbed his eyes again and no longer felt shame for the tears that were falling. "She'll choose whether to accept it or not, I now realize I can't control that, but I can control whether or not I make an effort to make things right."

He was so vulnerable right now she realized. She wanted to grab a hold of him and gently rock him back and forth, tell him that everything was fine but she knew she couldn't. She thought back of the hardened convict that had walked into her office the first time and now here he was in tears begging for her help. He had come far, he didn't know it yet, but he was becoming a man again. "All right," she finally said. "How long have you been thinking about this?"

"Remember when I called you from the bar?" he asked.

"Yes."

"Since then," He replied in nearly a whisper.

"Do you have any idea where she is?"

"None," he admitted and they both laughed softly at the absurdity of it all.

"Do you have any idea where to start? Do you know where your ex-wife is?"

"No idea whatsoever."

Margaret grabbed a writing book and began to jot down some notes. He finally felt some composure coming over him and wondered what she was writing. She glanced at him and smiled and then went back to her writing. He thought of asking her what she was doing but realized that he didn't care so he sat back in the chair and took some deep breaths.

"Jesse, I have some questions for you. I need to ask them to get an idea of where you're at so please don't be defensive or read anything into them, all right?" Jesse nodded but he could feel his defenses rising again and for an instant thought of just walking out. This was becoming hard, almost too hard. "So, you have no idea where your daughter is or ex-wife for that matter. How will you live? How will you pay the costs that it will take to find her? Your current job won't provide what you need."

"I know, but believe it or not I have actually thought of this and think I have a way."

"I'm listening."

"My parents, when they died, left me their estate sort of. I recently found out about it, last week to be exact. It isn't much, but it's enough to get me through the next year or so. If nothing else it gives me a good start. It was only after finding this out that I realized that maybe I could try to find Rebecca."

She wrote this down and then studied his face. She realized that for the first time since she had met him, he had hope in his eyes. He had found something, a purpose and he seemed to believe he had the means to go through with it. "Well, I won't say yes yet but I'm not saying no either," she said to him. "I need you to bring me proof of this estate and that it has been left to you. After I see it, I'll let you know, but I have to tell you I have to be convinced that you are doing this for the right reasons. Remember Jesse, I have worked with a lot of inmates. I'm not going to allow this young woman to be hurt by you again, but I'm firmly in your corner if you show me you are sincere, and right now I'm inclined to believe that you are."

Jesse stood up from the chair and walked toward the door. She wondered what was going through his mind or if she had been too harsh, but she knew that she had to lay the cards on the table immediately and now that she had it was up to him.

"That's fair," he said as he walked through the door. He felt strange, but it was good. He had hope, but he did not know it because it had been so long that he no longer recognized it.

*

As she walked into the office, she saw him sitting in the corner leafing through the morning newspaper. In the chair next to him was what appeared to be a shoebox with a strand of gray duct tape holding the lid to the box and she looked quizzically at him until he felt her stare and lowered the newspaper.

"How long have you been here?" she asked.

"Not long, maybe fifteen minutes," he replied. She smiled at him and walked to the receptionist's desk and looked at her schedule.

"You're in luck. I don't have anyone for the next hour. Let me get set up and then we'll talk." He smiled at her and went back to leafing through the paper as she walked into the hallway that led to her office. Five minutes later she called him back and he stood and grabbed the shoebox and nodded at the receptionist as he passed her.

As he walked in, Margaret poured some Sweet and Lo into her coffee and stirred it. He placed the box on her desk and pulled his customary cushiony chair in front of it and she took a sip and looked at him without saying a word. He stared back at her with a slight grin and she could see that he was feeling good about himself and she couldn't help herself any longer and her lips broke into a smile.

"OK, what have you got in the shoebox?" she asked playfully.

"The proof you asked for yesterday," he replied somewhat smugly as he handed it to her. "You didn't believe me, did you?" Her smile disappeared and she felt a little hurt by his comment. Had she given him a reason to think that she hadn't believed him? She remembered leaving the office yesterday and wondering if his story had been true. She had heard stories from paroled inmates. Most of those stories had been just that, stories, but she had always prided herself that she gave these men the benefit of the doubt.

"Why would you say that?" she asked. He just continued to look at her with a slight smile and she pulled the box close to her and carefully peeled back the tape and opened the top. Inside were papers that were obviously prepared by lawyers, deposits slip into a bank account and bank statements for the last five years.

"It was originally designed to be for Rebecca," Jesse told her as she continued to look at the paperwork in front of her.

"How did you end up with it?"

"It's kind of a long story," he replied.

"Tell me, we have some time," she said as she looked up at him and set the papers down neatly on top of her desk.

"Well, as I said, it was originally for Rebecca. Before I went inside Karla and I got divorced a few years before. Mom and Dad apparently forged a friendship with Karla while she was going to school and became close to Rebecca." Margaret stared at his eyes that now had a faraway look as if he were seeing something only he could make out. As he spoke, his voice became thinner and she leaned forward slightly without realizing she was. "Once I was inside, Karla was working here in Boise and my folks helped watch Rebecca while she worked. After a few years, Karla decided to go back to school and they moved somewhere out east I think," and he paused as he wondered where. "Anyway, while she was going to school my folks set up a trust for Rebecca because in part of their guilt over how I had treated them. They always assumed that after school she and Rebecca would move back to Boise."

Margaret took another sip of her coffee and Jesse stood up and walked to the window, looking down on the street below him. "After Karla graduated, she was offered a job somewhere down south, North Carolina, I think. Mom and Dad got angry because they felt they were going to lose Rebecca, which they had always been afraid of because of me. They apparently let Karla know they were upset. They told her some pretty pointed things about how ungrateful she was or something like that." He turned back toward Margaret and sat on the windowsill, the faraway look still in his eyes and Margaret wondered how he was feeling now that he was sharing this with her.

"Well, to make a long story short, Karla took the job and she and Rebecca moved east for good. My folks apparently blew their tops and really went off on Karla, especially my Dad. They tried to take her to court to get custody of Rebecca but of course, that failed. When it was thrown out Karla told them they could never see Rebecca again."

"Why would your parents go to those extremes?" asked Margaret, mesmerized by the story.

"Don't be too hard on them," he replied softly. "They had lost their son to drugs and prison and Dad had a bad heart and had been sick for a while. I don't think they were thinking of real rationally at the time."

"I guess not," she agreed.

"Anyway, Dad only lasted a few more years and after his death, Mom came to the prison. I think it was like the first time that I would agree to see her, I was still blaming them for everything. She told me about Dad's death and then told me about trust. She said she was probably going to die soon herself and was going to give me the trust but that I had to use it to help Rebecca. I agreed and signed some papers, not really intending to help anyone but myself once I got out. Anyway, after a while, I forgot all about it because it was about twenty years ago." He sat back down on the chair and grabbed the box.

"The other day I had a letter in my mailbox from some guy that runs the trust updating me on. I had completely forgotten about it. Anyway, there was a business card and I called the number and met with him. He gave me all of these which are copies. I took these papers to a lawyer to find out if it was real and how I could use it. He said as long as I use it for Rebecca, I can utilize it as I see fit. I asked if searching for her would fall under that category and he said I could as long as I documented every penny I spent."

Margaret scanned the front page of the trust and looked at the latest statement. "It's quite a lot of money, Jesse."

"It's not bad," he agreed.

"Did you ever talk to your mother again since that day in prison?"

"No. Once the trust was finalized, she kept her word and died shortly thereafter. I didn't find out she was dead until later."

"I'm sorry," Margaret said softly.

"Me too," he replied sincerely. He was actually missing her at this moment and the acknowledgment made his saliva thick and he swallowed hard.

"It does look legitimate," she said softly.

"It is."

"I'm going to have my lawyer look at it. If he says all are in the order, I will help you, all right?"

"It is all in order. I told you I went to a lawyer," he said, feeling his cheeks heating up and trying hard to not become angry.

"Jesse, I believe you, but I still have to have it checked out. Besides, it's always good to have a second opinion. I'll have him look it over this afternoon. I'll have peace of mind then, OK?"

"All right," he shrugged, but he could still feel the anger trying to boil.

"Once he gives the thumbs up, I'll help you, I promise." He relaxed some and gave a slight smile of relief. "But Jesse, this is a long shot at best and there is a good chance you won't find her, or worse, will and won't like what you find."

"I know," he nodded.

"You're sure you want to go ahead with this?" He nodded to her and again walked to the window and looked out into the day. The sun was shining through an opening in the clouds and he hoped that it was a good omen. "All right," she said. "I'll have my lawyer look at it today and will call you as soon as he lets me know."

"Thanks, Margaret," he said quietly and then he let himself out of the office. Margaret carefully put the papers back in the shoebox and pulled out her cell phone. She scanned through her contacts and settled on Dick Durbin. The phone rang twice and then his familiar voice came on the line.

"Dick, could you look at some papers for me as a favor?"

"Over dinner?" he asked.

"Sorry, I need an answer sooner than that, but I'm sure we can think of some way for me to thank you properly" she purred. "I'll bring them right over."

*

Dick Durbin finished checking the trust papers in front of him on his desk and picked up the phone and quickly dialed Margaret. After two rings she picked up and he playfully bantered with her about his sexual prowess. On the other end, Margaret rolled her eyes, but yes, he was telling the truth. In bed, he was quite the lover, probably the only reason he had been married so long to his wife. Margaret was sure that Mrs. Durbin had to know about her husband's philandering ways.

"So, tell me about the papers, please," Margaret cooed over the phone.

"When do I get payment?" he joked. Margaret felt a light tingling as she thought about the last encounter, she had with him. Though he was sixty years old, he had the looks of a man in his forties and the stamina of a vivacious twenty-year-old. He was wonderful to be with, but after the lovemaking, he would exit stage left and Margaret would feel pangs of guilt for his wife.

"Dick, please. This is important."

"All right," he laughed. He knew that if she wasn't interested, he had three more ladies he could call this evening. "The papers are all in order. Pretty standard, really; Jesse Rayburn is the executor and as long as he is spending the money in the best interests of his daughter there isn't a problem. Rayburn, that's a familiar name. Who is it?"

"He recently was released from prison. He served thirty years for attempted murder," she replied.

"So, his daughter must be of age. Why doesn't he just give it to her?"

"He doesn't know where she is. He wants to find her."

"You sure you should be doing this?" asked Dick, suddenly concerned. A convict, a trust, and a lost daughter; sounded like a perfect scam for someone who didn't have money but now suddenly had a trust.

"I trust him, Dick," she replied thoughtfully. "He's going to need some help though. Do you have any private investigators you could recommend?" Dick thought for a moment and then he remembered one that he had worked with years before.

"Good ones aren't cheap, Margaret. Looking at this trust, it's decent but not great. Money could dry up real fast with the private detective's we use."

"There must be someone. Please, Dick, think, you see what we have available financially. I like this guy. He's making a real effort. Surely you know someone that's decent that won't cost us an arm and a leg." Dick thought for a moment and one popped into his head. He was good, but he had some warts. He might be the perfect one for what Margaret was asking.

"I do," he said. "Raymond Albertson. He's a drunk, but he's good and cheap. Let me dig up his number and address. We used to use him a lot but he couldn't stay away from the bottle. Still, I've used him a few times to spy on Virginia to make sure she's doesn't have the same hobby as I."

"You're all heart," Margaret giggled. It was hard to feel too sorry for his wife. He provided her with a beautiful home, all the money she needed, and was a perfect gentleman when he was with her. Margaret didn't know the dynamics of the marriage, maybe Virginia really didn't mind, but deep down she knew she was only trying to justify herself and she knew that in all probability it was horrible knowing that your husband was a player.

He quickly gave her the private detective's number and address and flirted for another minute before hanging up. Margaret quickly called Jesse and made plans to meet him at Albertson's office later that afternoon. Today was going to be busy, and she still had five more clients to go. She rang the receptionist and soon a disheveled woman who was ready to give birth at any time walked into her office and sat and immediately began telling a story of woe.

Margaret looked at her watch, only five more hours to go.

*

Jesse stood in front of the old brick three-story building with the gray rock outlining the doorway that read *Magnuson Mining and Associates* chiseled on it. On the door were gold-painted numbers giving the address and the stain on the door was chipping and falling to the ground. Margaret drove up and saw him standing and pulled into the empty spot in front of the door. He nodded at her when she got out and she wasn't sure if he was disgusted with her or not.

He continued to look at her as they walked through the doorway and into the building. On the wall was a dusty directory with water stains running down the glass that covered the office numbers. She quickly scanned it and saw that Albertson's office was on the second floor in Suite 202.

"Upstairs," she said quietly, slightly unnerved by his continual staring at her. She walked to the elevator and pushed the button which turned on a red light behind it and heard the cranking of the mechanisms that made it go up and down. They seemed to groan at first and Jesse finally let out a disgusted sigh.

"Give it a chance," she said quietly.

"I'll meet you upstairs," he replied and he walked to the stairwell. She rolled her eyes as the elevator door opened and walked in, pushed the two on the panel, and slowly the doors closed and the clanking began again. She began to wonder if maybe she should have taken the stairs also as it slowly began to rise. Was Dick really serious about this guy or was this his way of getting even with her for not sleeping with him? The elevator jolted to a stop and for a moment she wasn't sure if the doors were going to slide open or not. Finally, they did, and standing in front of her was Jesse.

"Where to?" he asked dryly.

"Follow me," she said as she brushed past him and walked toward a brown door with a cloudy glass and gold, spray-painted numbers on it. She gingerly turned the handle and the door opened into an unlit reception area with two wooden chairs and a dusty desk for a receptionist that obviously did not exist. "Anyone here?" she asked and a grunt came from the office behind. She looked at Jesse and the two walked toward the office door. Sitting behind an old wooden desk was a disheveled man in tight jeans and a western shirt quickly trying to clean off the top of his desk.

"Just a minute," he grunted. The office was empty of furniture except for the desk and another set of wooden chairs that sat in front of it. There was nothing on the gray walls except for a water stain from a leak in the corner that went all the way down to the floor. In the other corner were three boxes filled with folders that now seemed to be used for nothing more than collecting dust. The man behind the desk was in his mid to late forties but he looked older. He had a couple of days' worth of graying whiskers growing on this face and a cup on his desk that smelled of cheap whiskey. His eyes were glassy and he appeared to have been sleeping off a hangover.

"Are you Raymond Albertson?" Margaret asked curtly.

"Depends on you, are you a customer or are you trying to serve Mr. Albertson with something from the court."

"We are potential customers," she replied.

"Then what can I do for you?" he asked as he rubbed his bloodshot eyes. Margaret sat down without asking and motioned for Jesse to do the same. He had not seen this side of her before and he sat before realizing that he was perturbed with her. She pulled some papers out of her briefcase and sat it down on her lap.

"We're looking for someone and we hear you have had previous success locating people," she said as she snapped the briefcase shut and set it down on the floor next to her.

"Who's we?" he asked, unimpressed with this gal that was trying to be Ms. Professional.

"I'm sorry," she replied. "My name is Margaret Taylor and this is Jesse Rayburn. Mr. Rayburn is looking for his daughter."

Raymond sat back and opened up a drawer and pulled out the cheap bottle of whiskey he had stashed and poured some into the paper cup on his desk. "Jesse Rayburn," he said thoughtfully after he had taken a sip, "rings a bell. Shoot anybody lately?"

"Not lately," Jesse replied as he struggled to control himself. How did this guy know? Maybe looks could be deceiving.

"Glad to hear it," Raymond laughed as he took out a pack of cigarettes from the pocket of his western shirt. "Been out long?" he asked as he lit the cigarette and took a long drag.

"Not really, few months. How do you know me?"

"I'm a good flat foot," he said as smoke came out of his nose.

"I guess so. I thought I was pretty old news."

"No, just old," he cackled, "so who are you looking for and why?"

"My daughter," replied Jesse.

"When you have seen her last?"

"Mr. Rayburn hasn't seen…"

"I'm not talking to you miss," he said sarcastically. This woman was a kick in the pants, obviously one of those broads that thought that by sounding official she could control the proceedings. He wasn't interested in playing her game. "When you see her last?" he asked Jesse again.

"I haven't seen in at least thirty years," replied Jesse in an even tone. He didn't like this guy.

"What makes you think she wants you to find her?"

"What's that got to do with it?" asked Margaret.

"Lady, I'll ask the questions, and again, I'm not talking to you. I'm talking to him. He's the client. I'm not sure what you are…cheerleader maybe?"

"I just want to see my daughter," answered Jesse, strangely enjoying seeing Margaret's cheeks turning crimson from the smackdown this guy just gave her.

"How nice," laughed Raymond again as he took another sip from the cup and then a quick drag from the cigarette. "Want to be a dad after shitting on her all her life, huh?"

"Gotta start sometime," Jesse replied, holding his composure in this chess game that was going on.

"Good answer," he replied with a smile. "But no, I don't think I can help. First of all, I'm pretty sure you can't afford me and second, I don't think you're the type of client I really want, convict."

Jesse smiled and slowly stood up. "Let's go, Margaret."

"Sit down Jesse," she said quietly. She opened the folder on her lap and grabbed some papers and quickly scanned them. Jesse looked at her, confused, but sat as directed and Raymond leaned back in his chair and put his feet up on the desk. His shoes were worn and dusty and one of the laces had been tied where it had broken.

"Come on Margaret, he's not interested," Jesse protested.

"Just wait a minute," replied Margaret as she continued looking at the papers in the folder.

"I'm a busy man," Raymond said as he took another sip.

"Not really, Mr. Albertson," she said with an even tone. "According to this, your business has been, shall we say, off?" Raymond continued looking at her as he took another drag from the cigarette and then dropped it into the old coffee can that now doubled as a butt holder.

"What have you got there?" he asked. Maybe he had underestimated this uppity bitch.

"I also am able to find things out, Mr. Albertson," she said coyly. "Let's see, you have a very delinquent phone bill, your cell phone is probably not working either, is it? You've recently lost your house, a charming little place on 2nd Street." She looked up from the papers and saw that his Hollywood tough guy detective act was vanishing. "Are you living here now?" He glared at her and downed the rest of the whiskey in the cup. "Shall I go on?" she goaded.

"If you want," he said dryly. What did she need him for? She seemed perfectly able to find things out on her own.

"All right, obviously you like to drink but it must be hard if you don't have any clients. I'm guessing that the local liquor stores probably want you to pay for your, shall we say, selection of fine whiskey's?" He laughed lightly and though he disliked her immensely he realized that she was quickly gaining his respect.

"So, I take it we are negotiating," he said.

"That's the spirit, Mr. Albertson," she replied.

"I'm not interested. I'm broke, have no clients, and I do spend my evenings here, but I'm still picky about my clients. Now get out." Margaret merely smiled sweetly at him.

"Will you be following me or have you not yet received your eviction notice?" He opened the middle drawer of his desk and pulled out the certified letter.

"I have it right here," he said defiantly. "Get out lady. Don't take this personally. It's a simple money issue. An old convict like Rayburn doesn't have any and I don't do charity work." Margaret grabbed the trust and set it down on his desk. "What's this?" he asked.

"I believe this is what you want to walk out the door," she replied as he grabbed it and started looking at its contents. He was silent for a few minutes as he studied the document and Margaret gave Jesse a slight nod. Jesse still wanted to leave, but he was enjoying the back and forth between Margaret and the burnout on the other side of the desk.

"Is this real?" Raymond finally asked.

"Yes."

"Maybe I was a little hasty," he replied.

"Would you like to reopen the negotiation?" He sat silently for a moment and looked coldly at Jesse. She knew everything about his money woes, and this trust would certainly help, but he didn't like the client at all. Above all, he didn't like this client.

"Two thousand a week plus expenses," he said finally.

"Is that negotiable?" she asked.

"No," he replied coldly.

"Let's go, Jesse," she said as she grabbed the trust from the desk and began putting the papers back into her briefcase.

"All right, maybe it is," he said quietly.

"Here's my offer, Mr. Albertson. Five hundred and expenses for one week; if you show me, we should continue with you we'll continue, otherwise, we'll move on." Raymond sat back in his chair and considered the counter offer. It was good, but he couldn't stand the thought of this lady dictating the terms to him.

"Too low miss," he said. "Seven-fifty and expenses but I'll need two weeks." Now it was Margaret's turn to consider. It wasn't a bad offer, but he had made her angry with the condescending tone he had used with her earlier.

"You have ten days. Here's seven-fifty," she said as she placed an envelope on his desk. He opened it and saw seven one-hundred-dollar bills and a fifty-dollar bill. "I want receipts for expenses and I won't be paying for your booze."

"Deal," he replied, still fingering the money. It felt good to the tips of his fingers. He would have a place to stay for another month now and the fifty would buy at least four bottles of cheap whiskey.

Margaret stood up and reached her hand across the desk and Raymond grabbed it and shook it. Jesse did the same but Albertson stared at him coldly and sat back down in his chair and grabbed a file out of the box next to the wall and began to go through it. Jesse slowly turned around and followed Margaret out the door.

Who was this guy, and what axe did he have to grind with him, Jesse wondered? Didn't matter though, the search had started.

Chapter 12

Jesse walked toward the bench where Raymond sat drinking out of a paper cup in the little park. He wondered if it was coffee or whiskey and as he came closer, he realized it was probably a little of both. The morning was overcast and the air felt heavy with precipitation but the rains had not yet fallen from the clouds overhead. The little park was a tribute to Idaho's warriors that battled in the jungles of Vietnam. Small plaques were attached to a brick wall that held the names of men who had left home at an early age and had come home in a simple, flag-draped, silver casket.

"That your ex-wife?" Raymond asked as he handed Jesse a photograph.

Jesse stared at the picture. She had aged, but the golden hair gave her away and she still held some of the beauty of her youth. It appeared she had done well for herself and from the picture, he saw a professional woman with a friendly grin but the warmth she had exhibited as a girl was now gone. "Yeah," he murmured, "where'd you get the picture?"

He thought back to the day before in Raymond's small office. It had been an uncomfortable meeting between the two of them. The private investigator made no secret of his disdain for him as he had struggled to pry information from a client who didn't want to cooperate. Jesse had finally had enough and walked out in a huff. Still, with the bits of information he had been able to coax out of the con, Raymond had enough to find the ex-wife.

"I'm just good I guess," Raymond replied. He wanted to get this over with. There was a bottle of whiskey waiting for him back at the office that needed his attention. Jesse continued to stare at the picture. The years had changed her. In prison, he had learned about people by staring at their faces. There was no such thing as a poker face he had learned early, and her face told him that the years had hardened her. He guessed that he was not the only one that had hurt her over the years. The face no longer showed innocent trust, instead, it was replaced by a cynicism that belied a lack of faith in anyone but herself. He realized that he had been the start of the pain he now saw in the stern eyes that no longer twinkling.

"I guess so," he responded to Raymond's bragging. "Seriously, how did you get this? We just talked yesterday and I'm pretty sure it wasn't a very good meeting."

"I googled her," Raymond responded. The fresh air seemed to clear his head from the whiskey he had pounded the evening before.

"What's that?"

"On the internet, I googled her."

"Internet?"

"Jesus Christ, do you know what a God damn computer is you dumb shit?" Jesse felt his cheeks reddening and he thought of socking the bastard in the mouth. So far, this partnership was not going well and he couldn't understand what Margaret saw in the guy.

"Of course, I know what a computer is. You better watch your smart mouth asshole. Remember, you work for me, not vice versa." Surely there had to be better private investigators out there, why didn't she get one of them?

"All right, I'm sorry. Maybe I was a little hard on you there. I went to the library and got on the computer. The internet is the world wide web…"

"Yeah, yeah…I know what you're talking about now. I've never been on it but I've heard. A lot of porn sites, you go there? Pretty sure that's the closest you'll get to a woman."

"Fuck you," Raymond snapped. "You want to know how I got her picture or not?"

"Enlighten me."

"I got on the internet, it has all sorts of websites, not just porn you sick bastard. I went to Google, it's what is known as a search engine and I plugged in the information you grudgingly gave me yesterday. Based on that and your description of her I narrowed down the choices and came up with this. This is her from her Facebook page."

"Facebook?"

"It's a social site…ah, never mind; just trust me."

"Wow," Jesse said. Raymond couldn't tell if he was serious or mocking him and decided that arguing about it would only prolong the time, he had to spend with the prick that made his skin crawl.

"Yeah," he said sarcastically, "amazing." He stared at Jesse who continued to look at the picture and suddenly felt a twinge of empathy for him. Jesse had a faraway look in his eyes and sadness seemed to come over his face and he sagged slightly into the bench.

"You were gone a long time," he said softly.

Jesse continued to stare at the picture, but what he saw was no longer the middle-aged woman but the girl he had so long ago dated. The picture of this woman was lifeless and the girl he had known had been a flower in bloom. "Didn't use computers on the inside," he murmured quietly, transfixed on the picture.

Raymond felt uncomfortable for feeling sorry for the convict. "Well anyway, she's in Massachusetts. She's a professor of Social Work or Psychology or something like that. Anyway, she's at Tufts University in Boston."

"So, what do we do now?"

"We go talk to her," replied Raymond. Jesse felt pins run through his spine. He hadn't spoken to Karla in decades and remembered the last time he had; her father had threatened to kill him. He wondered if he was still alive, still here in Boise.

"I can't go, my parole," stammered Jesse.

"Then I guess it ends here," replied Raymond in a matter-of-fact tone.

"Why can't you talk to her?" asked Jesse.

"It's best if you're there. Call your sugar-Mommy and tell her to take care of it. You're going. I'm interested now and besides; I'm hoping she hates you as much as I do. I'll enjoy watching her kick your ass."

"I don't think it's that easy," protested Jesse. The son-of-a-bitch needed a beating but Jesse knew that it would have to come at another time. He wasn't ready to go back in yet, not until he found Rebecca. In the meantime, he'd put up with the smarmy comments of this drunk. He had found Karla; that was saying something.

"Well, I don't know what to tell you. When you get it figured out, let me know?" Raymond grabbed the picture out of Jesse's hand and stood up. "You know how to reach me," he said as he walked away.

Jesse stared at him. There was no way his parole officer was going to let him leave Idaho and Raymond had to know this. Maybe it was over just as it was beginning. He had to talk to Margaret. Maybe Raymond was right, maybe 'sugar-mommy' could work something out. He stood and pulled his collar up as he walked away from the park.

*

Margaret hung up the phone and sighed. The man on the other end had been obstinate with her and she rubbed her forehead in the hopes that the massage would alleviate the headache she was feeling. He had been maddening to talk to, condescending in his tone, gruffly dismissing her arguments with what he considered deep anecdotes of expertise of the judicial system. Robert Jenkins was indeed a soured public servant who she realized had long ago forgotten his role in the rehabilitation and re-entry of those who had broken the laws of society. Now, he was simply a 'no' man.

As she recounted the conversation in her head it began to spin. She had been pleasant enough, explaining her work with Jesse and the positive strides he had made. She told him about his goal of finding his daughter and trying to make right with her to which he had answered with sardonic laughter. Still, she had soldiered on and updated him on the search and the need for Jesse to go to Massachusetts. He had no interest and had told her that she was nothing more than a bleeding heart being taken by a convict. With the conversation going nowhere she had politely ended it, keeping to herself the true feelings of what she really thought of him.

She didn't want to do it, but she had nowhere else to turn so she picked up the phone again and dialed Dick Durbin's personal cell.

"I need help," she said to him.

"This is becoming a habit Margaret, which is fine with me, but sooner or later you have to return the favor," he half-joked. Margaret wasn't in the mood as it had darkened since the encounter with Robert Jenkins just minutes before.

"Dick, this is really important," she said and she told him about the conversation with the parole officer. He listened attentively to her and jotted down notes as she continued. He could tell this was important to her and now he wanted to help. She was a good girl, really believed that she could help people change their lives. He knew it was naïve of her, but that was part of her beauty that so strongly attracted him. He appreciated that she didn't make demands on him and that she recognized their lovemaking was nothing more than a mutual act of self-gratification. Deep down he probably loved her more than his wife but he knew they would never be a couple. Besides, if that were to happen it would most certainly destroy a wonderful relationship.

"I'll make some calls for you," he told her as she finished with the details. "I know Jenkins, he's an asshole. Don't let him get you down. He's just filling time until he can retire. Guy's got no life so he tries to make everybody else's as mundane and empty as his. Don't worry about it."

The phone hung up and she smiled. Dick was a sharp lawyer and he was very good to her. She had once worked for him, right after college and they had enjoyed a short affair until a new job had taken her up north. She had stayed for three years but missed the bustle of the capital city and when a counseling position opened at Health and Welfare, she had jumped at it. Dick had made a few calls for her and she had secured the job. Since then she had moved on to bigger opportunities but always in Boise, near Dick. He was the closest she had come to a relationship and even though she had to share him with his wife and his other conquests, the relationship had evolved and she knew that he was the one man she could rely on.

Dick called about two hours later and gave her the number of the head of the State Parole Commission. He told her that he had 'smoothed the road and all she had to do now was lay down the asphalt.' She laughed at his cliché, marveling at how he could say something stupid and kind of make it seem chic. She called the number and spoke to the commissioner, explaining the situation to him, answering his questions, and putting some spin on it that made Jesse look a little more favorable than needed. The commissioner, Jack Taylor, knew he was being worked by this woman and Dick was right, she was scrumptious to listen to. Her voice both professional in tone but alluring, almost like listening to a phone sex professional, he thought to himself.

Jack and Dick had previously worked out a deal. He owed Dick for saving his ass a couple of years before when he had been nailed in a sting operation the police had run to cut down on prostitution. Dick had made a quick call to the DA, told him how this guy had cleaned up the parole messes the previous administration had made and wondered if he really wanted to deal with a new reformer now that the commission was doing so well and working so closely with the prosecutor's office. Within thirty minutes of arriving at the station, Jack had walked out, a case of mistaken identity by a rookie cop. Obviously, Jack had been at the wrong place at the wrong time and the rookie had been easy to convince. He waited a little longer before telling Margaret, enjoying her voice coming through the receiver and trying to picture in his mind what she looked like.

"I'm going to give you a chance with this guy," he finally said after she had finished making her pitch, "but you're responsible for him. If he runs, disappears, hurts someone, whatever, you'll be the one that will get thrown under the bus. Understand young lady?" She agreed, partly out of responsibility, but mostly because she wanted to stop talking to another condescending bureaucrat who had too much power and too little oversight over him.

She called Jesse and then reserved two airline tickets to Boston. The next morning Jesse met Raymond at the airport in the line to check-in and the men stood silently by each other, a coldness emanating off each man toward the other. Walking away from the counter, Jesse spied Margaret as she walked with a quickened pace through the sliding front doors of the airport, glancing upward at the schedule board searching for the gate. Hopefully, they had not passed through the security area she thought to herself as Jesse came silently up behind her.

"We're checked in," he said quietly, not wanting to startle her but being unsuccessful in the attempt. She let out a small squeal and whirled around and he couldn't help but laugh and she smiled in embarrassment. "I don't know how you pulled this off, but thanks," he said sincerely.

"Here," she stammered as she handed him an itinerary, she had put together for him and Raymond. He looked at it and smiled. That was Margaret, always professional, always prepared yet somehow a little disheveled at the same time. "I have a couple of rooms reserved for you at the Holiday Inn Express outside of the airport. It's under your name. I've already paid for it. I'll keep a ledger of costs and then you can pay me back after you get back."

"All right, well, I guess this is good-bye," he said, excited to go but scared now that the search was really underway.

"We gotta go," Raymond bellowed from the security station. He was clearly irritated and still in disbelief that the gal had pulled it off and gotten clearance for the convict to leave the state. The sooner he got on the plane, the sooner he could get a drink and fade off to sleep for the eight-hour trek across the skies.

"I'll call you when we get there," Jesse said quietly but avoiding eye contact. He turned and headed toward Raymond.

"Good luck," Margaret said quietly and Jesse turned and acknowledged her. She watched for a few more minutes until he and Raymond disappeared past security and headed toward their gate. It was now in their hands, she thought to herself, a drunk and a convict and she was lucky enough to be responsible if anything went wrong.

The plane rolled down the runway, picking up speed with each rotation of the tires until the front slowly lifted and the roughness of the asphalt became the smoothness of air and Jesse felt the sensation of his stomach coming up to his throat. He couldn't remember the last time he had flown and he felt both fear and exhilaration at the same time.

He looked out the window as the ground grew farther away. He was really doing this; the search was now real and he felt a surge of anxiety that at some point he would find her and would have to face what he had been. Raymond was already on his second whiskey and Jesse looked back out the window. He slowly closed his eyes and tried to picture what she must look like now and in his mind, the image he saw was a young Karla.

*

Jesse had endured a sleepless night on a lumpy mattress with Raymond's incessant snoring that sounded much like a sick foghorn followed by a low whistle. When the first light of the morning mercifully shown through the window that had not been cleaned in years, he got up and ambled over to a small coffee shop across from the motel.

The morning crowd that stopped in was filled with an Irish accent on their way to another mundane workday. The local's accent completely eliminated the use of the 'r' sound until one of the louts spoke of an 'idear about dealing with a fo' man who been unfai'a to the wo'kin' man.' Jesse couldn't help himself and snickered while acting as he had just read something funny in the newspaper he had before him.

He finished his coffee and walked back through the drizzle to his room, unlocking the door to the sound of a sick foghorn followed by a low whistle and he walked over to the television and turned it on with its volume loud enough to overtake the snoring and slowly bring the drunk out of his slumber. Raymond moaned and sat his feet on the floor, rubbing his eyes in an attempt to eliminate the hangover he had from the seven miniature bottles of whiskey he had drunk in the flight over.

After a shower and a gruff request to turn the television down or better yet, off, Raymond drank a quick cup of coffee from the little coffee maker provided by the motel. The men climbed into the rental, a maroon Toyota Camry, and merged on the thruway toward the city. Neither spoke to the other as they fought their way through the morning traffic. Raymond had a number of choice words for the drivers in front of him but eventually settled on 'Massholes' to describe his unhappiness with their driving abilities. Eventually, the road became less busy as they drove into the suburb of Medford and soon an urban oasis appeared. Old red brick buildings dotted the skyline and below them were numerous kids in their late teens and early twenties carrying book bags, riding mountain bikes, or just standing and debating with each other. Raymond slowed the car down when he realized the cars stopped for the kids, not vice versa. "Fuckin' brats," he cursed as three more darted out in front of him.

He pulled into a parking lot after nearly hitting another damn student who had just jumped out in front of him. He pulled out a campus map that he had downloaded from the internet and after some struggles with the balled-up paper found the Psychology Building.

"Looks like we have to walk to the other side of the campus," Raymond murmured, not something he wanted to do. He hadn't set foot on campus for years, his last experience ending sooner than he had expected many years before and being on this campus just reminded him of it. "You ready for this?" he asked.

Jesse nodded and opened the car door. He was nervous, no, scared. Soon he would be standing in front of a woman he had treated horribly in another time at another place. He felt panicky as he realized that maybe he couldn't go through with it and he continued to sit in the car.

"Come on, you've come this far," Raymond said quietly, "let's see what the professor has to say." Jesse looked at him and Raymond was unsure whether it was a look of resolve or doubt. Finally, he gingerly stepped out of the maroon Camry, and Raymond did the same.

"Where to?" asked Jesse and Raymond pointed and began walking while alternately checking the buildings to make sure he was heading in the right direction. Five minutes later they stood in front of a three-story brick building that appeared to have been built in the 1950s with a green metal sloping roof. They glanced at each other without saying anything and then began climbing the steps into the building. Raymond found the office for the Department of Psychology and purred to the receptionist, giving her a line about wanting to get back in school and if she could tell him where Karla Thompson's office was for their scheduled meeting. The woman had better things to do then talk to a kid in a middle-aged man's body. There was a stack of papers awaiting her that needed to be put into the computer so she quickly pointed toward a set of offices and told him that Karla's was the fourth one.

The two men walked to her office and the door was locked. Obviously, she was still teaching a class so they sat and waited for her to return. Jesse felt the tension grow inside of him. He wondered what her reaction would be if she would even recognize him. Slowly students began walking out of lecture halls and he knew that soon he would be face to face with her. He felt his throat tighten and his mouth became cotton as he sat.

"Oh my God…" he heard her say and he looked up. There she was, still stunning after all these years. Her hair was cropped short now but still stylish. She still had the petite figure of her youth but her hips were now wider from age. Her face had slight wrinkles around her eyes but her features were still sharp and only some sunspots on her arms gave away her age. She wore a skirt and blouse, both nondescript in nature but on her gave an elegant appeal of professionalism yet a softness that provided her students comfort to talk to her in a more informal setting.

"Hi Karla," he mumbled.

"You need to go…" she stammered and he could see that she still feared him. He was a nightmare that had re-appeared its ugly head after years of feeling safe that the beast was safely locked away.

"I need to talk to you," he croaked through a dry mouth and she saw that he was also nervous about the encounter. She unlocked her office door and walked in and he quickly followed her before she had a chance to shut it on him.

"No, you don't," she said as she set the book and papers she had with her on her desk. Now she was angry, angry that he had come back into her life and she intended to put an end to it immediately. "You need to go right now," she told him firmly, her eyes locked on him as Raymond slowly entered the office behind Jesse.

"Come on Karla," he groused, he was no longer nervous, just frustrated that she wasn't even giving him a chance. "I really need to talk to you. I've come a long way."

"I don't care," she said coldly. "I want you out of here now."

"Damn it, Karla, I'm here to talk about Rebecca," he replied tersely, the words burrowing his brow as he spoke and she felt the old fear that she had survived through during her youth and her anger grew because this selfish man would dare to put her through that ordeal again.

"You bastard, get out of here now or I'm calling security!" she yelled at him over the den of sound that was congregating out in the hallway. Raymond saw a crowd forming and knew that things were already out of hand.

"Come on Jesse," he said softly as he tried to pull him away from the front of the desk. Jesse broke away and continued to glare at Karla.

"No, I've come all the way here and she's going to talk to me!" he bellowed.

"Not right now she isn't," he said forcefully, "let's go."

"He's not to talk to me ever!"

"I'm sorry ma'am," Raymond apologized as he pulled Jesse away from the desk. Jesse was surprised by the old man's strength that the drunk showed. "Let's go, Jesse, you don't need the trouble."

"I should have known you'd be like this," he spat out in rage.

"Shut up Jesse," Raymond barked as he pulled him out of the office and led him out of the building. Security was on its way and Raymond waved them off and assured them that everything was fine and that they were leaving the campus. Two Tufts' policemen escorted them to the car and watched it leave the parking lot while radioing in the license number to the headquarters. In the car, Raymond privately enjoyed watching Jesse stew and waited for the blow-up that he knew was coming.

As they entered the city Jesse finally erupted. "Why'd you have me come here if that was going to happen?" He angrily stared at the large buildings outside the window. "C'mon Jesse..." he mimicked with a high pitch voice and Raymond couldn't help but laugh.

"She wasn't going to talk to you there, sport," he cackled through his laughter.

"So, now's it's over!" roared Jesse, realizing that he had probably been set up by this guy.

"Jesus, I thought you were once a big-time quarterback," Raymond laughed. "I 's'pose if something wasn't working you called it a game, eh?"

"Of course not," Jesse yelled but now that he had released his frustration, he felt himself calming down a little.

"No shit Sherlock. We go to plan B."

"You have one?"

"Of course, I'll get her phone number and address."

"How are WE going to do that?"

"Not we, me. That's my job. You just cool down," he said as he pulled into the parking lot of the motel. Raymond turned the ignition off and walked to the room. At the door, he realized that Jesse was still inside the car and he sighed and walked back and opened the passenger door. "Trust me, sport. I am good at what I do. Tonight, you'll be able to talk to her. By then the surprise will have worn off and then you can work your charm on her."

"All right, all right," Jesse relented as he pulled himself out of the car.

"You go inside and take a nap or something," Raymond ordered him. "I'm going to get a bite to eat and I'll be back in a while."

"No way, I'm not leaving you alone so you can get drunk," chided Jesse.

"I'm not going to drink. I need some food and then I have some work to do to make Plan B work, all right? Now go inside and get some sleep and calm down. I need you steady tonight." Jesse unlocked the motel door and looked suspiciously at Raymond but then walked into the room and closed the door behind him. He was tired he realized. It hadn't started as he had hoped but maybe Raymond actually could figure out another way. He lay on the bed and soon he was out, finally catching up on the sleep that he had missed out of the evening before.

Five hours later Raymond shook Jesse awake from his nap. Jesse immediately smelled the whiskey on his breath and bolted upright, angry that he had allowed himself to trust the damn drunk. "I told you not to drink," he seethed.

"I just had one about an hour ago. Calm down, I drink, all right? It doesn't mean I didn't take care of what we talked about. Clean up a little, we're going for a ride."

"You find her address?"

"What do you think? Come on, let's move."

Forty-five minutes later they sat parked in a quiet suburban neighborhood with older homes and little lawns. "Which one is hers?" asked Jessie. Raymond pointed to a single level home with a large porch in the front and an oak tree guarding the front lawn. "What are we waiting for?" asked Jesse.

"For her to come home," he replied. "Be patient." About fifteen minutes later a blue SUV, probably a blazer, but the lighting was poor and they couldn't make it out for sure, drove past them, and turned into the small driveway to the left of the house. It disappeared behind another house and Raymond cursed himself for not checking to see if there was a garage back there. After a minute or so a light went on in the kitchen area of the house and both men knew that Karla had arrived home. "Time to make a call, can you hold it together? This will probably be our only chance. Don't take no for an answer, but don't make her feel threatened either."

"I know how to talk to her," Jesse replied irritably.

"Yeah, you did a hell of a job this morning," Raymond replied in a serious tone and Jesse knew that he was probably right and this would be his last chance. He nodded to Raymond.

"How did you find it?" he asked.

"While you were busy arguing with her this morning, I saw the campus directory on her desk. Let's just say I borrowed it. It had both her home number and address in it and I came out earlier today to scope out the place." Jesse looked at him admiringly. He was proving to be pretty good after all. Maybe he had misjudged him. Maybe Margaret knew what she was doing after all when she hired this guy. Raymond took his cell phone out of his pocket and dialed the number. It rang once, then twice before she picked up. Her voice sounded a little out of breath.

"Ms. Thompson, my name is Raymond Albertson. I'm a private investigator…"

"How did you get this number," she demanded immediately, her voice turning to stone. "What do you want?"

"I'm hoping you'll agree to talk to your ex-husband. You'd be doing me a great service and I promise if you do, he'll be out of your hair for good."

"I have no interest in talking to him," she replied but Raymond knew that she was at least curious because she hadn't hung up on him yet.

"As is your right, ma'am, and I certainly understand. He is not the most agreeable fellow but he is my client and if you talk to him, I have a chance to finish my work." Jesse glared in anger at Raymond who smiled back, enjoying the opportunity of making him uncomfortable. "I sure would appreciate it."

The phone was quiet, but it wasn't dead and Raymond handed the phone to Jesse. Jesse looked back at him, a mixture of fear and hesitancy but he slowly put it to his ear. "Please don't hang up, Karla," he said quietly. Again, silence, but the line did not go dead. "I understand why you don't want to see me but I really need to talk to you. Can I come over?"

"Absolutely not," she replied firmly, breaking the silence.

"All right," he conceded. "That's fair. I wouldn't let me in either. I just really need to talk to you."

"I have nothing to say to you," she replied coldly and he could picture her in the house debating whether or not to just hang up the phone.

"Please Karla, just a half-hour." Again, there was silence for what seemed like an eternity. He expected to hear the line go dead but somehow, she remained on. As long as she remained on the phone, there was hope. "Please Karla."

"Then you will leave me alone?"

"I will."

"I mean it, Jesse, never again."

"Never again."

"There's a coffee shop, Ernie's, by the campus. I'll meet you there in an hour," and then the phone went dead. Jesse sat for a few more moments with the phone pressed against his ear and then slowly shut it and handed it back to Raymond.

"Ernie's, by the campus," he said simply and Raymond started the engine and pulled away from the curb. "God, I've caused a lot of damage, haven't I?" he said softly to himself. Raymond looked at him as he stared out the window. Damn right he'd caused a lot of damaged and Raymond cursed himself for feeling sorry for the bastard.

An hour later Jesse sat in a booth staring at the door, waiting for her to come in. He thought back to his youth when times were simpler and they had the whole world in front of them. He admired her now. She had found a way while he had wasted his. She was her own woman. He wondered how he had gone so wrong all those years ago. He could have been her, but he realized that all he had done was blame others to justify all the wrong moves he had made. She, on the other hand, had not accepted that as a teenage Mom she had nowhere to go. She was a strong woman. Suddenly she walked through the door and glanced around the nearly empty coffee shop until her eyes met his. He tentatively stood up and she slowly walked toward him with suspicious eyes of mistrust and her body language screamed that she wished to be anywhere but here with him.

"I appreciate you seeing me, Karla," he said quietly as she sat down. Her demeanor was cold.

"I'm not going to help you find Rebecca!" she stated emphatically.

"Just let me explain," he pleaded.

"No, you'll hurt her again."

"I won't," he protested but she continued to glare coldly at him and her stiffness told him that she abhorred him and the thought of him coming into her and Rebecca's life again.

"Leave her alone Jesse, just drop this," she demanded.

"I can't," he said softly. "Please let me explain."

"No Jesse, I don't want to hear 'how you've changed.' All you've ever cared about is what makes you happy. You don't care how other people feel or how your actions affect everyone around you."

"I didn't when I was young, that's true. I am different now and it doesn't matter if you believe me or not. You do change when you spend thirty years in prison. You realize that the world has passed you by and you're responsible for that. That becomes a very heavy burden to bear, but you accept it because it's true and you have no other choice. It usually takes ten or fifteen years inside to figure that out. Then you realize that you've driven away everything that you loved, loved you, and your heart becomes broken and then you learn the real truth."

"And what's that?" she asked, silently condemning herself for allowing him to interest her.

"You realize that there is only one thing more painful than a broken heart and that's one that was self-inflicted. When you reach that realization, you start to change everything about yourself because you don't want to be that man anymore. I have changed, Karla."

"I don't believe you," she said softly, but the coldness of her eyes softened a bit.

"Karla…" and he became silent for a moment and realized another truth. "I hurt you bad, didn't I," he said sadly.

"Don't flatter yourself," she replied, her eyes becoming cold again and her posture straightening in anger.

"I did, I know. No one should have to be treated the way I treated you. I'm really sorry about that."

"No, you're not," she hissed in defiance. "You're just trying to bring my defenses down so I'll give you what you want. Old habits don't change. You're a con man Jesse, a very dangerous one."

"I don't blame you for feeling that way…"

"Oh, that's big of you," and she could feel the anger build from the depth of her stomach and climb to her throbbing head as her cheeks crimsoned.

"I really am sorry," he said again and she noticed in her anger that there was a sadness in his eyes that she had never seen before. She wanted to believe it was a con, but the eyes had never deceived her, even during the most horrible times. His eyes were the windows to his soul and for so long they had been empty, void of anything, but these eyes that she was staring at had life, feelings, and she reluctantly realized that he was probably being somewhat truthful to her.

"I don't want you seeing Rebecca," she said, now calmer but still resolute. "If you thought saying sorry would work for you, you are sadly mistaken. You need to move on and leave Rebecca and me alone."

"Karla—"

"Leave her alone, Jesse, if you're truly sorry then this time think about what's best for somebody besides yourself." She stood up and turned toward the door. Jesse thought of chasing after her but he knew it would do no good. She didn't trust him, nor should she. He had been a terrifying blight on her life and he didn't deserve the help from her. He stayed seated in his chair and he realized that he wasn't going to find his daughter. Her mother would never let it happen and strength drained from his tired body and he knew that he was defeated.

*

Jesse sat on his bed and stared at the flickering screen of the television while Raymond nursed his whiskey on the rocks. In his mind, Jesse was reliving the conversation at the restaurant, and the image of Karla walking out played over and over in his head. Raymond stirred his drink absent-mindedly with a coffee straw not knowing what to say as Jesse continued to stare into the screen.

"She gives you any leads?" Raymond finally asked, breaking the silence.

"No," he replied quietly. "I hurt her pretty bad when I was younger. She doesn't want me anywhere near Rebecca."

"You didn't argue with her, did you?" Jesse gave him a disgusted look and then stared back at the screen.

"Doesn't matter now, I blew it. I just wanted to see my daughter." It was Raymond's turn to look disgusted now. He rolled his eyes in disdain toward the man on the bed whining again. He made him sick. This guy, who had caused so much angst for others, was trying to make himself out as the victim once again and Raymond felt nothing but disdain for him.

"Jesus," he exploded. "What the hell did you expect? You've been in jail for thirty years. Sounds like you were an asshole to her before when you were married. What'd you think she'd say…sure Jesse, here's the address. Christ man, grow up!"

"Well, you don't have to worry anymore, it's over now," Jesse growled back at him. Raymond stood up in disgust and glared at the con feeling sorry for himself and then stormed to the door.

"Good, I'm glad," he bellowed and he slammed the door behind him. He really was glad he was done with this pile of shit. The guy was as the old lady had said, nothing but selfish. Didn't care about what he had done to others, he just wanted everything to be his way. He was a spoiled brat who was now getting his comeuppance and he wanted to be pleased, but, damn it, he needed his money.

He went to the lobby which had an older computer that was slow and he googled Karla again. He went to the Tufts website and found her bio and started reading. As he read it, he jotted down some quick notes. Ms. Thompson was an interesting woman. He went back to the search engine and found more information about her and added to his notes, and then tracked her back a little more. He glanced at his notes and realized there was a possible trail to follow.

He took out his phone and made three quick phone calls, asking, more like begging some old acquaintances for a little help, and then he sat down on a lobby couch and waited. In thirty minutes the first phone call came back and he jotted down the information from a former cop who had a friend in the data entry section of the Ada County Sheriff's Office. Then the second call, an old partner who now worked with one of the top law firms in Las Vegas called and gave him a number of another P.I. in North Carolina to call. Raymond was getting excited and then the third call came back. It was from his son, an FBI agent in Miami.

The kid had done well despite the old man. He was truly a self-made man and had put himself through school because his old man had drunk his education away. After graduating summa cum laude from Portland State University, he had spent some time with the Portland PD before being accepted into Quantico and now he was a bona fide field agent. Even though Raymond had been a rotten father, the kid had always known the old man loved him and they remained on cordial terms.

The kid filled in some blanks that the old man had on Karla and soon Raymond had information on her dating back nearly seventeen years. He and the kid chatted for a few more minutes and Raymond finally understood why Jesse wanted to find his daughter. There's just something about your kid and he realized he hadn't understood that while he was underneath his roof. Once they leave a man realizes what is lost and will do about anything for another shot at doing it right. Jesse just wanted a shot. He had fucked up the first time and chances where he wasn't going to get another, but Raymond now understood the motive and he realized that it was probably pure.

After the kid hung up, Raymond thought of his financial portfolio, nothing but dust. He had spent most of the money upfront but had been at least sober enough to pay the rent for another month which would probably buy him two. But that was it and if he didn't come up with something, he had nothing waiting for him. He had to get Jesse to continue the search, had to, not for Jesse, but for him. He realized he wanted to see his kid again and that meant he needed some cash. If he could help Jesse find his kid that might put him back in business. He had everything to gain unless he lost the one client he had. He had to convince the con to continue. He looked at his notes one more time and headed back to the room.

"Look, I've been thinking," he said as he walked through the door. Jesse was still brooding on the bed and the television continued to flicker with the sound down low. "You really serious about finding your daughter or is it just bullshit?"

"Of course I am," snapped Jesse.

"I just ask because you seem to be giving up pretty easily. Did you really think this would be easy?"

"Fuck you," he growled, his eyes narrowing.

"I probably have that coming," grinned Raymond, and Jesse felt himself relax a bit. "I just think that since you've somehow managed to get this far you might as well see it through."

"There's nothing left to see through," replied Jesse quietly, but he sat upon his bed and seemed at least intrigued. "Karla doesn't want me to see her and she's not giving me any information. It's over."

"It could be," agreed Raymond and he lay on his bed and propped his head upon the worn pillows, "but maybe not. Is your daughter worth finding, is she worth the risk that you won't find her?"

"Of course she's worth it," Jesse said slowly, wondering where this was leading.

"Maybe we don't need Karla."

"We can't do it without her."

"I didn't say we were going to, but maybe if we follow her tracks, we'll be able to dig up some information. She's got a seventeen-year paper trail."

"She does?" Jesse said as he leaned toward Raymond. Now he was truly interested and he felt his hopes rising again.

"Yeah dumbass," retorted Raymond, amused at the childlike nature that Jesse was exhibiting. "Not everyone spent the last thirty years in the same address."

"That's a cheap-shot!" snapped Jesse.

"No, it's not," replied Raymond. "You want my help or are you going to give up?" Jesse was silent for a few moments and wondered if the drunk was serious. Jesse really did want to find her but he was afraid. He was petrified actually and he didn't want to cause Karla any more pain. But Rebecca was out there someplace and he knew that this was something he had to do.

"Can you really help or is this just you getting a couple more paychecks?"

"Sure, I want the paychecks," Raymond said truthfully. Boy did he want the money. "Hell, your sugar-Momma showed pretty effectively that I need the money. But I haven't had a good case in a while. Let's just say I like working again."

"So, what do we do?" asked Jesse. He believed him and the guy did seem to know what he was doing even when he was drunk.

"We have a deal?"

"Yes."

"All right," he said as he stood up and walked to the dresser and grabbed some papers out of his coat. He sat in the chair and turned on the light and told Jesse to come over.

"I've dug some stuff up on your ex-wife."

*

Jesse put fifty cents into the payphone by the waiting area of their gate at the airport. Raymond sat on a bench reading the newspaper and glanced quickly toward Jesse and motioned to his watch that time was short. Jesse nodded and heard the second ring and wondered why the asshole hadn't let him use his cell phone. He heard the click of a phone being answered and Margaret's familiar voice came into his ear and he couldn't help but smile. She was a good woman and he again tried to remember her from high school like he had done so many nights before but couldn't. Just as well, he probably would have screwed up her life too.

"We talked to Karla," he told her after some initial conversation.

"How did it go?" she asked, hoping for the best but expecting the worst.

"Not well," and she felt herself sag a little in her chair, "but Raymond got another idea that we're going to follow."

"Follow where?" she asked, perking up.

"We're heading to North Carolina. We're at the airport right now and we load in about ten minutes."

"But you're supposed to be back in Boise in two days," she said, suddenly concerned.

"I know," he conceded. "Can you talk to my parole officer?"

"You need to call him and I'll follow up. Can you call him once you get to North Carolina?" she asked, "by the way, where at in North Carolina?"

"I will. We'll be in the Fayetteville area. Karla got a job there after working in Boise. Raymond is hoping he can find someone who knew them or former friends of Rebecca."

"All right, do you need anything here?"

"Any information you can dig up about Karla or Rebecca would be great."

"I'll see what I can find. Don't forget to call your parole officer," she reminded him.

"I won't."

"Call me when you do, I'll follow up." He hung up the phone because Raymond was now giving him animated looks because the plane was loading. He walked toward him and they stood quietly in line until they were at the front and handing the gatekeeper their tickets. They made their way to their seats in the plane and buckled themselves in and soon they felt the wheels turn and the plane being pushed out of the gate.

Jesse looked out the window again and soon the plane was speeding down the runway and slowly lifting into the air and he felt his stomach rise into his throat again and he decided that he actually liked the feeling. The plane steadied out and Jesse pushed his seat back and stretched his legs as best he could and he looked into the clouds that now surrounded the plane and felt a peace that he had rarely felt in his life. He smiled as he thought of his daughter. She was out there and he was looking. He felt useful again, a man with a purpose and no longer a scared con trying to fit into a world he no longer knew.

The flight attendant walked down the aisle toward them and suddenly Raymond put his arm out to stop her.

"Ma'am, could I get a whiskey and water, please?"

Chapter 13

Dead ends; every time a path seemed to open it only ended in frustration. Raymond stared at his notes, trying to make sense of where the daughter could be, but all he saw was a jumbled jigsaw puzzle and he grabbed his cheap bottle whiskey and poured the brownish liquid into the Styrofoam cup sitting perilously close to the edge of the table he had his papers spread out on. He took a swig from the cup, hoping the alcohol would provide clarity but he knew that was unlikely.

He had followed the trail and she had left one that didn't seem difficult to follow. It wasn't like she was trying to hide from anyone and this only caused him to be more frustrated by the lack of available information on the daughter. Karla and Rebecca had moved from Fayetteville to Wilmington where Karla had spent two years earning a Master's degree in Psychology. She earned a Foundation Scholarship to go to UNC-Wilmington which had paid for her tuition costs and provided her with a Fellowship working with the department chair. She had moonlighted on the side, working for a local attorney doing filing and transcription. The lawyer was a sleaze who womanized and spent untold hours trying to get Karla in bed, but she had fought off his advances and earned her master's degree in less than two years.

With the degree, she had accepted a job in Tampa working for a local agency and had done some counseling with their poorer clients. According to the agency, she had been quiet and had kept to herself and her supervisor raved what a good worker she was and that, though at times aloof, had seemed friendly enough. No one knew of any friends she had there and after two years she had accepted another position with the company and moved to Jacksonville where they were opening a new shop. While there she began work on a PH.D. in Clinical Psychology at Jacksonville University while continuing to see clients for the company.

She kept a low profile at the company but her superiors remembered that she always had positive reviews. They marveled at how she had been able to work and go to school and most agreed that for two years there was no way she could have slept. Some remembered the precocious child, but only saw her in passing at the store or every once in a while, when she would bring her in to play in the office while she worked on notes or studied in the conference room.

After earning her degree at Jacksonville, the trail led to Coral Gables where she moved into higher education as a professor of Psychology at the University of Miami. Again, she didn't really stand out with former colleagues, most noting that she was very quiet and not necessarily the most popular professor in the department. But each agreed that she worked hard and was always getting positive reviews from her students and superiors. She stayed for four years and was due for tenure when she accepted a new job north of the Mason-Dixon Line.

Rebecca was a teenager by this time and one professor remembered a conversation with Karla in which she told him that she was worried about the kids her daughter was spending time with. He admitted that he was surprised when she told him she was taking a job at SUNY-Albany in New York because there was no question that she would be receiving tenure from Miami. Besides, UM was a much more prestigious school than Albany and he couldn't imagine the pay was anywhere near what she was receiving here. He surmised that she moved because of something that had to do with her daughter but admitted he had no way of knowing for sure.

Raymond tended to agree with this premise. Rebecca had been ticketed for underage drinking when she had been at a party that had been busted on the beach. Still, none of the other kids who had been ticketed had any type of future record that caught his attention and he realized that Karla had probably been an over-protective mother who had jumped at the chance to get away from a part of the country that for whatever reason she had not appeared to take to.

Raymond gulped down the whiskey that remained in the cup and unscrewed the bottle and poured more in. What was he missing? Somewhere in all the information he had acquired had to be a clue but he was missing it. He grabbed another yellow pad that had coffee stains and the smell of whiskey on it. He glanced through the pages and wondered what some of the things he had written had meant. Obviously, he had been drunk during some of his note-taking and he hoped he hadn't missed something important.

Then he found the tidbit he was looking for. The Albany years were interesting. She had spent two years working at the university in the Psychology Department and had apparently been quite the catch for the school. He saw that she had received a significant bump in pay during her second year there amid rumors that she and the department chair were having an affair. In truth, Karla had been involved in a serious relationship, but it wasn't the department chair but, instead, the provost of the school. He had recently divorced about the time she assumed her position there and according to some close acquaintances that knew of their relationship, had begun on the evening of her interview with the school and had been kept very quiet.

They spent time in New York City together but were never seen in Albany. Because she had received such a significant pay raise many in the department had assumed that she and the chair were romantically linked and these rumors had led to him getting divorced from his wife which only heightened the water cooler talk in the faculty room.

Karla seemed to have fallen hard for the provost but in March of her second year, the relationship began to sour, probably because of the unsubstantiated rumors about her and the chair of the department. When an opening in New York City became available Karla had quietly applied for it and the provost had pulled a few favors to get her an interview. That had been all she needed and in June she and Rebecca moved into an apartment overlooking Central Park in New York City.

Karla loved working at the City University of New York. It was the first place she developed actual friendships with her colleagues on the faculty. During her four-year tenure, she became a member of the faculty senate and participated in volunteer activities outside of the university. While things were burgeoning for her at CUNY, at home she and Rebecca began to have some cracks in their relationship. Rebecca had developed a bit of a rebel attitude and had begun to break curfew. Friends of Karla reported that it was not uncommon for the daughter to embarrass the mother in public with belligerent talk and disrespectful behavior.

Karla confided in friends that Rebecca had taken up with a rough crowd and expressed concern that she was slowly losing her daughter to the seedier side of the city. Close confidants reminded her that Rebecca was making good grades in school and that this was just a phase that all teenagers have to go through during the rite of passage from adolescence to adulthood. In her third year at CUNY, she had taken a sabbatical and she and Rebecca had left the city for a year or so. There was little information during this time to go on and Raymond suspected that maybe it was because she was working on a book or something academic. When she returned to New York, she was alone and her friends either didn't know or wouldn't say where Rebecca was.

Karla had met a businessman who worked on Wall Street and they had a romance that lasted a little over a year. Around the time that Rebecca moved out, Karla married him, but the marriage was short-lived. Turned out the guy was a scam artist who was working a Ponzi scheme and had apparently brought some folks in who didn't take kindly to their money disappearing. He had turned up in the Hudson River about a week after the SEC had come to ask him some questions. It was determined that the cause of death was suicide, but whispers had insinuated that he may have been a mafia hit as some members of the Bonomo Family had made heavy investments with him.

While all this had been going on Rebecca reappeared and moved back in with Karla for a time and they had appeared to have buried whatever hatchet had come between them. Another job offer had come for Karla, this one at Tufts, and with all the tumult she had experienced in the past year she quickly accepted and the two had moved, but then the trail turned cold because Rebecca had only stayed for two weeks and Raymond could not find any sign of her after she had left.

He sat staring at the papers. What could he possibly be missing? How does a person just disappear? Suddenly, it came to him and he stood up, eyes riveted straight ahead. Karla had anticipated this. After her experience with husband number two, she had realized that Jesse would be getting out a jail at some point and may want to find them. She had obviously realized that she had a trail that could be followed, but Rebecca didn't. She had made her daughter disappear.

Raymond fell back onto the bed and suddenly felt his headache. Jesse was right. They didn't have anything if Karla wasn't going to play ball. It was over.

*

"Give me another one barkeep," slurred Raymond. The bartender looked at the pathetic little man and shrugged his shoulders and walked away. "I asked for 'another,'" snarled Raymond.

"You've drunk me out of whiskey, my friend. It's time for you to go now," he replied and went back to his quiet conversation with the brunette wearing the low halter top so that he could all see of her voluminous breast except the nipple which he expected to see after his shift was over.

Raymond slowly pushed himself up from the bar. His head was swimming and his legs felt wobbly but he had felt this feeling many times and he knew that as soon as he got outside and breathed in some fresh city pollution, he would be all right. "Last chance to serve me, barkeep," he mumbled and he laughed at his joke as he turned and slowly staggered to the door. The barkeeper watched him walk out and quickly went back to staring at the brunette's boobs.

Outside Raymond summoned a cab and cursed it as it continued on without stopping. He waited for the next one and again put his hand up and this time the car stopped. He climbed in and wondered if the driver spoke any English. Another raghead, he thought to himself, the East Coast is full of them and he realized that he missed being home. He had done his best for the convict but the road had led to nowhere and now he was ready to get back to Boise. The cab pulled in front of the motel on the state line between New York and New Jersey. Raymond reached into his pocket and pulled out a twenty. "It'll have to do," he slurred. "It's all I got." The driver nodded and decided not to quibble over the final two dollars and Raymond handed it to him and nearly fell as he got out of the car. It sped away, spraying rocks as it left and Raymond cursed the Arab behind the wheel. He saw a sign for a liquor store across the street and slowly walked over. The night air was clearing his head and a nightcap would do him good.

Inside the store, Raymond found a cheap bottle and took it to the counter where another Arab rang it up to put it in a sack. He was glad the driver hadn't pushed him for the final two bucks or he would have been short a buck. He grabbed his brown bag and walked out, feeling more in control of his legs and crossed the road that was busy during the day but was now deserted. Inside his room he pulled his shoes off and turned on the television, removing the cap from the bottle and not bothering to get a glass. He took a sip and felt the burn going down his throat. Stuff didn't taste great but it did have a good kick to it, he thought to himself. Outside, Jesse knocked on the door and Raymond muttered to himself but got up and answered it. "Ah, it's the great quarterback…superstar…come on in," he slurred with a smile.

"You're drunk Raymond."

"I am, true," he stammered as he sat back down on the bed and took another drink from the bottle. "I'd offer you some, but you're on parole so I guess you probably can't have any. Kind of a tough deal for the fallen quarterback I'd say."

"What's your problem, Raymond?" Jesse groused as he wondered what the latest bout with the bottle was caused by.

"I don't have any problems. Everything is hunky-dory, superstar." He took another, longer sip from the bottle, looked at it, and noticed that it was already half empty.

"That's your problem," countered Jesse, pointing at the bottle. "I know, I had the same problem and then some. I liked drugs almost as much as the drink. I don't understand why you drink so much. You're good at what you do, why do you keep trying to destroy yourself with your drinking?"

"Oh, I see," laughed Raymond sarcastically, "you're an expert now. You probably got a lot of good counseling while you were in the clink. Obviously, all that good talk has made you an expert." Raymond took another drink and glared at the convict at the same time.

"No…I…"

"Come on the superstar. Save me…give me some words of convict wisdom," he spat at him in disdain.

"Ah, the hell with you," Jesse muttered. "No wonder you're a broken-down gumshoe, just make enough to buy the next bottle." He returned the glare and turned toward the door. "I'm out of here," he muttered and he put his hand on the knob and twisted it.

"Hey superstar, before you go why don't you take a load off. I have a little story I guess you ought to hear."

"Tell me tomorrow when you wake up," Jesse sniffed, looking back through the open door.

"You'll like this story," Raymond replied excitedly. "Come on, don't make me drink alone. Let me tell you a story."

"Tomorrow," sighed Jesse.

"Sit down dickhead, I gotta story you need to hear," he roared. Jesse saw how serious Raymond was and slowly closed the door.

"Fuck," he murmured as he grabbed a small chair from the table that had all the notes Raymond had made searching for Rebecca. "Fine, tell me your story." Raymond smiled at him and took another swig from the bottle as Jesse stared darkly at him.

"Once upon a time there was a kid who grew up in the sticks," began Raymond, putting his feet on the floor and leaning toward Jesse, "but he always had plans to get out, make a difference, live the good life…" and he took another drink from the bottle, but this time only a sip and he winced as the liquor went down his throat.

"This about me?" asked Jesse condescendingly.

"Shut up superstar, just listen."

"Fine."

"This kid did all the things that normal kids do. He went to school, got good grades, played some ball, and worked to save money for college. The big day arrives and he gets accepted into the school of his choice. Family is so proud, so happy…" and he took the last bit of liquid from the bottle but his eyes remained on the listener.

"Is there a point?" wondered Jesse.

"You really need to stop talking and listen, convict."

"You're walking a fine line right now Raymond," warned Jesse.

"Oh, I've been there before," laughed the drunk. "Anyway, back to my story. The kid goes off to college, does really well too; finds out that life in the big city suits him. He goes to class, takes good notes; studies at night, the whole shebang. Anyway, he takes a real interest in chemistry, biology. You know; the sciences; become infatuated with all the possibilities. He thinks that maybe he wants to teach or do research." Raymond looked longingly at the empty bottle and Jesse saw that his eyes were sad and realized that he was probably the kid he was talking about. "Thinks that maybe he wants to teach or do research," he repeated quietly.

Jesse stared at him and realized that he was grudgingly interested in the story. For so long all he had thought of was Rebecca and Raymond had been nothing more than a necessary tool to help him find her. Now he seemed almost human and Jesse couldn't help but listen.

"The kid really is getting into college," continued Raymond. "He finishes the first year and goes home for the summer but finds out that times have been tough in the sticks. The old man pulls him aside and informs him that there's no money for anymore college." Jesse could see a glint of anger in Raymond's eyes and lean forward toward him. "Kid can't accept it. Instead, he gets two jobs for the summer and gets himself a student loan. By the end of the summer he's got enough for another year of school but he has to find an apartment because he won't be able to afford the dorm and meals. He sucks it up and gets it done and finds a couple of other guys to live with him. The year is harder but he keeps his grades up even though he's now working nights to make ends meet." Jesse felt uncomfortable and was no longer sure if he wanted to hear the rest of Raymond's story. He was tired and not really in the mood for Raymond's excuse of being the drunk that he was.

"OK Raymond," he interrupted, "nice story. You need to pass out so we can—"

"Jesus convict, you're about to miss the best part!" he replied smugly knowing that Jesse wouldn't be able to help himself but to listen. The convict was a simpleton, much like all the others he had dealt with over his alcohol hazed life.

"Stop calling me convict," hissed Jesse.

"I'm sorry, don't want to hurt your feelings," he wisecracked.

"I'm going," Jesse said as he stood up.

"Sit down! You're going to hear the rest of this God damn story!"

"Make it fast," Jesse said through clenched teeth as he slowly sat back down. He should just get up and leave, but the drunk probably would just follow him and make a scene outside.

"So, at the end of the term the roommates decided to celebrate," Raymond said, again in a regular tone and with no slurring of his words. "All have gotten financial aid for the next year and all are doing well. So, before each goes their own way for the summer, they decide to go have a night out, blow off a little steam. They go to a local establishment and have a few brews and then decide to go somewhere else. At the next place, they find a pool table and play some eight-ball when a kid comes up to them and tries to sell them a little snort."

Jesse's eyes widened. Raymond obviously had gotten the story of the kid he had shot and now was throwing it back in his face. Jesse wanted to kill him right now, kill him as he should have the damn kid all those years ago.

"I don't need to hear the story, asshole!" he yelled as he stood up, his fists clenched. "Why are you doing this to me? I served my time!"

"There you go interrupting me again," laughed Raymond, ignoring the anger that Jesse was displaying and not afraid of the imposing figure of the convict standing over him with his fists clenched. "Anyway, the druggy starts telling the boys what a big-time football player he was, what a great player he should have been." Raymond stood up and walked to the chair Jesse had been sitting in. "Leaning over is hard on my back," he said. "Come on Jesse, sit down, we're just about there." Jesse knew that Raymond had no fear of him and he sat on the bed, again wondering why he didn't just leave, but the story was mesmerizing and for some reason that he could not explain he knew that he had to hear the rest of it.

"The kids are polite at first but eventually tire of the guy's mouth. They ask him to leave and he gets all high and mighty so they try to leave. He starts strutting' and pushes one of the guys, thinking that since he's a big drug dealer the guys will scare easily. Instead, the guys pop him around and the bouncers force him to leave." Jesse could see it unfolding in his mind, remembering back to the night that had been his final downfall.

"The guys go back to their game and enjoy the rest of the evening. Around midnight a couple of the guys get really tired. They've been packing all day to go home and want to get some sleep. But the third guy, well, he's having a good time. He's seen a girl, made some google eyes toward her, and has gotten some interest so he decides to hang out for a while longer, see if he can get lucky." Raymond reached into his pocket and pulled out his pack of cigarettes and put one to his mouth, lighting it and taking a long, hard drag before inhaling it and letting the smoke escape through his nostrils. "He follows her to another bar and buys her a drink which leads to a nice conversation and soon they're playing pool together. Everything's going really well but she had to go to the bathroom so he goes to the bar and orders two more. When she comes back, she says she doesn't really like playing pool and invites him to sit with her at the bar. All of a sudden there's a commotion. The boy turns around and there's the drug dealer." Raymond's eyes had a faraway look and his voice became low as Jesse squirmed uncomfortably in his chair. "Before he can say or do anything there's an explosion. He feels himself falling to the ground and everything becomes hollow. He hears some more pops and his body lurches as the bullets enter, then everything kind of fades away."

Both men sat in silence for a moment, Jesse stared at the ground as Raymond now looked directly at him, his eyes ablaze but his voice just barely over a whisper. "He's pretty sure he's dead," Raymond continued, "but feels as though he's stuck in a void, not part of the living but not really dead either." He took another long drag off his cigarette as Jesse lifted his eyes from the floor and stared at him, no longer seething, but numb. "A few days later he wakes up but can't move. Has tubes everywhere and is wracked in pain. He doesn't know it, but even though he's alive, he's actually nothing more than a zombie. Everything he dreamed of is gone. All the work he did is wasted."

Raymond stood up and walked directly in front of Jesse and slowly pulled his shirt up, displaying scars where the bullets had entered. Jesse gasped and felt himself go limp. "Here's your trophy superstar. I was the boy!"

"Oh my God," Jesse croaked, feeling as though he had just received a pipe to the side of the head.

"That's deep," laughed Raymond. "I thought it was time for you to see whose life you ruined."

"Raymond, I'm…sorry," he croaked again trying desperately to regain control of himself. He realized that he had never thought of the boy he had shot. Not during the trial, the years in prison. He had blocked it from his mind. He realized that when he thought back to it the boy had always been a faceless shadow. Now he was standing before him.

"Sure, you are," cackled Raymond. "I'm wondering, during those thirty years did you even think of who you shot?"

"Of course, I did," Jesse lied. "Ah shit, no I didn't. After I sobered up, I thought about the event, but you always were just a shadow, nothing more. I guess I did that so I wouldn't have to deal with what I had done."

"Stop the psycho-babble bullshit," Raymond said as he pulled the shirt down. "You fuckin' cons are all alike, you're all liars. Well, here's your handiwork. You didn't just fuck up your life; you fucked up a lot of lives. Do you ever think about what happened to all those kids you got hooked on your drugs, their families, or friends? You ruin lives, convict. That's all you do you piece of shit! You ruin lives."

"Raymond, I'm so sorry," he stammered. It was hitting him now, hitting him like nothing ever had before. All the counseling sessions, all the talks with spiritual people, they had all been just bullshit, not making him be accountable for the things he had done. This drunk had made him see it, feel it. There was no escape, he was right, he was nothing more than a horrible tornado that had ruined more lives than he could ever imagine.

"I don't want your fucking apology," hissed Raymond. "I just wanted to bring you to reality. I want you to go to hell! I have for a long time."

"Please Raymond," cried Jesse. "I've changed, I'm so sorry." He needed to be absolved for his sins but Raymond had no interest giving it to him.

"No, you haven't," he replied with a slight grin and an even tone. "You can go now superstar, but before you leave, I want you to ponder on something.' You've already ruined a lot of lives, but for the past thirty years, you haven't been able to fuck up your daughter's. It sounds like she was pretty young when you went in…maybe she doesn't even remember you. Do you really think it's necessary to ruin hers too? Now get the fuck out of my room." He walked toward the bathroom, a raging piss aching to get out.

"Raymond—"

"Get the fuck out convict!" he yelled as he walked into the bathroom and locked the door behind him. He listened as he urinated and smiled when he heard the room door close. He had done the right thing he thought to himself. The asshole needed to know.

Outside the door, Jesse leaned against the rail for support. He couldn't control the shaking of his body and he realized it wasn't from the coolness of the night. He was a bad man; he was the man that parents warned their kids about and he always would be. There was no such thing as rehabilitation. Not with what he had done.

*

He sat on his bed and stared at the ground. Sleep had done no good; the realization of the havoc he had wrought would not go away, even in slumber. His life had been a waste. He had caused nothing but pain for so many and last night he had heard from a man who he had literally destroyed so many years before. He buried his head in his hands and slumped forward, sobs now coming out, tears of anguish for the guilt he was finally accepting.

He thought of the destruction he had caused throughout his life. The drugs, the horrible words reigned upon those he loved, the utter disrespect for others. He shook as he cried, no longer able to contain himself. How could he ever make it up to those he had hurt so badly? He thought of his parents. They had been good, done their best to give him what he needed, always showing him the support that he craved, yet in the end, he had taken their hopes and destroyed them with his selfishness. He had been the reason the old man had died prematurely, and the old man's death had broken his mother's heart and she had followed soon after. He was responsible for it, just as surely as if he had put a gun to their heads and pulled the trigger.

He thought of Karla, now an untrusting woman who had become that way because of his many betrayals toward her. When they were together, he hadn't taken the time to realize how incredibly lucky he had been to have the love of such a true and caring woman. Instead, he had hurt her in every way possible. Because of him, she could no longer open her heart to another for fear that it would destroy her all over again. And Rebecca, his sweet child, long since grown up, had lived her life without the love and support of him as her father. He had screamed at her, terrified her with his unfeeling slaps against the face and roaring of his displeasure because she had made the innocent mistake of whimpering. All she knew of him was the hate he had cruelly shown her. And Raymond, a man who had now sunk into the depths of a bottle, had once been a boy with dreams and the work ethic needed to reach them. But they had been destroyed one evening because he, the monster, was angry that they wouldn't buy some drugs from him and had the nerve to sass him when he wouldn't leave them alone. He had put five bullets into him and left him for dead. But Raymond had been a fighter, and even though his dreams were gone he had stubbornly fought to stay alive, and now he had forced Jesse to recognize what a worthless piece of shit he actually was.

He stood up, tears streaming down his face. He looked into the mirror and the reflection disgusted him. Looking back at him was a broken man, in his fifties, crying like a baby. He couldn't stand himself and he wondered what to do. He had caused nothing but upheaval and Raymond had at long last made him realize this. Everything he had said was true, each word piercing him like a bullet that he could not dodge. His arms lay limply at his side as he stared into the mirror, wanting to look away but like being at a crash site, unable to avert his eyes from the carnage. He saw the glint of the belt buckle around his waist and immediately he knew there was only one thing to do. For once it was time for him to do the right thing and end all the misery he had caused. He unbuckled the belt and walked to the closet and felt the pipe the held the hangers. It was sturdy and the screws that held it to the wall were tight. He wondered if he could really go through with it but something inside of him kept telling him that he must and he took the belt off and looped it around his neck.

The tears continued to fall from his eyes and made it difficult for him to clearly see what he was doing but somehow, he tied a knot in the belt around the pipe. He said a silent prayer to a God he barely knew and he hoped that maybe in a few minutes that being would have mercy on his soul. Deep down he knew that as soon as he passed, he would be in a terrible place and he felt a deep fear inside of him and his courage began to wane. Then he realized that he must go through with it and finish what he had started. No one would care that a middle-aged con had exited stage left, he realized, and in a moment of clarity, he found the strength to collapse.

He forced himself to stay limp as his head began to feel as though it were bulging from the lack of air. Strangely, it did not hurt and as he began to fade, he felt almost light as if he were in a cloud up in the air. The sound of the fan became hollow and he knew that soon he would be passing out and that would be the end of it. In the hollowness came a strange sound that he couldn't quite make out but that sounded familiar to him. The sound was intermittent and he wondered what it could be. He felt blackness beginning to overtake him and he prayed that soon he would see a light as the sound continued to ring hollowly in his ears. Suddenly he realized what it was and he tried to push against his feet but his strength was now sapped. He pushed again with all of his might and fought to raise his arms to the bar. His hand felt the coldness of the steel and he grabbed it and pulled, his feet planting firmly against the floor as he stood and the darkness began to fade and stars began shooting toward him. He had a terrific headache now as he clumsily loosened the loop around his neck and he stumbled toward the sound emanating throughout the room.

"Helloooooo…" he managed to say as he lifted the phone off the receiver.

"Jesse!" he heard Margaret say in alarm. "Are you all right?"

"Yeah," he mumbled. "Just, uh, sleeping."

"You're not drinking, are you?" she demanded to know.

"No Margaret, honest, just sleeping," he lied.

"I have some news you will want to have." He tried to clear his head but the pain would not relapse as the air filled his lungs and he felt as if he were going to faint. He fought to stay conscious and concentrated on the woman's voice on the other end of the receiver.

"What is it?" he murmured.

"I think I've found Rebecca." Suddenly he no longer felt the pain from his head. His heart began beating faster and faster until it seemed as though it would explode out of his chest. Rebecca was within reach. The God he had prayed to had answered him. It wasn't time to go, it was time to make amends, accept what fate awaited him.

"Where?" he stammered. "How?"

"I can't go into detail," she replied. "I got some information from a friend and colleague and it seems to have checked out."

"What information? Margaret, you can't leave me hanging like this," and he thought of the irony of what he had just said and for the first time in a while, he felt himself smile.

"I can't tell you over the phone. Once you and Raymond get back, I'll fill you in. In the meantime, you two need to get back to Idaho as soon as you can and head to Coeur d'Alene. I'll meet you there and fill you in."

"All right," he replied. "I'll let Raymond know. We'll be back in Boise tomorrow."

"Good," she said.

"And Margaret—"

"Yes."

"Thank you. You have no idea how important this phone call is," he said quietly.

"Are you sure you're all right?" she asked.

"I am now," he replied. "I'll see you soon." He hung up the phone and grabbed a shirt and quickly put his shoes on. He had to see Raymond, but he was afraid and he thought for a moment of just packing his bags and sneaking out but he couldn't do that he realized. Once again, he would just be running away and he had to be better than that. He had been given a reprieve and now it was time to be a good man. It would start with going over to the next room and facing the man he had once tried to kill.

He knocked on the door and waited. There was no sound so he knocked again, this time louder and waited. He was just about to knock again when he heard some stirring inside and a muffled curse coming from one who had drunk too much the night before. The doorknob finally turned and Raymond faced him, smelling of whiskey and though the eyes were clouded, Jesse could see they were filled with hate.

"You all right?" he asked. Raymond nodded but made no move to allow the man that he abhorred into his room.

"Margaret called a few minutes ago. She says she has some pretty promising information back in Idaho." Raymond grunted and nodded again. His eyes squinted from the sun of the morning and the fresh air made his hangover that he had earned the night before begin to recede.

"I'll be ready in 20 minutes," he said as he closed the door.

Jesse slowly walked back to his room and grabbed his duffle bag and began stuffing his clothes into it. He walked to the bathroom mirror and out of the corner of his eye he saw the belt that was tied to the bar and he untied it and tossed it toward the bag and looked back into the mirror. This time he saw hope instead of despair. He felt fear, but he again had a reason to be alive. He splashed some water on his face, grabbed a towel, and dried it.

He looked closely at the mark around his neck that was now crimson. He touched it and felt a stinging sensation. He lightly touched it again but this time he silently thanked Margaret for keeping him alive

Chapter 14

Jesse lay in bed and stared at the darkened ceiling. He had tossed and turned all night and now he surrendered to the realization that he would not be getting any sleep and his mind wandered. He thought of the child he had abandoned so long ago and wondered what had become of her now that she was a woman. He cursed himself but for the life of him, he couldn't picture her as a child. In his mind, he could see a silhouette but it remained in the shadows and though he tried the child's face remained hidden from his view. He wondered if this was because of the drugs and alcohol he had ingested over the years or because of the hate he had felt for her for so long. Maybe he was a fool to be trying to find her now.

His thoughts turned to the nightmare that the flight back to Boise had been. Anything that could go wrong had. In New York, the plane had been delayed with engine problems which guaranteed the layover in Minneapolis. Raymond, who hated planes and abhorred being with him even more, had solaced himself with drinks from the cocktail lounge in the terminal until he had run out of money. He promptly passed out sitting in the waiting area rather than having to be with the one he loathed. Jesse had managed to get him conscious enough to walk onto the plane and get him buckled in but the ensuing five-hour flight had been a nightmare as Raymond had alternately snored and farted, sending a strong scent of foul whiskey into the pressurized air that made it slowly seep throughout the cabin.

They had arrived back in Boise in the wee hours of the morning and he had managed to get Raymond into his office after pillaging through the drunkard's clothes to find the keys. At last, he had made it home. Tomorrow, Margaret would meet them in Coeur d'Alene in the northern part of the state and update him on the information she had received about Rebecca.

He was frustrated she hadn't given him more information and wondered what the big secret could be. It didn't matter though; in a few hours the alarm would be going off and he and Raymond would be heading north and soon he would finally find Rebecca. He silently fretted over how she would react to him as the fear of the rejection grew in his stomach.

He looked at the clock for the umpteenth time, still two hours before he would be getting up and he closed his eyes and did his best to clear his mind, fighting the urge to think he slowly felt his body lighten and just as he was falling asleep he thought of his suicide attempt and he was again wide awake. He thought of the sensation he had felt of dying. He realized that he had been mere seconds from death and he wondered whether it was a coincidence that the phone had rang or if this had been part of a larger plan by a God he knew that he probably ought to get to know better. His thoughts turned to the one who had saved him and yet had no idea she had done so, nor of his feelings towards her.

She had become his secret crush and he thought of the irony of it all. As a youth, she had wanted him and he had barely known she existed, and now, as a man whose life had been best termed as a failure, he had to hide his feelings from her because he was sure she would never be interested in the likes of him.

She had grown on him slowly. He thought of the past months that he had been across the country trying to find Rebecca. His days filled with thoughts of his daughter, but the nights alone in bed had been of Margaret. At first, he hadn't realized that he cared for her and only thought he was fantasizing because it had been so long since he had been with a woman. But then he realized that he wasn't thinking of her in sexual terms, though he certainly could not help himself of thinking of her naked in his arms. It was her voice, soothing with a rich silkiness that he often thought of. Her voice had a softness to it yet was harmonic in its sound and he found himself slowly losing himself to her as she spoke to him in his mind.

If nothing else, he was a realistic man and he knew that she would never be with him, just as Karla never would be. His only hope was that somehow Rebecca would give him a chance to make things right. Rebecca, his last true hope for feeling a sense of normalcy in his life, was within his grasp, but so was the probable rejection from her and he tried to steel himself for that, knowing the pain he would feel would be more than he could ever imagine. He prayed that it would no longer matter if he felt that devastation of rejection, only that he followed through. If he did this, he would have a chance to move on with his life and maybe create something of himself. It was his chance to start over.

At last, the alarm sounded and he got up and jumped into the shower. Twenty minutes later he was walking out the door of his small apartment with the familiar duffle bag that carried some underwear, a couple of day's changes of clothes, his razor, and his toothbrush. He walked down to the parking lot of the complex and pulled the canvas off the old car he had bought days after getting the trust. It was an old Buick Rivera that had seen its best days long ago. Now the chrome was rusted and inside the once shiny seats were torn and covered by an old blanket, he had found at the Goodwill Store. Still, the car was his and though it cost an arm and a leg to keep it in gas he had thoughts of maybe someday trying to restore it to its former glory but he realized that the likelihood of that was as remote as him becoming the football star he had once believed he would be but still it felt good to actually have a goal.

He turned the key and the car made a couple of coughing sounds and then the engine roared to life, only to choke for a moment and die. He turned the key again and the result was the same. Finally, the third time was a charm and he pulled out of the driveway and headed toward Raymond's office to pick him up, wondering as he went whether he had yet awoken from another drunken slumber. To his surprise he was waiting outside, sitting against the front wall of the intrepid building.

"Ready to go?" Jesse asked as he pulled in behind a red Honda Civic.

"Not in that," snorted Raymond as he slowly stood up and grabbed his bag.

"You don't like my car?"

"Didn't know you had one," admitted Raymond. "You got some money, why didn't you get something' better?"

"It gets me from A to B," replied Jesse, already becoming annoyed with him yet feeling pangs of guilt because he was the reason he had become such a disagreeable man. Raymond sat his bag down on the ground and leaned into the window and Jesse was surprised that he didn't smell of whiskey. He had cleaned up and put on some sort of aftershave and actually looked presentable.

"You ever been to Coeur d'Alene?" asked Raymond, making eye contact with Jesse for the first time since the night he had told him his story.

"No," admitted Jesse.

"I'm not sure this old beater will make it to B."

"Come on Raymond, quit complaining. It will get us where we need to go."

"I doubt it," snickered Raymond. "Let's take my car," and he bent down and picked up his bag and walked to the trunk of the red, worn Honda in front of him that looked new compared to the Rivera.

"No," Jesse said firmly as he opened his door and stepped out, staring intently at Raymond.

"Yours will be lucky to make it halfway," snapped Raymond as he popped the hood. He felt refreshed from the shower he had taken earlier this morning and drinking his brand of coffee had made him feel alert and awake.

"No," Jesse said fiercely and Raymond turned around and looked at the convict and felt his blood begin to boil and the familiar craving of whiskey returned.

"Look, I don't want to spend any more time with you then I have to," he growled. "Let's take my car. We'll get to Coeur d'Alene, you'll be able to see your daughter, I'll get paid what's owed me and we'll all live happily ever after."

"No Raymond," Jesse replied resolutely. "We're taking mine. I'm going to find my daughter and I'm going to do it in my own car. Now shut the fuck up and get your things and let's go!"

Raymond stared at Jesse who glared back at him. The guy was an asshole and he was tired of being bossed by a convict who had shot him and killed his dreams. He thought of telling him to go to hell, do it on his own. He thought of killing him for the umpteenth time, being done with the bastard and doing society a favor at the same time.

"Jesus," he muttered and he grabbed his bag out of the trunk of his car and slammed it shut and walked to the passenger door of the piece of shit that Jesse was so insistent upon taking. "Fine, you're the boss," he said as he threw his bag into the back seat.

"Yes, I am," replied Jesse as he started the car and pulled away from the curb. "Yes, I am," he said again softly but Raymond did not hear nor cared.

*

The men drove west on I-84 and the car seemed to find its comfort zone at 67 miles per hour as the barren landscape of the rural Idaho desert stretched in all directions. Neither spoke as they drove through the quietness of the early morning with the slight chill in the air. Jesse thought of the inevitable meeting that was awaiting him and he felt knots form in his stomach. In the passenger seat, Raymond stared at the emptiness of the land passing before him and quietly contemplated the waste his life had become because of the driver beside him.

Strangely he no longer felt angry at him anymore. Telling the convict what his deed had done to him seemed to have alleviated the hatred that had built up for all these years. He had been lucky; he had been able to face the one that had victimized him and let him know of the damage that had been caused. He still wanted to hate him, but it was no longer there he realized. Now only a void where the hate had been for so long remained, waiting to be filled by something else but Raymond did not know what it would be and the emptiness seemed to sap him of the energy the hate had provided.

"Pretty country," Raymond said quietly. The desert country had its own certain beauty at this time of the morning. Dew glistened off the sagebrush and the stillness of the morning air allowed the sun to enlighten the area into a brilliant glow. Jesse stared silently around the land as he drove. "You really didn't know it was me, did you?" he heard Raymond say. Jesse stared at the gray pavement but he felt his hands tighten around the steering wheel.

"I've hated you for a long time," Raymond said, looking toward Jesse. Jesse could feel his eyes upon him and, not knowing what to say, realized there was really very little he could. "I'd sometimes get on the computer and look you up at the prison site. I wanted to kill you and when you got paroled, I actually thought about it seriously," he continued. "I followed you for about a month I guess, seeing your route, where you lived, what you did, where you worked."

Jesse looked at him, astonished that he had been hunted and not known. In prison he had learned to have eyes in the back of his head, knowing all the danger signs and signals. On the outside, though he now knew he had been a pigeon for the taking.

"I thought about it all the time. I was ready to go through with it and then I chickened out. I justified it that you weren't worth it, but in the end, the truth was that I was a chicken shit and didn't want to go to prison."

Neither spoke as they came upon the sleepy hamlet of Payette. The car rumbled down the ramp of the exit and soon they were heading north on Highway 95. Jesse tried to hide his surprise that Raymond had hunted him and wondered how he would have dealt with it had he decided to go through with it. Would he have done it up close or would it be from a distance? Would he have seen it coming or just been killed instantly, never knowing the attacker? Raymond had truly hated him because for a moment in time he had become him, the hunter.

"Then, out of the blue," Raymond finally spoke again, "you and Lady Margaret walked into my office. I was coming off a banger. At first, I was kinda stunned but then everything became clear, my moment of clarity I guess you could say." He looked out the window and his voice became low and Jesse felt himself leaning toward him to hear what he was saying, straining to catch his words over the purr of the engine of the old, beat-up Buick. "I had my gun in the desk and I thought about shooting you right then and there but then the chicken shit in me took over again."

Raymond looked toward Jesse who was afraid to look back at him. The man had stalked him, much like he had done to him on the fateful night that had ended his spiral on the outside. "I didn't want your case," he told him, "but Lady Margaret made an offer I couldn't refuse, so here we are."

"Here we are," agreed Jesse, his eyes looking at Raymond warily, wondering if he now had a gun and was ready to no longer be a chicken shit.

"Anyway, I've been doing a lot of thinking since the other night in the motel. You're a con, always will be, but, well, you're not the monster I always thought you were." Jesse stared at him in disbelief. Had he heard him, right? Raymond was letting him go, but why? He stared at the road, his hands taunt against the steering wheel, his mind confused. "I guess what I'm trying to say is I'm willing to move forward and leave the past behind, at least when I'm sober—" and he chuckled to himself and felt a freedom that he hadn't felt since the excitement of going off to college. "Can't say we'll be buddies, but you're not the enemy anymore."

Jesse looked at Raymond and the car began to slow. He pulled over on the side of the desolate road and put it into the park and opened the door, stepped out and walked behind it, and stared out into the open field behind the barb-wire fence. Raymond slowly got out of and walked next to him. Jesse stared at the mountain's way off in the distance, his mind was numb, so ashamed of himself for what he had done in the past, yet grateful toward the man who had found a way to forgive him. Raymond, the drunk bastard, was a better man than he.

"Come on Jesse, let's get back in the car and go," Raymond said quietly, gingerly reaching out and putting his hand on Jesse's back.

"I don't deserve it, Raymond," Jesse said as he continued to stare at the mountains and he felt his eyes burn as he fought against the tears that insistently continued to form. "Until the other night, I didn't truly understand how bad I fucked up. I always looked at how it affected me, never anyone else. The other night I saw that I got the good end of the deal."

"Look at me Jesse," Raymond instructed and Jesse slowly turned. "If it makes you feel better, I'm not doing this for you. I've carried a lot of anger for a long time. It wasn't the bullets that stopped me; it was the constant anger, being the victim. I finally figured that out when I talked to my son. Don't get me wrong, being the victim wasn't all bad, I got good attention for a while, but people eventually get tired of babying somebody who refuses to move on and eventually all that is left is the anger." Now it was Raymond who looked toward the mountains and he felt strength from them, an inner peace that he had forgotten existed. "It starts to control you, own you. It keeps you hostage and soon you're alone with your anger because no one wants to be around you. I'm a lot like you, I lost my wife and kid too, drove them out because they didn't want to be captive to an ogre. Well, I don't want to live that way anymore. So, it's not for you…it's me paroling myself I guess." He looked at Jesse and smiled, but it was different this time; peaceful, friendly.

"Makes sense," Jesse stammered as he wiped away a tear that had stubbornly escaped his eye. "Still, I'm really sorry Raymond, I really am—"

and then he broke down, unable to stay composed any longer. In the tears he felt the guilt and shame of his life and looked away from Raymond, not wanting him to see him this way.

"So am I," Raymond said quietly, rubbing Jesse's back. "But Jesse, we started out with nothing. Maybe we were supposed to come back together. Help us both to start living again. Lord knows we've been dead for a long time. Wasted a lot of years already."

Jesse rubbed the tears out of his eyes and smiled. "Yeah, you're right," he said quietly and he laughed embarrassingly.

"Daylight's burning," Raymond joked. "You ready?"

Jesse nodded and the men walked back to the car and pulled back onto the road. Though they did not speak, both noticed the tenseness had dissipated and in its place was a comfort of being with another who understood.

*

They drove into the little tourist town of McCall and found a gas station and filled the tank that was nothing more than fumes now. Looking down the main street, Jesse could see the beach in front of Payette Lake that was void of people. The sun shined brightly but there was a distinct chill in the air even though it was a spring day. After he had paid the attendant, they drove to the McCall Pancake House and Raymond looked at the local rag he had bought at the gas station.

"These are becoming antiques," he said to no one in particular as he finished the paper and folded it and set it on the table.

"What are?" asked Jesse.

"Newspapers; everybody goes to the web or television now for their news. The printed word is out of date as soon as it's printed. We live in a fast-food world, everybody wants it now."

Jesse looked at him quizzically for a moment as the waitress brought their orders and they hungrily downed the eggs and pancakes each had ordered. After the meal was finished Jesse pulled a five-dollar bill out of his pocket and threw it on the table and went to the lady behind the cash register and settled up. Raymond looked at his watch as he finished what remained of his deep, dark coffee in the stained cup. Still had a good five or six hours left to go before they rolled into Coeur d'Alene he realized. Barring any more stops, they should be getting in around seven or eight tonight. Jesse came back to the table and grabbed his keys and the two strolled out of the café and soon they were back on Highway 95 heading north.

"So, you really rehabilitated?" asked Raymond, whose stomach was starting to ache from all the food he had just inhaled, combined with the winding of the road they were following down the summit of White Bird Hill. He was hoping a little conversation would help him forget about it.

"Is there such a thing?" retorted Jesse. Raymond smirked and looked out his window at the cliff and the long drop without any trees to slow them down should Jesse lose control.

"So, what was it like in prison?" he asked. "You mind me asking? Not that I give a shit."

"I don't mind, I guess," Jesse said, concentrating on the road but enjoying the invitation of conversation. "I was there a long time."

"Twenty-nine years, 242 days," murmured Raymond.

"You knew? I thought only us cons kept count," laughed Jesse.

"I had a passing interest," Raymond replied in a serious tone and Jesse stopped laughing.

"I guess it's good to have someone interested in you…even if they do hate you," and this brought a snicker from Raymond, and Jesse smiled again.

"So, what was it like?" asked Raymond again as Jesse finally came to the bottom of the hill and the road evened out in front of him. "You're avoiding my question."

"Well, it's not something I really want to remember, to be honest. You are just kind of live day-to-day. Don't have any real purpose unless you're in the death house. The rest of us are just passing time," said Jesse in a matter-of-fact tone. Raymond looked at the con and saw that his face was hollow, almost ghost-like. His features screamed that he was protecting himself against something that Raymond could not fathom and he figured that Jesse wouldn't be able to explain.

"I suppose that's true," agreed Raymond but as he looked at Jesse, he saw that maybe he wanted to get it out in the open and he decided to press. "Ah, that's bullshit Jesse. Tell me what it's like in there. You were there for a long time. It's the least you could do for me, damn it! Tell me what it was like." Jesse looked at Raymond and for a moment he wanted to tell him to go to hell, to get the fuck out of the car. He wondered why the drunk wanted to know so badly, what he was digging for. Then again, the guy was probably right; it was the least he could do.

"I remember when I first went in," he said quietly, staring ahead at the road before him as Raymond looked intently at him. "I remember that really clearly. I had just gotten my time from the judge and they took me into the back room and started putting chains on me."

He stopped for a moment and remembered the feeling of the cold steel making him nothing more than a chained animal. Before the trial, it had just been handcuffs, but after the verdict, he remembered feeling like every part of his body was chained up. "They took me out to the bus behind the courthouse, that's where the jails were back then. There were six other guys and they put us on the bus. I got taken to my seat and they added another chain to me and attached it to a pipe on the floor. The old prison is only about a ten-minute drive from the courthouse and it seemed to go really fast."

He looked into the review mirror and thought of the kid that had been on that bus. It once seemed so long ago, yet now that he was out it was as though it were only yesterday. He felt as if he had gone to bed and slept for a week and when he awoke the whole world had changed without him.

"I didn't really get scared until we were about a mile or so from the pen. Then it dawned on me that I was going inside for a long time. Once we got there it was a whirl. I got dizzy and scared I was going to fall down but somehow I made it into the building." The road whirred underneath him as he drove but he did not notice. He was that stupid kid again who tried to not let anyone know of his fear, for that was the weakness to be preyed upon by the predators in this dark world he had just entered. "I got processed and they took me to a cell. I remember how small it was…and dirty. The old pen was overcrowded and most cells had two or three cons in them. The noise, it just never seemed to stop. I was really scared that first day and night. I didn't sleep at all and I wondered how the hell was I going to survive 35 years of this?"

He looked at Raymond and frowned sadly of the memory. Raymond's stomach was no longer bothering him and he was mesmerized by what he was hearing, picturing it in his mind. The con had suffered, he realized, justly so, but suffered all the same.

"Then I got moved to general pop. When you're a newbie, everyone wants to make you their bitch," he remembered. "You're the trophy they're fighting over. Well, they battled over me and the winner took me in the laundry room and broke me in so to speak." Raymond grimaced at this thought and wondered how Jesse could talk so nonchalantly about it as if it were nothing more than discussing the day's weather.

"At first you'll do anything to survive but eventually one of two things are going to happen. You become numb to it and accept it or you decide to get out of it. I couldn't take it anymore so I decided to get out. I thought of killing myself but I was afraid to die so one night I talked to an old-timer and told him my plight. He got me some batteries, the big ones you use in flashlights and a bag. He told me to put it in my pants, under my ass and balls. When lover boy came by and took me into the laundry room, I acted numb and he let his guard down and started stripping. That's when I pulled the bag out and cold-cocked him. He was stunned and dropped to a knee and I nailed him under the chin and he went all the way down. Then I beat his face over and over until it was hamburger and then I beat the shit out of his schlong and balls. After I got done, I cleaned up and found the clean clothes the old-timer had left me. I put them on and threw my soiled clothes into a bag he had told me too and went out into the yard."

"You get caught?"

"Nah, they didn't investigate those types of things really hard unless the guy dies. He got shipped to Orofino, brain damage; fuck him, I hope he's dead now." Raymond saw the hatred in Jesse's eyes as he thought of the man who had raped him and wondered what had become of him.

"Anyway, that was the end of the terror. After that you just kind of watch your back." Raymond shook his head and whistled. "You want to hear more?" Jesse asked, half hoping that he would and he was glad when Raymond nodded.

"For the next few years I just kind of tried to find things to pass the time. Everything is so routine. You get up, eat, bullshit job, eat, some sort of counseling, eat, bed…start over the next day. Over and over, never stops. You exist, don't live anymore. Still, better than being in the cage 23 out of 24 hours a day."

"Sounds like quite the life," Raymond said quietly.

"Yeah, great huh?" and Jesse gave an embarrassed smile. "So, my term was 35 years, 20 fixed. So, 20 years came and went and I went to my parole hearing. I really thought it would be a piece of cake but I walked in, sat down, and wham, they pounded me…what have you learned? What have you done to rehabilitate yourself?" Jesse smiled as he thought of himself walking in that first time all cocky and convinced that soon he would be back out on the streets. "The prosecutor was there and peppered the board about what a shitbird I had been," Jesse remembered the prosecutor thundering to the parole board like it was a damn trial all over again. "Found out I had a lot of dings on my record. I walked out and thirty seconds later was denied." Raymond saw the disdain in Jesse's face as he recounted this and remembered the same prosecutor calling him and telling him that Jesse was denied.

"I was pissed at the world and found ways to screw up the next three or four hearings over the years." Raymond leaned in, his interest all-encompassing, fascinated by the story of the man he had hated for all these years. "I remember when we moved from the old pen to the new house. It was bigger and cleaner and it's kind of started becoming home. I had my own little group I hung out with and since I was getting older no one really screwed with me anymore." He turned to Raymond and smiled. "Prison's kind of a young man's game. They still have lots of energy, you know? Us old guys, we're starting to realize that we fucked things up pretty good so we kind of start trying to figure out another way. We take things more seriously. We don't really like what we are and start trying to reinvent ourselves."

"Is that rehabilitation?" Raymond asked again.

"Nah, just age," mused Jesse. They sat in silence as the double-lane road passed under them, only an occasional car coming their way. The Buick rumbled through the flat land and Jesse saw the gas gauge was already down to half a tank. Lewiston couldn't be far, he thought to himself.

"I'd been in about 20 years," he said as Raymond turned from the window and looked at him again. "I met a guy named Ron Taylor. I didn't know his name at the time. Brain was still recovering from all those years of drugs, you know. He was a prison minister and he stopped by my cell one day. Told me he had seen me play when I was younger. We started talking that day and soon we started seeing each other weekly. He got me a bible and started trying to save me. At first, I faked it so he would keep coming by. It was nice to talk to someone different, someone from the outside." Jesse pictured Ron, his graying hair that he slicked back and rugged features. He had once been a lumberjack and then had worked at Simplot before going into the ministry.

"For some reason," Jesse continued, "he struck a chord with me about all this Jesus talk. Some of it started making sense to me."

"So, you're another saved con, huh?" but Raymond didn't sound convinced.

"Anyway," continued Jesse while ignoring the slight, "one day he comes in and tells me he won't be seeing me anymore. Tells me he had incurable brain cancer," and Raymond regretted the crack, "and that his days were numbered. I couldn't get over how calm he was. I asked him if he was afraid of dying and he said of course he was, but he was also at peace because he was a Christian. He told me there were two kinds of prison, the physical and the mental. We both were in a physical one; mine being the pen, his being cancer. He said that we can't get away from it, but we could get out of the mental one through God's love and acceptance of Jesus. Then he got up, shook my hand and told me it was time to get out of my mental prison, expand my mind, and start living." Jesse glanced at Raymond and he nodded. He understood and Jesse patted his leg lightly.

"He told me as he was walking out that I was the lucky one because if I did that eventually I would get out of my physical prison. I asked him about his and he smiled and said that since he was out of his mental prison already when he died, he would be released from his physical one. Then he left. He just turned and walked out and never looked back. I swore to change right then and there. He died two months later I heard. I started meeting with the prison chaplain a lot and he got me to start taking some responsibility and accountability for what I've done. Thought I had done a pretty good job of it too until I met you, then I realized I hadn't done shit."

Raymond smiled at him and looked out the window. "One thing the chaplain did a good job of was for the first time in my life I started realizing I wasn't the victim here. I started to get some goals, little ones like reading a book, keeping a journal, keeping my cell clean. I had another hearing coming up and I wanted out. Wanted to make Ron proud. I had this feeling he was watching me."

"So, you got out?"

"Not the first time, but they said I was making good progress so I kept doing the same thing. At nights I started thinking about my little girl. At first, I'm sorry to say I had trouble remembering her name, isn't that the dumbest thing you've ever heard?" Tinges of guilt shot through him as he thought of those nights lying in his bunk and trying like hell to remember it. "After I finally figured out it was Rebecca, I started to wonder what she looked like, what she was doing. That's when I first started toying with the idea of finding her. Anyway, the next time I went before the board they said I was sufficiently rehabilitated to go back into society. I thought I'd be ecstatic, but instead, I was scared. Almost wanted to turn them down. You know the old saying, don't you?"

"What?"

"Be careful what you wish for."

"Ain't that the truth," laughed Raymond, thinking back to the first time Jesse had walked into the office with Lady Margaret.

They continued to drive as the sun fell behind the mountains and neither man noticed that while they had been talking, they had already climbed the hill overlooking Lewiston and gone through the spruces on the way to Moscow. The car was nearly empty of gas when they entered the sleepy college town and Jesse pulled into a convenience store and filled the car while Raymond used the restroom and grabbed a couple of coffees for the road. He realized he had not had a drink today nor had felt the need to imbibe and he tried to remember the last time that had happened. Jesse walked in and paid the cashier and soon they were on the road again toward Coeur d'Alene.

Jesse turned on the radio and fumbled with the knob looking for a station. Raymond chastised him lightheartedly and took over the radio. He found a country station but Jesse frowned at him so Raymond continued to look until both agreed on a classic rock station emanating from Spokane. They sat in silence the rest of the way, only chatting to point out a sight they saw or one of the little towns they drove through. At last, they saw the waters of Lake Coeur d'Alene as they came into the city and crossed the bridge that spanned the Spokane River that flows out of the lake. They exited onto the boulevard that led toward the large resort on the lake and drove slowly through the main drag downtown until they were at the intersection of 15th and Sherman.

"What's the name of the motel?" asked Raymond.

"The State Motel. Suppose to have a chimney in the shape of Idaho. I think it's off to the right."

Raymond looked and soon he saw the chimney and pointed it to Jesse. He slowed the car down and turned into the little parking lot. It was like going back in time. The type of motel that you saw in the 1950s. Raymond looked at Jesse and started laughing as he turned the car off. Jesse shrugged and got out and walked into the little office. In five minutes, he was back out with the keys that were attached to a green four-inch state of Idaho. He grabbed his bag out of the backseat and tossed Raymond his key. He ignored Raymond's muffled laughter coming out of his car as he unlocked the door and walked into his room.

Rebecca was near, but where?

*

She knocked on the door and waited for him to open it. When he did, he smiled, and though tired from driving all day he found some energy that had disappeared earlier. She walked in and looked around the cozy room. She felt as though she had walked into a small forest. The bed and the tables were of knotty pine and the wooden chairs were stained the same color. He invited her to his bed and she backed away from him.

"Please Margaret, you've got to check this out," he pleaded and he led her to the bed and instructed her to lie down. She did so tentatively and then he put a quarter into a contraption on the bedside table and suddenly there was a whirring sound and she slightly arched her back in alarm but immediately relaxed as the massaging bed worked its magic fingers on her. He smiled and laughed at her contentment and enjoyed the sight of her relaxation until five minutes later when it finally shut down. She smiled contently, the body now completely relaxed and she slowly sat up.

"Very nice," she cooed and he nodded and felt aroused by her.

"So, where's Rebecca?" he asked knowing he could not act on his animalistic instincts.

Margaret quickly sobered and his fantasy faded as she told him about the surprise phone call from Karla. Jesse listened intently as she spoke of the conversation and his brow furrowed as she informed him of the conditions Karla had set. As he listened, he fought to control the anger growing inside of him and feared that at any moment he was going to explode. Why wouldn't she just let him know where Rebecca was?

"You need to hear what she has to say," she told Jesse as he stood and paced the small room.

"Why can't I talk to her now?" he demanded.

"It's not time, Jesse. It's three hours difference between here and Boston, to begin with, but more importantly, you need a good night's rest because you have some very big decisions you are going to have to make."

"What decisions?" he demanded to know.

"Tomorrow," she replied as she walked to the door.

"Come on, Margaret," he pleaded.

"I'm tired Jesse, I'm going to my room now," she said as she opened the door.

"Margaret—"

"Good night Jesse," she replied as she walked out.

He was alone. Rebecca was so close but he had no idea where and it nearly made him crazy. Good night sleep? What was that he wondered to himself? He was tired though, to the bone in fact and he succumbed to the temptation of the bed. Ten minutes later he was sound asleep.

Chapter 15

She heard the pounding on the door and groaned and pulled the pillow over her head. The sharp knocks continued against the wooden door and her eyes slowly open, exasperated with each rap, yet still understanding of the man who on the other side who was growing ever more frustrated.

"Margaret," he called impatiently and he banged against the door again. She groggily pushed the covers back and found her robe lying on the circular table and put it on as she stubbed her toe against the leg of the chair in front of it. She silently cursed him as the sharp pain climbed her leg and the knocking continued.

"I'm coming," she shouted irritably as she hopped her way to the incessant pounding and she pulled the chain back from the door and opened it. Jesse saw her contorted face and smiled. "What time is it?" she asked in a hoarse whisper, surprised by the light since her blinds had been closed and her room remained dark.

"Six o'clock, I guess," he answered. "So, tell me what Karla said."

"Jesse, slow down…go back to your room," she murmured as she attempted to rub the sleep out of her eyes while leaning against the doorway.

"Come on Margaret, you're killing me, what'd Karla say? Where's Rebecca—"

"Jesse, I'm going to close the door," she replied testily and he could see she was clearly perturbed with him for waking her so early. "I'm going to take a shower and I need some coffee!" her voice rising and she stood straight and glared at him and he smirked at her but saw that this was not negotiable.

"All right, all right," he surrendered to the woman in the doorway. She was truly beautiful he realized and he wanted to grab her, pull her close to him, but he knew he wasn't good enough for her and that they would never be together and it caused him some sorrow because it was just one more thing that was out of his grasp. "I'll meet you across the street," he said with a smile, covering the ache he was feeling. "Hurry! I'll be at the coffee shop."

She closed the door and breathed a sigh of relief as he stood outside for a moment longer fantasizing of her. He realized that he probably looked suspicious and he laughed at himself and slowly walked down the small driveway in front of the office with the brick chimney shaped like the state of Idaho. The street was empty and he crossed the four lanes and walked into the small restaurant.

The hostess smiled at him. "One?" she asked.

"For now," he replied, "but another will be joining me at least, maybe two." She led him to a booth by the window and handed him a menu as he scooted into the shiny green booth. "Could I get a coffee please?" he asked and she nodded. "Cream too," he called after her as she walked toward the coffee pot that was simmering behind the long bar at the front of the cafe. He looked at the menu but didn't feel especially hungry but the food smelled good and he silently debated whether or not to order. She brought the steaming coffee to him and set a little dish down that had six liquid creamers sitting in it.

"Would you like something?" she asked. She was a tad overweight but still had a decent figure. She was probably in her late thirties, he thought to himself, but her face showed that the years had probably not been easy. Her auburn hair was in a bun and had blonde streaks in it and he wondered what it looked like when it was down. She was pleasant enough, he observed, as he ordered some eggs and hash-browns which pleased her because now she knew she would get a tip. As she walked toward the kitchen, he stole another look at her and realized that lately he was doing a lot of staring at women and for a moment he became disgusted with himself. Then he realized how long it had been since he had been with one and against his will, he began to fantasize again.

The bell that hung over the door clanged as another customer walked in and the waitress called him by name and Jesse knew that he was a regular because he made a joke that wasn't funny that caused her to laugh as if it was the most hilarious thing she had ever heard. He realized that being a waitress was probably a most thankless job and he forced himself to stop fantasizing about her out of respect.

He wondered what was taking Margaret for so long. Had she snuggled back under the covers? He thought of going over and knocking on the damn door again. It would serve her right for not giving him the details last night. Instead, he looked out the window and stared at the chimney and wondered how difficult it had been to make it look like the state. He thought of Rebecca again. Rebecca, she had become a compulsion to him. In the past months, he had felt like he had finally gotten to know her a bit but still knew very little. Karla had done a bang-up job shielding her, protecting her against men like him, actually, protecting her against him. But still, tiny shards of her life had been exposed to him. She had worn braces when she was young, played some volleyball in middle school, been a good student. But then she had disappeared and he wondered what she had become.

He looked at his watch as the waitress brought the food to him and he glanced toward the motel to see if Margaret was coming yet. Still, no sign of her and he tried to remain patient. As he nibbled on his food, he thought of the daughter he had lost. He remembered being in the hospital when she was born and walking in the birthing room, the child lying on the mother and he cursed himself for having no feelings for her at that time. He had been so selfish, only seeing the child as another barrier between him and his dreams. He thought of the few times he hadn't been high or drunk and remembered she had a delightful little laugh that he had not to allow her to share with him. Now it rang in his ears as he remembered it coming through the hallway of the apartment they lived in while she played innocently in her room. It made him sad and he hated that he had not realized as a young man the gift of being a father.

He wondered how close he was to her right now. Maybe a block, maybe miles; he only knew that the search was nearing its end, and relief was mixed with the trepidation of the reunion that he knew she would probably end as soon as she realized who he was. For God's sake, he thought to himself, why would she want to see him again? Surely all she could remember of him was some monster that continually screamed and hurt her. Maybe he shouldn't find her, maybe Raymond was right and it was better not to see her, screw up her life any more than what he already had. The bell over the door rang again and jolted him out of his thoughts and he saw Margaret walking over to him. She ordered a cup of coffee, black, and sat down across from him.

"Damn woman," he groused as he looked at the clock on the wall. "I was afraid you went back to bed."

"I thought about it," she smiled as she gulped the first cup of coffee that had been placed on the table earlier and was now lukewarm. "I need a warm-up," and she signaled to the waitress who smiled and brought the glass coffee pot over and refilled her cup. "I'll have a bowl of oatmeal," she said to the waitress. "Put it on his tab."

After she walked away to place the order, Jesse leaned forward toward Margaret. "So, you talked to Karla," he said quietly like it was some big secret.

"I talked to her, yes."

"Well," he said impatiently, wondering why she wasn't filling him in.

"Jesse, Karla is really torn up about this," she said and his shoulders slumped momentarily. "She wants to believe that you've changed, but she has a lot or reservations also."

Jesse sat back against the booth and looked out the window. This was not starting out well. But she was nearby; he could feel it and he knew he had to somehow hold it together. "I know," he finally acknowledged, "but she must have told you something or we wouldn't be here." He leaned forward again, buoyed by a hope that he didn't know where it was coming from. "We're here, that's something, isn't it?"

"Yes, she did tell me things."

"Well, what? Where is Rebecca? Come on Margaret, quit playing games," he said harshly.

"I'm not Jesse, I know you're excited, but…well, I understand Karla's nervousness."

"So, what; you had me come to Coeur d'Alene for this? Come on Margaret. I've stuck to this. I've searched all over the country. I've shown I'm serious." He stared at her for a minute and he felt his chin begin to quiver. She knew something, but she wasn't telling him. Why?

"I need this," he pleaded in a barely audible tone. "Please…" Margaret looked at him, her empathy growing, but Karla had made some requests and she was going to honor them.

"Karla hasn't spoken to Rebecca for approximately five years," she finally said. "They're estranged."

"What?" In shock, he fell back against the booth again and stared at her with his mouth open. He felt as though he had been hit by a thunderbolt. How could they be estranged? What could have possibly happened that would have made Karla deliberately remove herself from Rebecca's life?

"That's why she's so afraid," continued Margaret. "She's afraid if you find her, she'll lose her forever. Do you understand now?"

"Not really," he admitted as he looked at her in confusion. He couldn't understand the fears of the woman who so long ago he had nearly destroyed. He couldn't understand the guilt she now felt for turning her back on Rebecca as her parents had done to her. He only knew that another brick wall had appeared and he didn't know if he had the strength anymore to break through this last one.

"It's hard to explain," Margaret said quietly to him. "I guess the best way for you to understand is that it's something only a woman can feel because the child came from her." He looked at her, his eyes pleading, wanting to figure it out but she knew that he never would be able to. "Maybe I should start at the beginning."

"Margaret, tell me about my daughter," he said, realizing that the feelings of the mother were beyond him and it was best not to condemn her. She had raised her, protected her from him and the world. No, Margaret was right, it was not something that he would ever be able to grasp, but it didn't change the fact that he needed to find her, try to make things right. Most of all, he desperately wanted to see her again, if only for a moment. "Tell me about her," he whispered. "We'll figure it out after that."

She nodded reluctantly. "Let me eat my breakfast and then we'll go back to my room. My notes are over there,"

He stared at the chimney again, but he didn't see it. Instead, he thought of Karla, still protecting her child from him, even from afar.

*

Margaret laid out the papers on her bed carefully putting them in chronological order. In the corner of the room, Jesse watched her and tried to control his impatience with her and wondered why she was keeping him on edge like this. She could feel his eyes boring through her and realized that she felt vulnerable. She was alone in a motel room with a man who had done many bad things a generation before and she wondered if she were truly safe with him.

Once the papers were in order, she looked at him and the fear she had felt evaporated. Looking back at her were the eyes of a child, eager to learn yet afraid of what he was about to find out. He no longer seemed like the aged convict, but a young, expectant father realizing he may be in over his head. She gave him a sympathetic smile and he exhaled and tried to relax as he settled into the chair by the window.

"What do you know about your daughter?" she asked and he admitted he knew little. He told her of what he had found out through his and Raymond's snooping and how the trail had seemed to evaporate after New York.

"She graduated from a high school in Syracuse at the Faith Heritage School," she began and he leaned forward, unaware that they had been there. "Karla spent a year in Syracuse as a visiting professor from CCNY, apparently some sort of program they offer in New York as part of a Public/Private School Education grant. When Karla returned after the completion of the year, Rebecca remained behind with a family so that she could get her diploma there. Karla said those two years were her best as a student. Because Faith Heritage is a private school she just disappeared because they are not required to post enrollment information." He nodded; it made sense now why they hadn't been able to find anything. Once the trail had ended there was no way to know which direction to go from there.

After Rebecca had graduated, she moved back to New York City and enrolled at Hunter College where she had earned an academic scholarship. She was a typical student, wide-eyed and excited to be in the city and studying at such a prestigious college. She had decent grades, all A's and B's in a science-heavy load and was a pledge to one of the sororities on campus. She spent the Christmas seasons with her mother and they had a wonderful time, going to Rockefeller Center to skate, riding the train from Grand Central Station into New England, and holidaying on the slopes of Vermont. Karla spoiled her, feeling the empty nest syndrome heavily and was always quietly heartbroken when school resumed and Rebecca went back.

The second semester of her senior year seemed to be going well until Spring Break when she came back home and shocked Karla, telling her she was pregnant. Rebecca had found out in late January and had withdrawn from school almost immediately but because she was afraid to tell her mother. She stayed with a friend who lived in a flat near the campus. When school let out for the break she had nowhere to go so with her options limited she went to her mother's and broke the news to her.

"This was the start of the unraveling of their relationship," Margaret told Jesse quietly. "Karla felt betrayed because she hadn't initially told her, especially since she had been through this experience herself, and of course because she had dropped out of school so near to graduating."

During this time Rebecca and the father had continued to see each other. His name was Ernesto Fambragino. They had met in the nightclubs around the college. Ernesto was actually a lowly soldier in one of the so-called crime families of the New York mafia, and his territory that he worked in was in the area of the college. Rebecca had met him during her junior year in one of the nightclubs, The Copper Club, which was actually owned by one of the Family's members and was used to launder money. They had been dating since then.

By the time Karla found out about the pregnancy they were engaged to be married. She was adamantly against it.

"She sounds a lot like her mother," Jesse noted, "headstrong, bent on doing the right thing."

"There's something about having a baby that changes a woman, Jesse," Margaret observed though she had not experienced it personally.

"What happened to the father?" asked Jesse. Margaret resumed the story, telling him how one of Rebecca's friends told Karla about Ernesto's involvement in the mafia, and of course, she was horrified. The two fought ferociously, Karla desperately trying to talk Rebecca out of the marriage, but the daughter was in love with the dashing young man who showered gifts on her and would hear nothing of it.

"Soon they were married," Margaret said softly, imagining Karla's pain as she told Jesse. "Much like the mother did years before. That was when the estrangement began."

In November, Rebecca had a daughter which the new couple christened Chelsea Michelle. By this time Karla had thrown her hands up and the two of them were barely communicating. "In fact," Margaret noted, "Karla found out about the birth of her granddaughter from one of Rebecca's friends who had found out from another who still kept in touch with her." Jesse wondered how Karla must have felt to find out that her child had given birth and she had not been a part of it. It must have been devastating, knowing her child chose the criminal over her.

The young couple seemed happy and even Karla admitted that Ernesto had actually been a good father and husband. Three years after Chelsea had been born Ernesto had been sent as part of an outfit to deal with a Mexican group that was trying to muscle into their territory. Ernesto had cased the joint that the Mexican Gang sold their cocaine from and the Capo had decided that a message needed to be sent to the newcomers. Ernesto and two other members of the outfit had been selected to do the job and the plan had gone off without a hitch. But unbeknownst to the Capo, Ernesto did not feel he had been getting what he deserved so he kept one bag of the kilo they had stolen from the Mexican Gang and proceeded to make a small fortune. He began to freelance more and eventually, word got out of his enterprise. The Mexican Gang was not happy that he was selling on their turf, even less so that it was their cocaine he was selling.

One evening Ernesto was set to meet with some 'investors' from out of town to expand his new business. He went to the meeting with two kilos and waited at the abandoned shop where the meeting was to take place. He and his lookout sat on their car inside the shop when the lookout spotted headlights slowly approaching. Ernesto signaled to them and the car drove into the shop. They waited for them to get out of their car and when they didn't, he walked slowly toward the car until all four doors burst open. He backed away slowly but it was too late. The four 'investors' jumped out of the car and immediately shot and killed the lookout. Ernesto raised his hands in surrender and out of the back seat came the leader of the gang. Ernesto was savagely beaten before being mercifully shot; a clear message sent to the Family Ernesto had soldiered for.

Ernesto's ties to the Mafia screamed in the headlines of the tabloids, Rebecca and Chelsea were on their own. The Family would have nothing to do with them. Ernesto had betrayed them by going out on his own and not sharing the profits. Now in death, he was bringing unwanted publicity to them. Rebecca had nowhere to turn for help.

"Karla said that Rebecca called her asking for help," Margaret explained. "Karla wanted to but didn't have the means at the time." The problem was that Karla had lost some money from some bad business advice from her former husband and was trying to get back on her feet herself. She had no resources to help Rebecca and Chelsea but she was too proud to tell them.

"She told me how angry she was because Rebecca seemed to have her taste in men and was making the same mistakes she had." Jesse could only glumly nod in agreement. "She immediately regretted it but something kept stopping her from picking up the phone and talking to her daughter and the estrangement became permanent."

"She should have known better," Jesse complained bitterly.

"Stop it, Jesse," Margaret chastised him. "Karla has done an admirable job, by herself mind you. I'm sure it was extremely difficult for her."

"I know," he said sadly, "I'm sorry."

With Ernesto's death, the police and Feds had questioned Rebecca. The more she was questioned the more vulnerable she felt. One night she had received a call, the unknown voice warning her that she was being watched. Terrified she called the police but they ignored her pleas because she hadn't any information to trade with them for her protection. The next day a dead fish wrapped in a newspaper was in the backseat of her car. Terrified, she called the FBI and begged for help. Again, her pleas fell on deaf ears. She knew she had to get out so she packed what few belongings she could into a suitcase and then went to the basement behind the old furnace where Ernesto had kept his drug money and pulled out ten thousand dollars and called a cab. Early the next morning she and Chelsea were on a train heading to Chicago. In Chicago, they switched to a Greyhound and four days later she was in Spokane.

She settled in Coeur d'Alene and she began work on an RN degree from the local community college. It only took her a year and a half to obtain it. She utilized the daycare the school offered for Chelsea and they lived quietly in a subsidized apartment within walking distance of the campus. After receiving her degree, she received an offer from the Shoshone Medical Center down the road in Kellogg and began her career as a nurse.

"She was named Employee of the Month three times during the two years she was there," Margaret bragged to Jesse and he smiled with pride. He saw that she took as much pleasure in his daughter's success as he did and he was grateful.

"Eventually an opening at the larger Kootenai Medical Center led her and Chelsea back to Coeur d'Alene." Margaret smiled. "Your granddaughter is seven years old now and is finishing up the first grade." Jesse felt his chest tighten and he felt out of breath. He was right, she was here. He was close and he felt fear and trepidation yet joy all at the same time.

"Where is she Margaret?" he asked. "What's the address?"

"There's still more," she replied. "Karla, of course, kept track of her. She told me losing her baby has been devastating but she also has tremendous pride in her because Rebecca made it without her, something she doesn't feel she was able to accomplish when she was younger. Let's take a little break, get some lunch." He hadn't realized that it was nearing noon but he didn't care; he wanted to see his little girl.

"Margaret, what's her address?"

"After lunch," she replied calmly. "She's not going anywhere Jesse, and there is still more you need to know." He wanted to argue with her but he knew it would do no good. He let out a large sigh and gave a half-smile. She was running the show he knew, and deep inside he found it sexy. He silently cursed himself. His thoughts needed to be on his daughter, not Margaret's pants.

"All right," he said in resignation as he followed her out the door of the motel room. She walked ahead of him, unaware that he was staring at her ass and secretly wanting her.

"The same place?" she asked and he reddened as he realized that he had caught him gawking.

"That's fine," he stammered and she turned forward, smiling to herself but knowing it could go no further. She thought back to the boy in high school and how she had always wanted to be noticed by him. After all these years, she finally had him wanting her, but it was now too late.

*

"She's forgiven you," she said as he stared at the uneaten salad in front of him.

"Karla?" he asked, surprised.

"Yes," Margaret said as he turned and looked out across the street toward the chimney shaped like Idaho for the umpteenth time. "She wanted you to know that." He didn't know how to feel. It had been so long ago and he had been so awful to her. He thought of the woman he had seen back in Massachusetts, so distrusting, so angry to see him walk back into her life and then being horrified what he wanted from her.

"She's a good woman," he said quietly, staring out into the sun-drenched street. "Better than me..." and his voice trailed off for a moment. "She was once mine and I didn't know what I had," he finally continued, his eyes staring into another place during a more innocent time. "God, to be young again and to do it right, take the things I've learned and do it right. I do love her," and he looked at Margaret and she could see the pain and guilt in his eyes, "always will I guess…"

They sat in silence amid the chaos of the lunch crowd at the busy little café off the main street. He remembered her as she once was, young, beautiful and she had loved him, him! How could he have gone so far to the dark side with this angel at his side, he wondered? Margaret stared in endearment at him, knowing that he was experiencing so many emotions felt he had forgotten he had.

He looked at her and tried to speak but remained silent. She reached across and lightly put her hand on his and he smiled slightly. "Don't you understand, Margaret?" he finally asked. "I think I just realized what this is for me. This is my second chance, I don't know if I deserve one, but this is it. I know I've lost Karla for good, but maybe, if I'm incredibly lucky because lord knows, I don't deserve it, but maybe I will be fortunate enough to establish something with Rebecca and take these things I've learned and do it right with her…and my granddaughter…" Suddenly his eyes lit up and he laughed and Margaret felt the joy of the sound he made. "Shit, I'm a grandfather," he said in wonderment. "Please let me know where she's at."

She smiled and felt his joy but knew it wasn't time yet. There was still more he needed to know and she steeled herself for the frustration he would feel.

"Jesse," she said delicately, "even though Karla has forgiven you and sees the change, she still has misgivings…" His smile immediately disappeared into a look of nervousness, fearing for the worst. He had felt it many times and he knew that the fear was nearly always justified.

"Are you going to give me the address or what?"

"You still need to listen right now. This isn't only about you," she scolded him and she stood, dropped a twenty on the table to cover the lunch, and walked out into the day. His breathing was harder and he felt the old anger again. Was she playing a game with him? He took a deep breath and stood and walked out of the café. She was already across the street and walking calmly to her room and he waited for a car to pass and then raced across the four lanes, his anger causing him to tremble.

She stood at the door as he ran toward her and opened it as he breathlessly came to her. She motioned for him to go inside and he did as instructed but he would not sit. She calmly came in behind him and sat down on the piney chair and silently waited for him to calm down. At last, he quit pacing and collapsed against the wall and glared at her.

"Karla forgives you, but she doesn't want you to see Rebecca, nor does she want you and her to see each other anymore," Margaret said calmly. He continued to glare at her and he rubbed his hands and felt every muscle in his body tensing. "She's afraid," continued Margaret, "this is uncharted territory for her, Rebecca and you. You need to consider this. You need to look at the whole portrait, not just the snapshot with you in it!"

"So I've come all this way and now it's over," he whined bitterly. "That's bullshit, Margaret!"

"Please lower your voice, Jesse, I'm right here, you don't need to yell."

"If you're not going to tell me where she's at because Karla doesn't want you too, what was this all about then? It's bullshit. I've done everything I was supposed to do. This is bullshit what you're doing!"

Margaret's face remained passive and she sat quietly while he shook in anger, acting like a willful child who was not allowed to have his way. She wanted to tell him, but she had to be sure he knew everything; then he could decide what the next step was.

"Maybe it wasn't about finding your daughter," she said softly and he looked away. "Maybe it was about finding yourself, the real you, warts and all." He looked at her again but this time the glare softened. "Maybe you should listen to Karla, maybe you should drop the search because you have found what you were searching for." His eyes looked to the floor and he tried to think but he couldn't. His mind was spinning, so close, yet he might as well be on the moon. "Maybe that's Rebecca's gift to you," she said softly.

"Maybe I want more," he growled defiantly, lifting his eyes from the floor and finding a strength that hadn't been their moments before. He was going to fight for her. It wasn't about him; it was about her. He was fighting for something other than himself he realized and he felt a new passion growing inside of him. "I'll take the answer…but I gotta know the answer," he said as he slowly stood up. "Karla shouldn't hold that power. Hell, she's estranged. She's basically me with tits."

"Stop it, Jesse, she raised that girl, you didn't. She sacrificed. You didn't. She was there, you weren't. For God's sake, did you really expect her to say 'Oh Jesse, here she is'?"

"Just give me the damn address!" he yelled.

"Absolutely not!" she replied angrily. "Not when you're like this!" She moved toward him and for a moment he felt a strange fear of her. She wasn't afraid of him, didn't care what he had done in the past. She was protecting someone far away that she barely knew. "There is more to it than just letting you have your way. Can't you see that Karla has opened up an opportunity for you to have some dialogue about this? Wouldn't it be better if you two were on the same page instead of having Rebecca become a wall between the two of you?"

She was now right in front of him and her anger seethed through her pores. He really didn't care about others, just himself. He was nothing more than a typical convict and she had bought into the 'I've changed' bullshit and now she was as furious with herself as she was with him.

"Don't you realize that if you handle this correctly your daughter may finally have both a mother and father and her child, grandparents? I won't give you the address, not until you calm down, start to rationalize…"

Jesse glared at her. She was a typical woman who had let him spend his money on a search that was never meant to get this far. Well, he had shown her. Fuck her, he thought and he stormed past her and slammed the door behind him as he left the room. He stood outside and in the warmth of the day realized that he was shaking.

Inside she wondered what he would do, but then she no longer cared. He was…and then she began to calm down. He had needed this, needed to hear the things that were said. He knew he had hurt many, but over the years he had found a way to minimize and place the blame on others.

Not today though, no, he had faced it and she realized that now he needed time to himself to process it, deal with the multiple feelings he had to go through. She sat down on the bed and quietly began picking up the piles of paper that were strewn over it and she knew that now it was time to wait it out and see what would come of it.

Chapter 16

Jesse paced around his room before collapsing on the bed. They had conspired against him. Given him hope that at last, he would be finding Rebecca only to have the two of them orchestrate this cruel façade and leave him grasping for something that was just past his fingertips. Why? What was their game, he wondered to himself angrily? If Karla had her way, and she controlled all the cards, there was no way she was ever going to let him anywhere near her. For all he knew maybe Rebecca wasn't even in Coeur d'Alene. Hell, she was probably someplace back east. She might even be in on it, he thought to himself bitterly.

These fucking women made him so damn angry. It had been a wild goose chase. His pacing quickened and with each step, his heart beat harder and he wanted to break something, anything…no, he wanted to hurt someone. Make them feel what he was feeling. His teeth gritted and his muscles were taunted, coiled; ready to explode. Suddenly, out of the corner of his eye, he caught his reflection in the mirror above the dresser in the knotty pined room. His breathing was deep and his brow was soaked with sweat. He stared at the reflection, at the man who stared back at him, and he caught a glimpse of a younger man, angry, wanting to lash out at all that had caused him pain. He stared, dumbfounded at the stupidity of the young man that glared back angrily at him and he wondered what to do next. The image was motioning to him, ordering him to come with him but he couldn't move. He wasn't that young man anymore, he suddenly realized. That boy was gone now, he had tried to come back one last time but the older man had found a way to subdue him. He realized it wasn't Rebecca that had stopped the young man from succeeding, it was him…Jessie Rayburn. He knew that if he was truly serious about finding and building a relationship with her, he had to let go of the monster from the past. The young man had no relationship with the daughter, didn't want one. He loathed her; she was responsible for everything bad that had happened to him. The old man knew better, she was a gift, one he didn't deserve but was still willing to fight for and as he thought of this, the younger man finally disappeared from the mirror and in his place stood Jesse, older and afraid, but it was him again.

Suddenly his chest heaved and his eyes burned. The sobs came loudly, sounds of loss emanating from him. He couldn't fight them anymore and he wailed and as he did the tension in his body dissipated and in its place was pure, unadulterated pain. Pain from within that for years he had kept under lock and key was now free and his body writhed in the guilt he felt for all the horrible things he had done to his family, Karla, Raymond, and especially to Rebecca.

The tears came and wouldn't stop. He clutched a pillow in his hand and held it with all his might against his upper body as he collapsed to the floor and fell into the fetal position. His body rocked and the force of the sobs brought an ache to his muscles yet at the same time it was liberating, iron doors long ago locked now bursting open and he felt as though he could see into his own soul and though he despaired of the ugliness that he found he felt a cleansing sense overcome him and he wished for this feeling to never end. He was new again, the monster no longer had anywhere to hide and he felt it dying now that it was in the light, the clutches that had held him for so long now falling away, disappearing into a hell he had once been so sure he was destined to spend eternity in.

Slowly he felt himself regaining control of his emotions. The anger now was gone and only the hurt remained but it was manageable and it felt good because it was real and it had been earned. An overwhelming calmness set in that everything was as it should be and that hope still remained. He dried his eyes and laughed to himself, amazed at the transformation he had just gone through and though he was alone he no longer felt empty as he had so many times before. He stood up and walked to the basin and turned on the taps, splashing the water over and over against his face. The coolness felt good against the skin and it brought refreshment, new energy. He looked in the mirror and for the first time in decades, he didn't hate the reflection and instead saw a glimpse of joy. Karla had nothing to worry about any longer but he had to convince her of that. He could do this, he coaxed himself; he had to.

He dried his face and his hands and stood up straight and proud, feeling a new strength and walked over to the phone. He wondered if she would pick up and prepared himself for disappointment if she didn't. He dialed her number and waited, barely breathing. He heard the first ring. He wasn't sure if he really wanted her to answer or not as the second ring rang in his ear. For a moment he thought of hanging up but somehow kept his nerve as the third ring finished.

"Karla Thompson," he heard her say and his heart leaped.

"Hi Karla, this is Jesse. Can we talk?" he asked; his mouth dry and his voice slightly weak. There was no answer and he waited for the inevitable click of the phone being hung up, but it didn't. There was only silence. "I know this is hard for you, it's also hard for me too," he said softly and he prayed she would stay on the line.

"Is it?" she asked rhetorically but without malice in her voice. He breathed softly, relieved that she wasn't hanging up.

"Yeah, I guess I'm finally at an age where I see how my screw-ups hurt everyone else. I'm really sorry Karla, I know I hurt you badly, for the first time I really do," he said apologetically and he was still afraid that at any moment the line would go dead.

"You're just saying that Jesse. I've heard it many times before," she said pointedly and he realized how deeply he had affected her so many years before.

"I really am Karla, and I don't blame you for not believing me. I was so bad to you, you and Rebecca, my parents—"

"So, I suppose you're a whole new man now," she said in a quiet voice, not wanting to let her defenses down. She hated talking to him because it brought everything in the past back and though the anger was now gone, the hurt remained unhealed.

"No, just older," replied Jesse, fighting the urge to strike back. "I see what I was now. I'll be honest with you, I didn't see it until a few moments ago, but I see it now…"

As he spoke, she closed her eyes and saw someone else, someone young and vibrant and she remembered how much she had loved him before the storm. He was such fun, so full of himself yet still endearing and a slight smile came to her face. She thought of the dates they had gone on, the laughter they had shared. She remembered his cockiness yet the innocence he possessed. Mostly she remembered the boy with such hopes and desires that had she sat next to in the car with her head on his shoulder as they drove through the lights of the city, just the two of them against the world, hoping that someday their dreams would become true as teenagers do.

"Karla, you still there?"

"I am," she said softly. "I suppose you want me to give you my blessing to see Rebecca, well I can't Jesse. I want to believe you I guess but I don't."

"I understand," he said sadly but he wasn't ready to give up and he realized that he was truly different. In the past, he would have fought with her, call her awful names, and then slammed the phone and blame her and everyone else for his perceived injustices. "When I called, I guess I did, but now I think I just want to talk. I—"

"What did you say?" she asked surprised.

"It doesn't matter," he replied quietly.

"Tell me," she said. "Convince me that you've changed."

"Well, I guess I'm at a point where I see that everything I once had is gone and I'm responsible for that…no one else did it to me. I drove you away, pissed away my dreams, killed my parents, I did it, I know that now." He was silent for a moment and he felt his eyes beginning to burn as the enormity of actually verbalizing it felt like a knife piercing his heart. "Anyway," he said trying to compose himself, "you reach a point where you finally realize how destructive you were, that you have nothing left, and it's scary." He looked up at the ceiling as a tear began to fall from his eye and he wiped it away as another began to form. On the other end of the line, Karla felt the hardened resolve begin to melt away. "You don't know what to do and all of a sudden whacking yourself off starts to make a lot of sense. But I got lucky. I found myself something, something important." He wiped another tear away. "During the course of searching for that, Rebecca, I guess I've found something else…me."

"And who are you?" she asked softly.

"I'm somebody that finally woke up and recognized how bad I was before, how selfish. When Margaret told me about your conversation, I was so angry. I had all this pity for myself, wondering why you were being the way you were. I came back here to my motel room angry at the world again, blaming everyone else—" and his voice choked in shame as he thought about it. "Then I looked in the mirror and finally, after all these years, realized why you don't want me anywhere near our daughter, I haven't introduced you to me yet." He heard her exhale in non-belief but he didn't care, it was no longer in his control whether she believed it or not, only that he tell her. "You only know the younger version of me, the one that hurt you, ran out on Rebecca. You only know the one that hurt everyone who loved me. I realized that I could be him again, but I don't want that. I'm tired of being alone, of seeing hurt or fear in everyone's eyes when I come around."

He rubbed his eyes while she reminisced of a more innocent time. She no longer hated him, she realized, but she knew that she would never again trust him and he was asking for permission to have access to try to create a relationship with her most precious gift and she was terrified. She would never be able to forgive herself if he hurt Rebecca and why should she really believe him. But he did sound different, deeper…

"I want to be someone people are glad to see. I want to be someone that I'm glad to see when I look in the mirror. I don't want to be a zombie anymore…subsisting day-to-day. I want to live my life, be a part of the game again so to speak. I understand who you hate Karla…I hate him too, but I'm not that person anymore."

She wanted to believe him; he was being so sincere and personal. She thought back to when he was the monster and she realized that even at his worst he hadn't ever lied to her. He had basked in hurting her but he had never tried to convince her that he was anything but what he was. Maybe she could believe him, maybe he had actually changed. She was conflicted and she knew that she still loved the young man he had once been before it had all gone awry.

"Karla," he said, interrupting her thoughts. "Let's talk face to face. I know you're against me seeing Rebecca, but I need this—"

"Why Jesse? Why is seeing Rebecca so important to you? You ran out on the both of us. You never showed any inkling of caring, much less loving her. Why now? Why?" she demanded.

"Why?" he said slowly, "because I do. I need to try to re-establish, oh hell, who am I kidding. I need to establish some sort of relationship with her if I can. I know there's a damn good chance she'll want nothing to do with me. I can't control that and I accept it. But I can at least let her know I'm here and I'm ready and willing to do whatever it takes."

She was silent and he wondered what she was thinking. He tried to picture her in his mind. He thought of her hardened demeanor and realized he hadn't seen her smile in decades and he was the reason for the sadness that emanated from her eyes. Why should she believe him, what had he ever done to give her a reason? It was hopeless.

No, it wasn't! She was still on the line; she was still listening. She was still giving him a chance. "I'm ready and willing to do whatever it takes," he said, "within the law of course," and they both laughed and he could feel the tension lighten just a bit. "Seriously though, it means nothing if you don't at least understand. Maybe I can't make you understand but I can look you in the eye if you're here and hopefully you will be able to see I'm sincere and I won't harm our daughter."

She didn't reply, but she didn't hang up either and it gave him the courage to continue. "Karla, I need to do this. I need to finish what I've started. I haven't done that in a long, long time. Please come out."

She listened to him and realized that if truth be told she didn't want to share Rebecca with him. He had given that up long ago and now he was asking them to come back into his life. She wasn't ready, Rebecca never would be.

"I don't think so, Jesse," she said softly and her heart hurt and she wondered why what had he done to earn that right?

"Please Karla, if for no other reason than to consider seeing her yourself. I don't want you to go through what I am and you will if you continue to not see her." He winced knowing that he was going somewhere that he shouldn't be but she had to hear it and he was the person to let her know what exile would be like.

"Don't tell me that," she snapped. "You have no idea what you're talking about or what has happened."

"I know what it's like to be out of one's life. I know that better than anyone." He wondered if he had blown it but he knew it was something she had to hear. Maybe she would end the exile and realize that she was letting Rebecca slip away from her. He had done right in telling her, even if it was the final nail in the coffin guaranteeing he would never see Rebecca.

"Look," he said, finally ending the awkward silence between the two, "I promise you I won't see Rebecca until you and I talk face to face if you'll come out."

"You swear?" she asked and for a moment he felt as though they were high school kids again.

"I do, please come out."

She was silent again and she could hear his breathing and could feel his anticipation, hope, that she would change her mind. But there was so much to do, the school was coming to an end, tests needed to be given, grades figured out. On the other hand, maybe if she were there, she could talk some sense into him, stop him from changing everything.

"All right," she heard herself saying, "but don't expect my mind to change. I'm not ready to let you see her, but I'll hear you out."

"Thank you, Karla."

"I'll call you with my ticket information," she said.

The line went dead, but Jesse felt alive. Alive with hope and he hung up the phone, stood up, and raised his hands in elation. Karla was giving him a chance, a chance he probably did not deserve, but one that he promised himself he would make the most of.

*

The closest airport for commercial jets from Coeur d'Alene is in Washington just to the west of Spokane. It's only a forty-mile drive on mostly interstate and Jesse rehearsed in his mind what he was going to tell Karla to convince her to give him her blessing. With each passing mile, he became more nervous and he could feel the perspiration forming above his lip even though the evening weather felt cool. It had been a day since she had called with the ticket information but had seemed like a lifetime. As he came closer to the airport time moved at a dizzying speed, like he was on a roller coaster.

He turned off the exit that headed toward the airport. It wasn't large, but it was probably a little bigger than Boise's. He turned toward the parking garage and took his ticket so the gate would raise and drove his car to the second level. The garage had a number of spots open and appeared desolate. He pulled in and stepped out into the night and instinctively pulled his collar up. It was cold inside the large structure and he felt a slight wind coming through the openings. He hurriedly crossed the overpass walk and rode the escalator down into the heart of the airport where the airlines provided their tickets and took the luggage. He walked up the stairs toward the tarmac and found a chair to sit and wait for her to debark.

He nervously checked his watch; she should be arriving any time now and his stomach made a gurgling sound that he hoped that no one noticed. He looked toward the empty opening where she would be coming through. He tried to relax but couldn't. What if she said no, what would he do? Raymond would be able to find Rebecca quickly. Hell, he probably already knew where she was. Could he go against Karla's wishes after all he had done to her? But on the other hand, could he really just walk away after all the time he had put in to find his child? Suddenly he saw a glint of blond hair and he knew she was here. He stood up and walked toward the entrance.

She looked tired, haggard to be honest. She had probably been flying for at least eight hours. He tentatively lifted his hand when she came through and she gave something halfway between a smile and a frown and walked toward him. They both felt the awkwardness of the moment and silently waited for her luggage. He stood with his hands in his pockets and they watched the conveyer belt as the bags began tumbling through the opening, an invisible wall separating them. At last, her bag started coming down the chute and she reached for it but he gently nudged her aside and grabbed it, pulling it off the belt. They walked to the escalator and she gave him her hotel information. She had reservations for the Red Lion at the Airport and within five minutes of getting in the car, they were parked in front of the hotel.

She checked in and took her bag upstairs while he waited in the lobby. Fifteen minutes later she returned to him and they walked quietly toward the hotel restaurant and walked into the nearly empty establishment. It was after nine and the sounds of a piano coming from the lounge next door drowned out their silence toward each other. She ordered a salad and when it came ate it daintily, not wanting to talk to him about what they had to decide.

"I still don't think you should see Rebecca," she finally said without looking up.

"I know, but you're here so I have to believe that you're at least willing to entertain the idea," he replied.

"I wouldn't say that," she replied irritably. She sensed him looking at her but she would not lift her eyes to return it. She was tired and regretted coming here in the first place. She remembered realizing she had made a mistake as soon as she sat down on the plane in Boston but somehow, she had stayed rather than getting up and walking off.

"Then why have you come?"

She pondered for a moment, wondering the same thing. "I guess because you do seem different. Maybe you have grown up," and she saw the hurt in his face. "I'm sorry, maybe that was wrong to say. I'm just tired; it's been a long day." She finally looked at him and smiled and he returned it, relieved that she was at least now becoming civil. "I'm just afraid, Jesse," she confessed and he saw the sincerity of the statement in her eyes.

"I don't know what I am," he replied, "I only know I'm not the young man you once knew. I know what I want to become and I'm hoping I'm doing the right things to become him." They stared at each other in silence and this time it was Jesse's eyes that looked away, trying to hide the shame he felt for the things he had done to cause her fear.

"I'm scared too," he confessed. "I'm scared that I'm going to fail and go back to prison. I'm scared that being on the outside is too much for me because the thirty years made me institutionalized. I'm scared of the future and the unknown." She listened to him as he poured out his fears and she no longer saw a hardened criminal but a scared boy trying to find the light. For a moment the mother in her wanted to grab him, pull him close.

"My choice is to succumb to the darkness or try to find the end of the tunnel," he said resolutely. "Right now, I'm looking for the light."

"So, when did you become a philosopher?" she asked with a smile.

"I went to the prison library once," he responded and they both giggled. "This is kind of nice, isn't it?"

"I suppose it is Jesse, but I can't help wondering if you are just softening me up, getting my guard down."

"Is it working?" he asked and they both laughed again.

"I had forgotten about your wonderful dry sense of humor."

"So had I," he confessed. They sat quietly and enjoyed the strains of the piano coming from the other room. The song sounded familiar but neither could remember its name.

"I really need to find her Karla," he said as the song ended. "I need it so I can be the man I was supposed to be."

"That's quite dramatic Jesse, but I suppose it could be true. You know, she may not want to see you have you thought of that scenario?"

"I know. I accept that, but I have to follow through. I won't hurt Rebecca; I promise I won't. I'm done hurting others, on purpose anyway." Karla stared at him and he could not tell what she was thinking. Her eyes stared through him as if she were looking to see what was on the inside and he hoped that it was good. "Please Karla." Suddenly her eyes reddened and became wet. He stared at her and she remained passive except for her eyes. He could sense the fear she was feeling. The desperateness of the moment caused her eyes to tear up until it became too heavy and slowly trickled down her cheek.

"I won't stop you," she said in a broken voice as she wiped it away with her hand. He reached across the table and grabbed her hand and to his surprise, she did not pull it away.

"I know how hard that was for you," he said quietly as he caressed the top of her hand with his thumb. "Thank you."

"I don't know if I'm doing the right thing," she said as another tear escaped her eye. "I just know I want to believe you. Please don't let me down again."

He nodded and squeezed her hand. "I don't know if it's the right thing either, but I believe it is. I have to try."

After dinner, he walked her back to her room and turned to leave but she stopped him and invited him in. He couldn't help but show his surprise and she teased him and he blushed in embarrassment. They spoke of the old times and reminisced over what once was and it was delightful.

"Why won't you talk to Rebecca?" asked Jesse. "Margaret told me that you haven't talked to her in some time." Karla's face hardened and she glared at him and he immediately regretted asking her and prepared to be escorted out.

"Don't start with me Jesse, it's none of your business!" she replied angrily.

"I know," he agreed. "So why won't you talk to her?"

"Jesse, don't presume because I had a nice dinner with you and we have been enjoying each other's company for the past hour that you can talk to me about my relationship with my daughter. It's complicated and you haven't earned the right to even be called her father just yet."

"I'm not presuming anything Karla, it's only a question. Now, why won't you speak to your daughter?"

"Damn it, Jesse," she exploded. "Get out of this room and leave me alone. I will not have this conversation with you. You were gone, you left us…remember? I did the best I could. I made all the difficult choices…just stop it!" He turned and walked toward the door.

"You did well Karla, I know you did your best which is why I can't understand why you won't talk to her now." He turned the handle and opened the door and looked back to her standing in the middle of the room seething.

"Before I go just let me say this, you're going down a dangerous path. One day turns into a week, then a month, then a year and all of a sudden you realize that thirty have gone by and you missed everything. Seriously, how long has it been since you talked to her?"

"I don't know," she confessed and she walked toward him.

"Time gets away Karla. You're better than me, you're smarter, but that doesn't make you immune from doing stupid things. Letting life get between you and your daughter is stupid, worse, it's a damn tragedy. That is one thing that I do know. Believe me, Karla, you don't want to go down that path."

"Maybe," she conceded quietly.

"Just think about it?" She sighed and nodded and reached out for his hand. He grabbed it and gave it a slight squeeze and she smiled. They slowly walked out of the room toward the elevator and he pushed the button. The light whir of the elevator filled the air as they stood in silence awaiting the car. The doors opened and he looked at her. She pulled a slip of paper out of her pocket and handed it to him. He opened it and saw it was a Coeur d'Alene address and phone number.

"You would have found it anyway," she said.

"Means more coming from you," he replied and he walked into the car and pushed the lobby button. She stared at him as the doors closed and the whirring sound filled the air again and she slowly walked back to her room. She entered her room and sat on the bed. She was so tired but was thankful she no longer felt afraid. The anxiousness still remained but her fear was now gone. Suddenly there was a quiet knock on her door and she walked to the door and looked through the peephole. It was Jesse. She opened it and he was breathing heavily.

"Come with me tomorrow," he said breathlessly.

"I can't Jesse."

"You can come with me. We'll see her together," he said to her with hope in his voice.

"I leave for the airport at five in the morning. I have to get back to Boston. I'm sorry Jesse, this is something you'll have to do by yourself," she said to him. He nodded and smiled sadly and then began walking down the hallway back toward the elevator. "Jesse," she called out and he stopped and turned toward her. "Thank you."

She closed the door and smiled to herself. He had changed. It would be all right. He was ready for whatever was going to happen. The monster was dead. He didn't know it but he was finally becoming the man she had been searching for.

*

She stood in the lobby and waited for the van to take her back to the airport. It had been a short night but she felt rested and refreshed. The van pulled up in front of the lobby and she grabbed her bag and walked into the dark morning and climbed into the van. Two more joined her, another woman and a man and they waited quietly for the driver. Soon the van left the hotel for the short ride to the airport and Karla replayed the previous evening with Jesse.

It was amazing how much he had changed. It was in his eyes, she realized. They were no longer angry, hurtful. Now they were soft, almost childlike, as though he were discovering the world all over again. He was finding it scary yet somehow enticing. She remembered that she had once been like that and for a moment felt a tinge of jealousy.

She arrived at the airport and checked her bag. She went through the security area and felt self-conscious as she always had to go through. Relieved to be through she walked to the Seattle Coffee kiosk and bought a black coffee. She poured some cream and opened a packet of honey and squeezed it into the cup and slowly stirred it into the mocha-colored liquid. She glanced at her watch as she walked to the magazine store and bought a copy of the morning newspaper and then walked to her gate.

With the paper read and the coffee cup now empty, she waited quietly for the flight to be called. A woman's voice came over the loudspeaker and Karla grabbed her ticket to check her seat for what seemed like the tenth time in the last hour. It was still the same, 34B, and the gatekeeper announced her row. She stood and joined the line that had already formed. As she came closer to the entrance, she looked at her boarding pass again, checked her watch, and sighed. She wanted to be with Jesse. She wanted to see her daughter; tell her it was all right. She wanted to be Rebecca's Mom again and Jesse was giving her that chance. She stepped out of the line and sat down. She had to think.

The line dwindled until there were only a few passengers left. She had her cellphone and she kept thinking of calling Jesse but for some reason, something was stopping her. She needed to see Rebecca she decided. She needed to support Jesse. She stood up and tried to walk but she couldn't. There was only one person left in the line and then there were none.

"Ma'am?" asked the gatekeeper.

Karla looked at her desperately and reluctantly walked toward the gate. Inside she was screaming to stop and turn around, but her feet continued forward, beyond her control. She was suddenly face to face with her and she just stared.

"Are you all right ma'am?" Karla continued to stare at her and wanted to turn and run down the tarmac but she felt as though she was in cement.

"I'm sorry," Karla said quietly as she finally handed her the ticket. The gatekeeper took it and ran it through the ticket machine and handed it back to her and smiled.

"Have a wonderful day," Karla heard her say as she passed.

Chapter 17

Tom Petty belted out the lyrics of *Learning to Fly* that roared through the radio speakers as the beat-up car rumbled toward Coeur d'Alene. Jesse listened to the chorus of the song and thought that maybe that was him but then he reminded himself that he wasn't a kid anymore and life wasn't a jingle. Still, his mood was one of expectancy as he tried to sing along with a song whose lyrics he did not know. He exited the freeway and headed toward Sherman Avenue to the little motel with the State of Idaho chimney and suddenly it hit him. He had found her and the realization felt more like a weight than a relief. The end game had arrived and he wasn't sure if he was ready for the probable rejection as he had thought he would be.

He pulled into the motel and saw Margaret's light was still on. He turned off the engine and sat in the car staring at the light and he wondered whether to knock on her door. She answered it for him as she walked out into the twilight in her gown and robe. She smiled at him and walked to the passenger side of the car and climbed in and he remained stoic, staring at the light. She reached over and turned the key and then turned the radio knob until music came softly out of the side panels of the old car's door.

"Eighties music, I still think that's the best," she said with a smile as she settled back in the seat. "Now the kids just listen to people rapping with a bass drum banging in the background." He laughed lightly and they listened to the *Finer Things* that played on the radio.

"Who sings that?" asked Jesse. "Music kind of ended around the mid-'80s for me you know."

"You didn't have music in prison?" asked Margaret. "I think this is Boz Scaggs…no wait, it's the Little River Band, I remember now, I saw their concert and they played this I think."

"No, wasn't really like that before television cameras came into the prisons. I was watching some news channel and they were showing different prisons and you hear music being played all the time but I'm telling you, it wasn't like that at the joint I was at. Hey, why the hell does anyone want to watch a show about prisons anyway?" The song ended and the disc jockey announced that Steve Winwood was the singer and Jesse gave Margaret a raised eyebrow looks and she giggled.

"Maybe I didn't hear that song after all," and he laughed. "It's a different world now," she sighed as another song came on the radio. "So, how did it go with Karla?"

"Fine," he replied. "I think she finally understands what I'm doing, more importantly, I think she believes me when I say I'm not who I was."

"Are you going to move forward?" she asked.

"Yeah, I've come this far, it's time to finish the search and see if…well, you know."

They sat silently and listened to the soft music and the windows began to fog and Margaret giggled and looked at Jesse and he smiled back at her. "When I was younger, I use to have fantasies of being with you in a foggy car with soft music playing," she said and he smiled and felt a physical sensation, wanton in need, something he had not felt in ages with a woman next to him and his cheeks crimsoned as she lightly placed her hand on his. "Why don't you turn the car off and let's continue our conversation in my room."

He swallowed hard and turned the key and stepped out of the car. He walked around the beaten-up Rivera and opened her door. She stepped out and grabbed his hand and pulled him toward her. They walked into the small room with the piney knot furniture and she led him to her bed and turned out the light and then turned toward him and embraced him. Their lips slowly met and he pulled her tighter to him, anxiously opening his mouth as she did and kissed more urgently. Her hands went through his hair as he rubbed her back furiously and she backed away for a moment and he was afraid that he had hurt her somehow. She untied her robe and it fell softly to the floor and then he pulled the straps of the nightgown down over her shoulders and it dropped as well and they fell to the bed. She pushed him onto his back and pulled his shirt off and lightly ran her hands across his chest as he pulled her head to his and kissed her frantically.

It had been so long since he had been with a woman and even as he fervently loved her he feared that he was inadequate but her motions and sighs of passion propelled him to continue until he, at last, had nothing more to give of himself to her and they collapsed into each other's arms, and he relished her breath upon his chest as she draped her arm over him and he pulled her tighter to himself. At last, she looked up and gingerly ran her finger over his lips and then softly touched them with hers before laying her head again on his chest. He rubbed his fingers through her hair as a tear ran out of his eye because he realized that after all these years, he could love another and show it passionately. He knew she probably didn't love him the way he loved her at this moment and that was as it should be for, he still hadn't earned her unconditionally.

"Margaret," he said softly as he continued stroking her hair.

"Yes," she said as she softly nibbled on his nipple.

"I'm sorry about the other day, you don't deserve that from me after all you've done."

"Accepted," she giggled.

"I just, well, you said some things that—"

"Jesse," she purred as she put her finger over his lips, "sometimes you don't have to explain," and she smiled as his face crimsoned in embarrassment. They lay in each other's arms and she moved up to his ear and whispered into it. "I suppose you want an address."

"Karla gave it to me," he smiled and then they kissed again.

*

He sat in his room staring out the open door at the rain falling from the sky. It smelled good, new, and everything seemed greener as the freshness of the precipitation softly landed from the heavens. He felt good today, renewed, but also nervous. It was coming to an end and he feared for the worst and didn't know whether to complete the journey knowing that failure was such a strong likelihood. He walked back to his bed and sat down on it and stared out the open door, listening to the softness of the water and he noticed that tensions he had felt in his muscles were loosening. Margaret appeared in the doorway and he smiled sheepishly as she walked in and Raymond followed behind her with a cup of coffee in his hand, looking grumpy and a little unkempt and he collapsed in a chair and cursed when the liquid spattered on his pants.

"Are you nervous?" asked Margaret after she had gotten a towel for Raymond who busily was brushing the coffee deeper into his pants.

"Very," replied Jesse, trying to let the soothing sounds of the rain chase the butterflies out of his stomach.

"I wish I could tell you it'll be all right, but there's a good chance she is going to reject you."

"I know."

"Do you have a plan if that happens?"

"No," he admitted.

"Maybe you should wait," she said softly as Raymond finished the last remnants of the cup and walked over to the door, staring out at the gray clouds. He reached into his shirt pocket and pulled out his Marlboro's and stuck one in his mouth and lit it, blowing the hazy smoke toward the parking lot. "Maybe you've accomplished what you set out to do," she continued as Raymond took another drag.

"I have to go through with this, Margaret," insisted Jesse, becoming a little irritated with her and failing to hide it.

"I'm not saying you shouldn't," she replied evenly, "I just want to make sure you understand what you're facing," and she pulled out a binder from her bag and opened it.

Margaret began reading Jesse some statistics she had pulled up about first meetings and Raymond continued to puff on his cigarette. She got up and sat next to Jesse and showed him some charts and handed him some testimonials to read. Jesse looked at them, he owed her that he reasoned, but they meant nothing to him and he wondered why she was doing this. Could Karla have had a change of heart he wondered? Maybe she had called and begged Margaret to talk him out of seeing Rebecca. Raymond took one last drag of his cigarette which was now nothing more than a filter and a tiche of tobacco and then dropped it on the sidewalk and stamped it out.

"Miss Taylor, could I speak to Jesse alone for a minute?" he asked as he came back into the room. She looked up at him, surprised, but quietly stood up and walked out into the rain. "She means well," he said when they were alone and Jesse nodded.

"When I was young, another young man changed my life," Raymond said as he sat back down in the chair and looked at Jesse on the bed. "He shot me, left me for dead," and Jesse squirmed uncomfortably. "For years and years, I couldn't figure out why and I hated that young man for all that he had robbed me of." Jesse looked down at the floor and Raymond walked over to the bed and sat beside him.

"I hated him so much that I became dead even though I was still alive," he continued as he leaned back on his hands. "The young man that shot me had a daughter that was so low on his priority list that he just abandoned her. He blamed her for his woes and lamented that she was the cause of all his lost dreams." Jesse wondered where this was going. Was he in cahoots with Margaret? He was now sure that Karla had had a change of heart.

"He became more and more bitter and eventually did something that put him in the pen for a long period of time. That little girl grew up without her dad. She probably knew from the beginning she wasn't wanted and if she sees that man, she will probably hate him too."

"Hell, of a pep talk, Raymond," Jesse said curtly.

"Jesus, there you go again. Why do you always have to interrupt me before I'm done? If you keep your damn mouth shut you might learn something..." Jesse stared at him and shook his head.

"About six months ago I met a man I knew and hated. That man hired me to do a job for him. I didn't want to because I hated him, blamed him for my plight, but I needed the money so I took it. As the days went by this guy, I hated became harder to hate. He was different than I expected. I kept trying to hate him and then one day I realized that instead of hating him I just hated myself." He stood up and walked to the door and took out another cigarette and lit it.

"This guy, whose hand had pulled the trigger that changed my world, had died I realized, and in the shell was a man who was trying to change, who was understanding the havoc the younger man had made and was trying to fix it. He didn't always do a very good job at it," he said as he took a deep drag out of the cigarette he had just lit and blew it out of his nose, "but he was trying and kept chugging forward even as doors continued to close in front of him."

"Against my better judgment, I started to like this guy which really pissed me off. I became awful to him but it didn't deter him, son-of-a-bitch kept plugging away." He opened the door and dropped the half-smoked cigarette onto the cement and stamped it out with his foot and turned back toward Jesse.

"I recently got to know this man and he is now my friend. That's a big deal to me because I don't have any besides him. I would never be friends with the man who shot me but he is dead and you remain. Your daughter may hate you; Lord knows Lady Margaret has the stats that say that will happen, but it doesn't matter. The younger man would quit now because the hard part begins as soon as she answers the door." He walked over to Jesse and sat down beside him. "You know this, but you, the older and wiser man that took over from the boy know that it's time to be a father."

"She may not know it, but she needs you, even if it's only for a minute," he said and he stood back up and walked toward the door.

"I'm scared, Raymond…"

Raymond turned around and looked at Jesse, whose eyes were filled with the fear of the unknown, the child desperately looking for the light. "I know," he replied, "but you're not afraid of the moment. You would have quit if you were. It's time to become a father."

Jesse stood up and walked toward him and put his hand out. Raymond grabbed him and suddenly pulled him close and wrapped his arms around him. Jesse, taken aback, slowly put his around the shorter man and they squeezed awkwardly and broke away quickly, but it had been real and they realized that a new bond now connected them.

"Jesse," Raymond smiled, "you'll need a job. Daughters are expensive I hear."

They both laughed and Raymond walked out the door but turned and looked at him. "You can work for me," he said sincerely.

"One thing at a time Raymond," Jesse replied.

"I'm serious," he said.

"Thanks, I'll take it, but not until after tomorrow," Jesse said and Raymond smiled and walked toward his room. Jesse watched him and quietly said a prayer of thanks. He was ready. Tomorrow morning, he would meet the woman he had abandoned as a child.

The fear was gone and in its place was anticipation.

*

He forced himself to step out of the car and trudge forward toward the gray house with the blue door. The front walk was uneven, the cracks of the century-old cement bending one way and then another. He focused on it, forcing himself to move toward it until he was walking upon it. His breathing became difficult, air seemingly fleeing from him and he gulped it in with all of his might. The world was slow motion now and he felt as though he were floating over his shell and watching.

The cement steps stood before him and he lifted a foot and placed it down, forcing himself closer and closer to the door. He stood on the small porch with the wooden planks painted gray and he continued forward. He was here now, in front of the screen door and his mind battled with him, debating whether or not to open it and knock. He continued this battle in his mind as his hand reached out and opened it and he knocked on the blue door with his other, four times he counted and he wondered if it was loud enough or too soft and she had not heard it. He debated whether to knock again but instead, he closed the screen door and stepped back, his eyes staring intently into the blue of the wooden structure that obstructed him from knowing what was happening inside and his ears strained to hear something, anything.

Footsteps, at first soft but continually growing louder filled his ears and as they did his breathing is no longer was labored, but now shallow, barely audible as his hearing senses struggled to determine where she was as the sound of the steps came closer. His chest tightened and he wondered if he was maybe suffering a heart attack. The pain grew as the sound became louder but he didn't collapse and he determined that it was not his fate to die on this porch at this moment.

He wanted to run, what has he done? He must be crazy to have tried to find her. What could he offer? He had to get away, find a place to hide but his feet stubbornly refused to move and he realized in his paralyzing fear that he was eager for the door to open.

Suddenly everything became quiet as the knob creaked and turned and the door slowly opened. His eyes strained and then she was there, behind the screen, directly in front of him and she is beautiful, more beautiful than he could have ever imagined. Her face is young-looking though she is into her thirties; a softness still stubbornly fighting off the wrinkles of age unlike those that now engulfed him. Her skin a silky white and her hair, the hair of her mother; the golden blond of a wheat field as it sways to the soft wind right before it is harvested.

She has sereneness emanating from her, a quiet dignity that produces a majestic look and he found himself hypnotized by the beauty of something that he had a part of creating yet in truth had nothing to do with. Her voice is soft as she speaks with a shyness she cannot hide but she does not seem afraid.

She smiles as she greets him but he realized immediately it is a smile out of politeness and that she doesn't know who he is. He stared in silence, unable to move or think or speak but he realized that he was right to come here. Though he may never see her again, he was right to come here because she is the angel he dreamed she would be.

He tried to speak, but the words from his mouth were guttural and with each attempt his tongue became thick. She gently opened the screen door and stepped out so that now she was merely a foot away from him and gingerly she placed her hand on his shoulder, quieting his attempts at speech.

"Mom called," she said softly. "I've been waiting for you."